Love is Forever

NATALIE FOX

Heartline
Books

NATALIE FOX

Of *Love is Forever* best-selling author Natalie Fox says: 'Guiding my hero and heroine through the pages of this book was, for me, a true labour of love. The location of the Greek isles is my idea of heaven. Sun, blue skies, white-washed villas, lush countryside and warm, relaxing beaches lapped by the Aegean Sea. To say nothing of a dark, fiery and passionate hero!'

International acclaim for Natalie Fox's previous novels: 'Fast paced and full of steamy tension…' and 'You'll admire her heroines, and lust after her charismatic heroes!'

Rendezvous Magazine

chapter one

He was there as usual. Watching them from the cliff top.

Far below, from the terrace of the beachside villa, Sara Anderson lifted a hand to shield her narrowed blue eyes from the white-hot sun as she gazed up at him. He was all Greek male. Dark, strong-featured, tall, strikingly beautiful. At her first sight of him, a week ago, he had taken her breath away. Not in fear – she had simply been awestruck. Her heart had given a sudden lurch, and she had felt almost ashamed for allowing herself to admire another man when she had vowed to stay true to Spiros forever.

His routine was unwavering in its execution. The white limousine would come to a smooth halt at precisely the same spot every afternoon, just three metres beyond the last olive tree on the dirt track above the villa, which nestled in a rocky cove. He would switch off the engine and get out of the car and lean back against it to look down on them. Then, very slowly and deliberately, he would remove the dark sunglasses from his eyes and slide them into the breast pocket of his white silk shirt. His golden arms would fold cross his chest and there he would stay for another ten minutes, motionless, soundless, just watching them in whatever activity they were pursuing at the time.

Sara and her five year old daughter Thea, reading on the terrace overlooking the sea; Thea drawing at the rustic patio table; Sara outside preparing vegetables for the evening meal while Thea dozed in a lounger under a shady olive tree. Anything and everything he drank in with his dark penetrating eyes, saying and doing nothing till Sara wanted to scream at him in frustration, '*Why are you doing this,*

Alexander Karakou – and what do you want from us?'

But she never did cry out to him. Because of her small daughter, she just waited patiently for him to make the first move, which he must do eventually, because why else had he gone to so much trouble to get them here, to this remote Greek island?

'Mama, why doesn't he come down?' Thea asked as she slid her small warm hand into Sara's. 'I don't understand why he comes every day. He just stares at us and then goes away.'

Sara smiled down at her daughter. As always, when she looked at her, Sara thought how lucky she was to have her. Thea was a joy. Dark-haired and olive-skinned, her deep brown eyes a stunning feature of her heart-shaped face, and with a nature so uncomplicated that Sara felt privileged to be her mother and to be loved by her.

'The villa belongs to him, and he just comes to see if we are safe and well,' Sara suggested softly.

Maybe he did. But there was more, of course. The wealthy Greek hadn't sent flight tickets, money and a yacht to pick them up at Kos before delivering them here, to his beachside villa on this hot dry island, for nothing.

Sara hadn't set foot in Greece since her daughter Thea had been born on the small island of Zanos, on a dark and stormy night which had destroyed so many people's lives. In fact, until a month ago, she had never heard of Alexander Karakou. However, she had been intrigued by both his letter of introduction and the travel arrangements he had made for her and her daughter.

The letter had contained an offer of temporary employment – a very welcome prospect for a single mother struggling to get by on a small income. Alexander Karakou had, he explained, recently taken over the Athens based tour company for whom Sara had once worked. She had been highly recommended, thanks to her previous experience, as someone qualified to judge whether or not his island home would provide a suitable exclusive location for wealthy British holidaymakers. Particularly those wishing to 'get away from it all'.

In return for her report, Sara and her small daughter had been offered the free use of a villa for the duration of their stay, and there was the possibility of similar work for Sara in the future.

Naturally, Sara had been cautious. She certainly hadn't leapt up and down with excitement at the prospect of a free holiday in Greece, courtesy of a complete stranger. She had contacts in the Greek islands, and the Athens travel company she'd used to work for had proved to be very helpful. After careful checks, Sara had discovered that Alexander Karakou was a very well-respected Greek citizen, a man of both old and new wealth, successful, charismatic, and apparently a bit of a womaniser until he'd married and settled down. Then, unfortunately, he had been struck by tragedy. His young wife had died of leukaemia a few years ago, since when Alexander Karakou had gone to ground like a wounded fox. Although his businesses had continued to flourish, it seemed that for some years he had become a virtual recluse.

'So what do you want with us?' Sara muttered under her breath as she watched him move back towards his car and start up the engine.

With every day that passed she was growing more and more frustrated by her employer's behaviour. She didn't feel threatened by him. In fact, if Sara had felt he posed a threat to her or Thea she would have immediately left the island. No...it was his strange behaviour, the way he spent part of every day gazing down at them from the cliff top, which she was finding increasingly odd and disturbing.

At one point she had wondered if the job she'd been offered had something to do with Thea and her father,

Spiros? It was, after all, the only connection Sara had with
Greece. But she had eventually dismissed that notion. As far
as she knew Spiros had been an only child, whose parents
had died in his teens. Besides which, he certainly hadn't
moved in the same circles as the wealthy Alexander
Karakou.

No...Sara shrugged her doubts away. This was, after all,
her host's private island, and he had every right to check that
she wasn't abusing his hospitality. All the same...it was
about time that her new employer got his act together.
Otherwise it was beginning to look as if he wasn't going to
speak to her before she returned home to England!

'He's going,' Thea said in a small voice. 'Do you think he
will come down to the beach tomorrow? He looks nice,
Mama, but a little sad.'

'Yes...yes, he does,' Sara agreed thoughtfully, surprised
by her daughter's perception. But then, she shouldn't be
surprised. Thea was her father's daughter: sensitive, intelligent, thoughtful, and just about everything else that was
good in the world, Sara told herself with a heavy sigh. If
only Spiros were here to see his daughter growing up
so beautifully. If only...

'So, what is it to be?' Sara said quickly, swinging her
daughter's hand, which was still tightly clutching her own.
'Swimming, snorkelling, beachcombing or —'

'Or playing with Stefios and Chloe in the village?' Thea
pleaded hopefully, twisting the side of her yellow cotton
sundress in excited expectation that her mother would say
yes.

Sara laughed and shook her head. 'OK, we'll go into the
village and you can play with the children. But you mustn't
get under Maria's feet. She has quite enough to do with her
job, the taverna and her family.'

'Maria says that I am always welcome,' Thea said

happily. 'She says it is good for my Greek to be with them. And I am half-Greek, Mama. So...'

'OK, OK!' Sara laughed. 'I'm not arguing with you. We'll go. But let me get changed first, because I need to see Maria.

'About the strange man on the cliff top?' Thea asked as she sat on her hands on the edge of the bed, watching Sara slip into a white sundress.

'No, not him.' Sara grinned. 'We need some more honey. And Maria knows just where to get the best,' she added absently, scowling at her reflection in the mirror. Her skin wasn't as dark as Thea's, and though her skin had taken on a golden tan, the tip of her nose was just a trifle overdone. Sara quickly dabbed sun block on it. Although she feared that it was too late. It was entirely her own fault, of course. She ought to have known better, especially after having lived in Greece for so long. As for her hair, that should have been bundled under a bandanna from day one! As it was, the sun had bleached the tips, but mercifully there was little other damage. It was still long and glossy – and as straight as Thea's hair was curly.

As they strolled leisurely along the cliff path, and down the hot winding dirt track road that led to the village, Sara was buried in thought. Up to now she'd been reluctant to question Maria, or try to pump her for more information about her employer, Alexander Karakou. But it was beginning to look as if she was going to have to do something about this increasingly odd situation.

Maria had introduced herself on the first day they had arrived, explaining her role in their lives as maid to the villa. She came every day, to clean and change the linen, and she shopped for them too – so keenly and obligingly that Sara hadn't the heart to tell her she was longing to do her own shopping in the small open market in the centre of the town, just a few kilometres away.

Sara, of course, spoke fluent Greek. Which meant that the

'maid and house guest' status had soon been abandoned, with the two young mothers forming a cosy friendship after just one week of meeting each other.

And that was why Sara hadn't wanted to bring up the subject of Alexander Karakou and his mysterious behaviour. After all, the villa belonged to Maria's employer, and whenever she spoke of him it was always in warm, glowing terms. Sara certainly didn't want to put the maid's loyalties to the test by asking awkward and personal questions. But…but, as far as she was concerned matters had gone on long enough. Perhaps Maria could throw some light on the situation?

Maria and her family lived in a row of tilted white terraced houses, with vibrant blue shutters and a blue front door that was always open to the street. Her husband, Forte, ran a small taverna at the end of the terrace.

As Sara and Thea approached the taverna, they saw that Forte was sitting outside under an awning, his children Stefios and Chloe playing a board game on the cobbles at his feet. Thea ran towards them as they called out, waving her over to join them. And Sara, satisfied that her daughter was in safe hands, pushed through the bead curtain that covered the doorway of the house, calling for Maria.

'She is not here,' a deep voice drawled coolly from the dim interior of Maria's tiny main room.

Sara jumped in fright, peering nervously through the darkness.

'I believe she is visiting a neighbour,' the dark voice continued as Alexander Karakou moved out of the shadows to stand by the open door, where there was more light through the beaded curtain.

Sara's first impression was that his tall, powerful figure was far too big for this tiny house. He filled it physically with his height, and with his strong and dominant presence. This was the closest she had been to him, and if she had thought him beautiful from a distance, close up he was more so. Dark and intense, he gazed at her with eyes so liquid brown you could almost drown in them.

Her daughter had been quite right, Sara thought reflectively as she met his scrutiny, her eyes, as blue as the Aegean, a soft contrast to his dark liquid pools. He did have an air of sadness about him. It dragged at his handsome features, but somehow didn't distract from his basic good looks. Sara couldn't help thinking that if he smiled she might faint with surprise and emotion.

'You must be Alexander Karakou,' she said softly. She smiled hesitantly and raised her hand to take his in introduction, but his hands remained firmly clenched at his side.

'Must I?' he murmured coolly.

Sara frowned. Now that they were finally face to face, close enough to speak – and certainly close enough to scrutinise one another seriously – he still appeared to be maintaining his air of mystery. She lifted her small chin, and her lovely blue eyes flashed with irritation as she gazed up at him.

'I think I've had enough of your puzzling behaviour,' she pointed out grimly. 'Quite frankly, I'm running out of patience. If you are not who I think you are, why don't you say so?'

His dark eyes narrowed warily. Greek men were used to being in charge of any confrontation with a woman – and he was clearly no exception.

'Yes, I am Alexander Karakou,' he admitted slowly. 'But whether or not I am *precisely* who you think I am, is possibly another matter entirely.'

Sara gave a slight shake of her head. She had already surmised that this meeting, when it happened, was likely to be a difficult one. However, she still had a niggling feeling that this situation somehow involved Thea. Which didn't make any sense. There was no way this wealthy man could have had anything to do with Thea's father, Spiros – a poor Greek fisherman. So what *did* Alexander Karakou want from her?

'Why have you done all this?' she asked quietly. 'You've gone to considerable expense to bring us to this island, where I am supposed to be working for you. But you just come and watch us every day. Saying nothing – and doing nothing!'

As she gave a helpless shrug the fine strap of her white sundress slid down her arm. She lifted the strap back on to her golden tanned shoulder, and a brief glinting expression in his dark eyes had the effect of suddenly making her feel nervous, her cheeks reddening beneath his gaze.

'This isn't the time or the place to discuss my intentions,' he said smoothly, before nodding his dark head towards the door. 'Should you not be with your daughter? The street outside a taverna, is hardly the ideal place for a child to be playing.'

Sara's lips parted as she gazed at him in surprise. And then she realised that he must have been spying on them as she and Thea had walked down the narrow village street to the taverna.

'Where I see fit to let my daughter play is no concern of yours,' she retorted quickly.

As his dark brows drew together in a deep frown, Sara told herself that Thea was utterly wrong in her belief that this was a nice man. He clearly wasn't at all 'nice' – and Sara was astonished to find herself feeling a jolt of deep disappointment.

'I will call on you later,' was all he said as he pushed the bead curtain aside, before his elegant figure strode out into the searing heat of the village street.

Sara was still clenching her fists fiercely, muttering grimly under her breath, as Maria bounced in at the same doorway some moments later.

'Ah, he has been!' Maria exclaimed excitedly, quickly scooping up a pile of money from a small circular table in the middle of the room. 'He is such a good man to work for. He pays every month, but sometimes *she* comes and spoils my day. Nothing is ever right for *her*. She goes to the villa and does this…' Maria disdainfully whipped an index finger over the gleaming surface of her own table and then scrutinised the tip haughtily.

'"*Really, Maria! What is this? Could it be dirt? I hope not. Oh dear, Maria, you really must do better!*"'

Sara burst out laughing at her friend's mimicry. Whoever *she* might be, the woman was clearly a pain in the neck as far as Maria was concerned!

'She is a *beetch!*' Maria stated emphatically in English, grinning from ear to ear.

'Who is "*she*"?' Sara asked.

Maria waved her hands dismissively. 'She acts like a wife – but he has no wife. She looks like a mistress – and I think she must be. She's certainly *not* his mother!' Maria added with a mischievous sparkle in her dark eyes, before giving a shrug of her shoulders. 'It does not matter. She is a *beetch* – and she lives with him and his daughter. That is all I know. Now, come – Thea tells me you want more honey. I will take you to Padras and the bees.'

So, Alexander had a daughter! Sara was surprised to hear it, because there had been nothing about a child during her enquiries back in England and out in Athens. And there had been no mention of the fact that Alexander had a mistress. Not that it mattered, of course. In fact, it made him appear slightly more human. However, Maria's information had done nothing to help solve the mystery of why he had summoned her and Thea to Greece. Or why he'd virtually ignored them both ever since.

Some hours later, Sara and Thea slowly made their way back to the beachside villa, where a cooler breeze from the sea was waiting to greet them. They'd had a lovely afternoon with Maria and her family. Sara had helped in the kitchen of the small restaurant when a sudden rush of tourists had descended on them, and the children had continued to play happily in the street and in the shady garden at the back of the taverna.

Now they were nearly home: Sara clutching a huge earthenware jar of honey – and none the wiser as to why Alexander Karakou had summoned them to Greece – and Thea skipping ahead on the rough road flanked by aged olive trees and scrubby rosemary which filled the air with a heavy perfume.

Sara briefly closed her eyes as she took a deep breath of the heady scent. She hadn't realised just how much she had missed Greece.

She had lived and worked on the islands for two years as a travel courier before meeting Spiros, falling deeply in love and deciding to live together. It hadn't been long before she'd realised that she was expecting his child. As Spiros had had no family, and her parents were divorced with new partners of their own – and little interest in her, now that she was an adult and living abroad – there had been no outside pressure for them to marry in a hurry.

They had been so happy together, living each day to the full in what now seemed such a carefree, lotus-eating existence, idly making plans for the future, but doing little or nothing about them. And oh, *how* she wished she could turn the clock back. To have been legally married to Spiros before…before disaster had struck, might possibly be important in her current situation. But for the life of her she couldn't imagine how or why. When fate was against you there was nothing you could do to prevent a tragedy, she told herself with a deep sigh of sadness and regret.

Married or not, Spiros would still have taken his boat out in that rough, storm-whipped sea, to rescue some shipwrecked fishermen. There was nothing anyone could have done to prevent the raging storm that night, when Thea had decided to enter the world three weeks early and with dire complications. In a matter of hours Sara had survived an emergency Caesarean, given life to her daughter – and lost her lover forever.

Tragically, Spiros had never known that his child had been born. He had gone down with his boat, together with the boats belonging to three other fishermen, in one of the worst tragedies that small Greek island had ever experienced.

'Do you still miss Papa?' Thea asked later that evening as she lay in bed, Sara having just finished reading her a story.

Sara closed the book and smiled down at her. Brushing the dark curls from the child's wide brow, she thought how proud Spiros would be of his beautiful daughter, who appeared to have inherited most of her father's genes. Strangers were always taken aback by the sight of her ethnic beauty, especially since Sara, though fairly dark haired herself, had startling large blue eyes and a much fairer complexion.

'Yes, I miss him very much. More so, somehow, now that we are here in Greece,' Sara told her softly. 'It brings back so many happy memories. Your father was a wonderful man, Thea. He was so warm and gentle. Such a good man – and very brave, too. Because, although so many lives were lost that night, many others were saved because of your papa. A friend wrote to me and said there is a plaque on the harbour wall in his memory now. Maybe, when we leave here, we'll be able to go and see it.'

'Is it far?' Thea asked sleepily.

'Only a few islands away. In fact, we could easily take a boat there, and even maybe stay for a few days.'

As she heard herself saying the words, Sara decided that she was definitely going to make plans to visit the island where she had once been so happy. Just as soon as she'd sorted out the vexing problem of Alexander Karakou.

'Will that man be there?'

Before Sara had a chance to reply, Thea had fallen fast asleep. Lovingly kissing the child's forehead, and tucking the thin cotton sheet under her chin, Sara found herself wondering if Alexander's strange behaviour was somehow beginning to worry her daughter. Although the whole affair was deeply puzzling, Sara certainly wasn't afraid of him. But maybe a child would be likely to view the situation from a different perspective from that of an adult?

So, why *was* the man behaving so oddly? Sara asked herself yet again, as she quietly closed Thea's bedroom door behind her.

Although she was staying in the only villa in this craggy cove, it certainly wasn't a palatial building. But the setting was exceptionally beautiful – its wide terrace providing a perfect spot to view the spectacular sunsets over the sea at night.

However, as she now made her way out on to the terrace overlooking the beach, Sara was unable to prevent herself from giving a sudden gasp of startled surprise.

Goodness knows how he had managed to enter the house without her being aware of the fact. But there was no mistaking the identity of the tall, powerful figure, whose dark silhouette was framed by the glittering fiery rays of the dying sun.

Alexander Karakou certainly believed in making himself at home, she thought grimly, viewing with a jaundiced eye the lithe body and long legs of the man lounging in a cane chair. Motionless. Waiting.

He turned to look at her, not affording her a smile, just that odd gaze of his, part curious, part unsure, part disapproving.

'Can I get you a drink?' she asked. 'Some coffee, per-haps? Or wine? I also have a bottle of ouzo in the fridge.'

He nodded. 'Yes, ouzo. With water.'

A few minutes later she handed him a glass, before lean-ing across the table to light a citronella-scented candle, both to ward off the mosquitoes and to illuminate the gathering darkness. The sudden flame from the match threw into relief the firm bone structure of his face, accentuating his drawn expression.

This was not a happy man, Sara thought pensively, more curious than ever about his motive in bringing her and her daughter to this island. He was reputedly wealthy and successful, but he now looked as if he was carrying the woes of the world on his broad shoulders.

'Don't you think it's about time you told me what this is all about?' she said as she sat across from him, sipping a glass of iced water with slices of lime floating in it. 'Your letter stated that you wanted me to visit this island to see if it was suitable for tourists. But I'm definitely coming to the conclusion that you've brought me here under false pretences.'

He lowered his glass to the bleached wood table and gazed out to sea. 'I need to know everything about you and Thea,' he stated quietly, without looking at her. 'Your life together, how you spend your days with her. I want to know everything about the child from the minute she was...' His voice suddenly faltered, and he swallowed before con-tinuing, 'I want to know everything about Thea.'

The night was hot, but a sudden cold chill snapped at Sara's spine. Why such a fervent interest in Thea? *Was* he some distant relative of Spiros, who'd found out about their love-child? But Spiros had always said there was no one, that he had no family.

'I thought this must be something to do with Thea,' she said, quietly but strongly. 'Especially since she's my only connection with Greece now that I don't live and work here any more. Are you some distant relative of her father?' she added when he made no reply. 'If so, you must be very distant, because he always told me that he had no immediate family.'

At last he turned to look at her, and now she saw that his eyes had lost their dark intensity, becoming subtly softer and more gentle.

'Would it come as very much of a shock to you to hear that Spiros *did* have immediate family: parents, brothers and sisters?'

Sara's insides clenched. So he knew Spiros by name, but obviously not intimately.

However, she managed a shaky laugh and shook her head. 'Yes, it would surprise me,' she retorted. 'In fact, I'm astonished that a man of substance, such as yourself, would bother to tell such a blatant lie. Because I happen to *know* that Spiros had no one – no family at all.'

'Spiros would obviously have denied a family, to save you anxiety and humiliation, Sara,' he told her softly. 'He was a simple fisherman and —'

Sara's defence of the man she had loved burst forth quickly. 'He was far from a *simple* fisherman,' she ground out, glaring at the stranger who'd had the nerve to invade her private life. 'If you met him, you *must* know that.'

'I never knew him personally,' Alexander admitted slowly.

Sara frowned. But she was more concerned with defending Spiros than questioning Alexander's motives in snooping into her past.

'He was intelligent, warm and loving, gentle and caring. Spiros was my *life* for the short time I had him!' she cried, her voice trembling with passion.

The man who had insulted her lover ran a tanned, weary hand over his forehead. 'I'm sorry...I didn't mean...'

'I don't care what you mean!' Sara snapped tersely. 'You've already started to tell me a pack of lies. Just what *is* your game, Alexander? And why on earth have you gone to such lengths to get us here?'

He glared at her darkly, furious with her for being so angry with him.

'This is no game,' he told her firmly. 'This is life – which can be hard and cruel – and which is something you are going to have to face, head-on. All my so-called intentions are going to tear you apart – as I have been torn apart these last months. Indeed, our lives are so deeply and inexplicably intertwined that you are going to wish you had never succumbed to a passionate, brief holiday affair with a Greek over five years ago!'

Sara was momentarily stunned by his angry outburst. And it was a moment or two before she was able to rally her forces.

'How…how *dare* you bring my affair down to the pitiful level of a holiday fling? I was living here in Greece, working amongst people I loved and in a country about which I cared deeply. If you must know, I lived with Spiros for two years and—'

'And yet you apparently never knew that he had a family in Crete, consisting of three grandparents, two parents and five brothers and sisters?' Alexander drawled sardonically.

'*Stop it!*' Sara hissed, clutching the edge of the table to steady her anger. 'Why are you saying these things?' she pleaded, her heart thudding wildly. 'You must know that none of it is true!'

Alexander didn't reply, but gazed at her intently for a long time.

During those agonising moments Sara tried to pull herself together and get a firm grip on reality. Whatever this man might say, she knew that she must somehow find the strength to be strong – if only for Thea's sake. So, what was likely to be the worst-case scenario? That some dim and distant relative of Spiros, whom he had known nothing about, might now be trying to lay claim to her daughter? If so, she would fight them through every court in the land, she told herself defiantly.

'As I said, I never knew Spiros,' Alexander said at last. 'I used to own the fishing fleet for which he worked, though I had sold out long before the tragedy. And, although you may not wish to believe what I say, the records show quite clearly that Spiros had a family living in Crete.'

Sara felt as if a deafening bombshell had exploded inside her, shaking the ground at her feet, leaving her stunned and dazed. Oh, my God – Alexander *must* be telling the truth. Spiros really *had* possessed a mother, father, sisters and brothers. And she had never known.

'If you never knew about his family, it can only be because he wanted to protect you,' Alexander continued quietly. 'Some Greeks do not want their sons to marry foreigners. Perhaps Spiros, as the eldest son, was expected to marry a Greek girl of the family's choice? Who knows?' He shrugged, before adding softly, 'I'm sure he never intended you to be hurt by his deception.'

Sara lifted her chin and glared at him. Deeply wounded and trembling with the pain of Spiros's deception, she could only shake her head, desperately trying to deny what she knew must be the truth.

'I'm not hurt because…because I don't believe it,' she stormed. 'You don't live with a man for two years, share a life with him, and not know if he is living a lie.'

But in own her mind she had already moved on from her passionate outburst, and was attempting to come to terms with the situation. Because it was no good trying to fool herself any longer. Due to his work, Spiros had frequently been away at times, long trips that could well have taken him as far as Crete…

Sara stared intently at Alexander, attempting to fathom what lay behind the bland, impassive expression on his face.

In the space of a few minutes she had gone from never doubting Spiros to the dreadful revelation that their life together had been founded on deception. So, why was Alexander – a man she hardly knew – apparently so determined to bring her small world crashing down about her ears? He didn't look the sort of man to lie, cause trouble, or upset someone simply for the fun of it. His credentials were impeccable. According to Maria, he was an exemplary employer. He'd been married, survived the tragic loss of his wife, and had a daughter of his own...

Damn you, Alexander Karakou! Damn you for putting doubt where there had never been doubt before.

'Was there a reason for you never marrying?' Alexander asked her quietly.

Suddenly feeling weak and exhausted, Sara slumped back in her seat. Slowly lifting her glass to her trembling lips, she took a sip of water before giving a heavy sigh. He was clearly waiting for an answer. But she couldn't bring herself to look at him.

'It...it didn't seem to matter at the time,' she murmured desolately.

How could she possibly begin to try and explain the happy, joyous life she and Spiros had shared with one another? Especially to a macho Greek male, whose countrymen were generally very strong on family values?

Slowly she lifted her head to look at him as a light gradually dawned in her head. Alexander had said that he'd once been Spiros's employer. Was this about compensation to the families of those lost in the tragedy? If so, he could have already paid some money to Spiros's family – and only just found out that Spiros had an illegitimate daughter. Which would explain his interest in her, and why he had brought them here, to this island.

'We talked of it, and would have got married eventually,' Sara told him dully. 'But somehow the time was never quite right,' she added with a slight shrug of her slim shoulders. 'I was working as a courier on the islands, the season was frantically busy, and Spiros was working hard. Our time together was precious, and we…we were just enjoying our life together. When I discovered I was pregnant, we were both delighted. Spiros said we must marry immediately, but…'

Sara gave a heavy sigh. She could now understand Spiros's sudden desire for them to get married. His family might be against mixed marriages, but if his English lover was carrying his child, his family would *have* to accept the marriage.

'There has never been any doubt in my mind that Spiros loved me,' Sara continued pensively. 'If he kept his family from me, and me from them, then he had his reasons and it doesn't matter to me now. Why did you have to destroy my happy memories?' she demanded, her eyes glinting with unshed tears in the darkness of the night. 'If there is money involved, I'm not interested. Nothing can compensate for my loss.'

'This has nothing to do with money,' he told her wearily. 'I only wish that it was that simple.'

Sara frowned. 'So what *is* this about? Do…do Spiros's family know about my daughter? Did…did they ask you to bring me here? '

He shook his head, staring down at his empty glass. 'So many questions,' he murmured thickly. 'Where do I start?'

'You start at the beginning,' she told him firmly. 'But before you do so, I want to make something very clear.'

Sara leaned across the table, her quietly determined voice rising above the trill of cicadas in the olive trees and the gentle pounding of the sea on the rocks far below.

'Whatever your reasons for bringing me here, whatever your reasons for delving into my life, I want you to understand that Thea is *my* daughter,' she told him steadily. 'Spiros is dead,' she continued, her voice thick with feeling. 'He never even had the chance to see her. He never knew that Thea had been born on that terrible night. And I love her with a passion only a mother can feel for a daughter who has been so cruelly robbed of a loving father. I just wanted you to know that before you start something you can never win. Because if Spiros's family have asked you to take Thea from me you can tell them I will fight them till the day I die. She is *mine*, and no one, no one in the whole world, has any claim on her but me. Have I made myself clear?'

As her words died away in the deep and profound silence surrounding their two figures, it suddenly seemed as if time itself was somehow standing still. She could barely hear the sound of the sea beating against the rocks, and the familiar noise of the cicadas had become hushed in the darkness. Alexander Karakou was hardly breathing, only gazing at her so intently that she almost shivered. The feeling of some sort of catastrophe looming in her future was so overwhelming that her stomach clenched in fear and alarm.

Sara struggled to pull herself together and ignore her strange sense of deep apprehension. She was merely guilty of slightly overreacting to the strange situation in which she'd found herself – as would any caring mother who was also a single parent.

'I'm not going to apologise for anything I've said,' she told him firmly. 'I meant every word. I've built a life for myself and Thea since Spiros died. But I've read about cases of tug-of-love children. If Spiros's family have found out that he had a child before he died, I can understand their interest in Thea's welfare. But they have absolutely *no* claim on her, because we were never married.'

Sara sighed deeply, and gave a brief shrug of her tense

shoulders. 'However, if…if Spiros's family want to see his daughter, I…I won't deny them access. And…and perhaps we could come to some arrangement regarding visits to Greece.'

All the same, the thought filled her with dread. There might be some loophole in the law which would allow the family of a part-Greek national to lay full claim to Thea. She was such a beautiful child, they were bound to fall in love with her…want her, and…

'They have no knowledge of Thea's existence.' Alexander suddenly interjected coldly.

Sara's heart momentarily eased with relief, before she raised her head to gaze at him in surprise. If Spiros's family didn't know that he'd had a child, what was all this about?

'They don't even know *you* exist, Sara,' he continued. 'And, that is the way it is going to stay – unless you decide to contact them at some time in the future.' His eyes levelled with hers. 'Neither you or Thea have anything to fear from Spiros's family. And you have nothing to fear from me either.'

'So why…*why* all this mystery?' Sara demanded bitterly. 'You've brought my daughter and me to this island. You have watched us ever since our arrival. And you're here now, casting doubts on my relationship with Spiros and filling my head with desperate worries about my daughter. Just what do you *want* from us?'

She glared at him. The damned man wasn't making any attempt to give her an explanation for his actions. He was merely gazing out over the sea. Admittedly, he was looking troubled. But so what? What right had he to look that way, when *she* was the one having to face all these problems?

Jumping abruptly to her feet, Sara declared, 'This is a totally ridiculous situation – and I won't put up with it any longer! I intend to pack up and leave tomorrow.'

But, to her intense annoyance, there was no reaction to

her words from Alexander. The man seemed to be buried in a world of his own, continuing to stare fixedly out to sea.

'I think it's time you left,' she told him bluntly. 'You obviously have nothing more to say. Although, thanks to you, I'm going to have a sleepless night trying to come to terms with what you've told me. So why don't you go home to your mistress – and leave me in peace!'

Suddenly she had his full attention, his dark head turning as he stared at her in astonishment.

'What "mistress"?' he rasped as he rose slowly to his feet.

Sara raised a dark brow, wishing she hadn't lost her temper and let that slip out. It really had nothing to do with her. 'Well – you do have a mistress, don't you?' she muttered.

His dark eyes narrowed angrily, as if he was insulted by the suggestion. Sara didn't want to get in any deeper than she was already, but she guessed she owed him something.

'Look,' she sighed heavily, 'you seem to know all about me, Alexander, but I'm no fool. Did you really think I would be stupid enough to accept your invitation to come here to Greece with my daughter without checking up on you?'

He looked taken aback, his dark eyes startled.

'Yes, of course I did my homework on you before I came out here,' she went on in response to his unspoken question. 'I'd have been an idiot not to. In fact, as I have contacts out here on the Greek islands. I probably know as much about you as you know of me,' she added defiantly.

He frowned at her for a moment, before giving a harsh rumble of sardonic laughter.

'If you have indeed made enquiries about me, it would seem that you know very little,' he told her grimly. 'If you did, you certainly would never have come anywhere near this island!'

Sara gave a sigh of both impatience and frustration. This man did nothing but speak in riddles.

'Quite frankly, Alexander, I've now got to the point where I simply don't care why you brought us to this island,' she told him bluntly. 'In fact, I'm sick and tired of your dramatic games.'

For the first time his mouth creased into a smile. Although heavily sardonic, it nevertheless relaxed the harsh lines of his features. For the first time in their acquaintance he seemed almost human, but the words that came from his thinned lips were to Sara's ears mysteriously *inhuman*.

'If you knew the truth, you wouldn't sound so cynically dismissive of me.'

'You give me no choice,' she retorted, lifting her chin. 'You talk in riddles, act very strangely and then, when I ask you what this is all about, I get nothing but evasive answers. I think you live such a shallow life that you have to invent mysteries – just to amuse yourself! Well, I'm now thoroughly bored with all this nonsense,' she added, raising a hand to cover her lips as she pretended to yawn with boredom.

In a flash, his hand snaked out to clasp hold of her wrist. His fingers tightened in an iron grip as he pulled her roughly towards him, and her heart thudded in her chest at the sudden proximity of his tall figure.

His black eyes glinted angrily down at her. 'This is no joking matter. Both our lives are going to change drastically in the next few weeks,' he growled, his voice heavy with menace. 'Believe me, Sara, there will be times when you'll wish that you had never been born. And I must tell you that my heart is full of dread for our future.'

'What future?' Sara couldn't help giving a snort of nervous laughter. 'We are not likely to have any "future" – especially as I have every intention of leaving this villa first thing tomorrow!'

'You will never leave this island,' he said flatly, the note of utter certainty in his voice causing Sara to stiffen. 'I'm afraid that you are now trapped here. We are both trapped.'

Suddenly he let her go, almost flinging her hand back at her.

'When I discovered your existence, I hoped that you would prove to be a sweet English rose. I prayed that you would be the sort of woman to make it easier for me.' His lips thinned. 'Sadly, my prayers have not been answered. You have, unfortunately, turned out to be a feisty beauty with fire in your blood, and you are clearly already threatening to make my life a living hell. But I will get what I want in the end. It is my right!' His fist came down hard on the table, as if to emphasise his determination.

It was such a dramatic gesture, and his words were so astonishingly bizarre, that Sara simply refused to take him seriously.

She shook her head, her long dark hair a moving curtain around her face. 'You have no rights where I am concerned. So stop trying to frighten me. But if you insist on playing this absurd game of yours you might at least tell me what you *do* want. Not that it will make any difference to *my* life,' she added hurriedly. 'But it's obviously deeply troubling *you*!'

She wondered whether she had gone too far. His fists clenched at his sides, and the muscles of his broad shoulders and strong, muscular arms were clearly taut and strained beneath his shirt as he tensed his whole body. His face was stiff with suppressed anger.

'Thea is what I want,' he said lethally.

The words echoed in Sara's head, until she swayed and had to close her eyes to steady herself. She had been right. He wanted to take her daughter away from her. He *must* be working for Spiros's family after all. He meant to take her, and…

She felt Alexander's body against hers, her senses spinning at the heat and firmness of his tall figure. Her blue eyes widened with alarm as he moved his hands up to tighten his grip her upper arms. His face was still taut and strained, his eyes still darkly threatening. When he spoke, the tone of his voice was low and almost emotional, but the words were terrifying.

'Both you and Thea come as a package. It is the only way,' he told her flatly. 'You deny that we have a future – but I can assure you that we have. Not the future of our choice, of course. The fates are not likely to be that generous. Both of us must surely have sinned somewhere in the past,' he mused quietly, almost to himself. 'Why else should we now find ourselves facing such punishment?'

Sara, confused and disorientated, tried to move away from him. She didn't understand one word of what Alexander was saying. But she had not the slightest doubt that he was deadly serious. His whole being seemed filled with a deep turmoil, his features so deeply etched with pain that she couldn't help responding to his inner agony and pain.

'I don't understand you,' she whispered faintly. She didn't struggle against him any more. He was still holding her, head bent now, so she couldn't see into his eyes. She asked herself why she wasn't afraid of him when she clearly had every reason to be. Alexander was, after all, threatening to take her daughter away from her! No...she checked herself quickly, that wasn't quite right. He'd never actually *said* that he was going to do so. But...but he obviously seemed to want Thea, so what was the difference? What did all this mean?

Slowly he lifted his hand to cup her chin, holding it firmly as if to steady her. His dark eyes stared intently down into hers.

'You will learn, in the future, that I do not take marriage lightly,' he whispered softly. 'It is a serious commitment. Although in our case, of course, it will have little to do with love. But it is necessary. And it is inevitable.'

Sara tried to move her chin from his fingers. She didn't

know whether to laugh or cry. Whether this was a deadly serious situation – or a hysterically funny one. Either way, Alexander Karakou seemed to have lost all grip on reality.

'I don't know what you're talking about!' she seethed through clenched teeth. 'I'm not interested in any talk of marriage – or listening to your views on the subject. What the devil has it to do with me?'

He bent his head and pressed his mouth to hers, holding her chin so firmly that she had no chance of escape. Shocked, her whole body frozen in panic, Sara endured the kiss which was charged with fire.

It was a kiss without end. Long and slow, falling between passionate feeling and sheer experimentation as to how far to push her. Sara couldn't respond to it, *wouldn't* respond. No man had kissed her so intimately since Spiros. She had thought she was dead inside, but...but, oh, God – she wasn't! A spark blazed between them, but Sara *wouldn't* acknowledge it. He was a stranger. Nothing and no one to her. While Spiros had been her only love...

'Cold,' he murmured with dissatisfaction as he drew back from her at last.

Sara gazed up at him in grim amusement. 'What on earth did you expect?' she retorted. 'Flaming passion, from a complete stranger? We mean nothing to each other, Alexander. So why should there be any feeling?'

His thumb brushed over her tremulous hot lips, wiping away the moisture. He smiled thinly. 'I suppose it isn't necessary, of course. But the thought of some fiery passion might help us through the long, dark nights that are going to be our life in the future.'

Her eyes narrowed, not amused any more. 'You know, I'm beginning to think that you are quite mad – and this is one of my more vivid nightmares.'

'I am not mad and, as you will learn, I'm also very serious,' he stated firmly, before turning and walking away, towards the steps on the edge of the terrace, leading down to the beach. 'I'm leaving now. Tomorrow I will be back in your life, *and* the day after that. I don't want to rush you.'

'Huh?' Sara gave a caustic laugh. 'Rush me into what?' she called angrily after his fast disappearing figure.

He didn't respond in any way. Wide shoulders hunched, dark head slightly bent, he strode rapidly away.

Sara watched him disappear into the dark of the night, heading along the beach towards the next cove. When he had finally gone, like a fading apparition, she seriously began to wonder about her sanity. Had this evening really happened? Had he actually been here?

As Sara sat on the terrace into the early hours of the morning, the burning impression of his mouth on hers was the only confirmation that Alexander *had* been there – that he *had* been real. She desperately tried to make sense of everything he'd said, but it was almost impossible to do so.

However, one thing he had done, and which was causing her such deep pain, had been to raise so many awful doubts in her mind about Spiros. All these years she had kept him alive as a part of her life – both for her own sanity and for the sake of her daughter. And now, and in one short evening, Alexander Karakou had destroyed that faith. Because she now knew that, for whatever reason, Spiros had lied to her about his family.

Well, Alexander would be back tomorrow, and perhaps then… Almost without thought, she brushed a hand over her lips, but there was little she could do to banish the feeling that she had somehow been branded by that kiss, still feeling shocked and disturbed by the touch of his mouth on hers. Strangely, the after-effect of his embrace was somehow becoming more intense, rather than fading with time.

He had said she was cold. Which, of course, she wasn't. But she was damned if she was going to let him know *just* how disturbing she found his dark, powerful body. But he hadn't been cold. His whole being had clearly responded to hers, showing that underneath his cool and sophisticated aura there lay a deeply passionate nature.

At last Sara went to bed. Lying motionless under her thin cotton sheet, she tried to ignore her strange mixture of feelings about Alexander Karakou. There was no doubt that he was a very attractive man. But her instinctive response to his potent mixture of sensuality and suppressed passion meant that he was also high dangerous as far as she was concerned. As for all the business about marriage…and a future life together? What utter nonsense! she told herself with a tired yawn, before slowly slipping into a deep sleep.

chapter two

'I heard voices last night,' Thea said, as they were having breakfast on the terrace.

It was another scorching hot day, which was quite normal for this time of the year in Greece. But Sara found herself wishing for a summer storm, to clear her aching head of all the troubling thoughts and emotions which had been raised last night by her visitor.

'It was Alexander Karakou,' Sara told her, spooning sugar into her coffee and stirring it thoughtfully. 'He's the man on the cliff top: the man who owns this villa. He came here to see how we are enjoying our holiday. He said he would come again.'

'And he has!'

Sara jumped. Thea giggled through a mouthful of yoghurt as Alexander appeared around the side of the villa. He was wearing white cotton trousers, which emphasised his slim waist and lean hips, with the sleeves of his mint-green short-sleeved shirt rolled up to display his muscular arms, and dusty white espadrilles on his feet. He looked far more casual and relaxed than they had seen him before.

'Wipe the yoghurt from your mouth, Thea,' Sara told her, quickly handing her a napkin as Alexander smiled down at the small girl before pulling out a cane chair from the table – and proceeding to sit down, just as if he had every right to be here. Which he had, of course, Sara thought dejectedly. It was his villa, after all.

'So – you are Thea?'

'Yes. And you're Alexander Kar...Kara...' Thea giggled again and went pink.

'Karakou,' he finished for her. 'It isn't an easy name to say. So, you may call me Alex,' he added, giving Thea the sort of warm, intimate smile he had never bothered to bestow on her mother.

She should lose sleep over that! Sara told herself sardonically, watching as Thea reached out to shake Alexander's hand over the rustic breakfast table. 'Pleased to meet you,' they both said together...*and* laughed at one other.

Sara found herself feeling unaccountably annoyed to see that they were obviously getting on so well together. She was also equally annoyed to find herself instinctively responding to the warmth of his engaging smile. It had the effect of almost instantly transforming his usual expression of dark, brooding menace into one of a very relaxed and amiable, good-looking man.

'Thea, would you go into the kitchen for a coffee cup for Alexander? They are on the top shelf, so you will have to climb up on a chair to get it. Be careful.'

Thea was about to do as she was told, but as she got up from the table Alexander did too. 'I'll get it,' he said quickly.

'No,' Sara said, motioning her daughter to the house with a wave of her hand.

Alexander glared at her as Thea skipped off inside the villa. 'She could easily fall and hurt herself,' he pointed out sternly.

Sara glared back, not appreciating his concern. 'She's five years old, going on for six, and —'

'I know exactly how old she is,' Alexander snapped.

Sara felt her insides going cold again. 'Will you stop this?' she hissed at him across the table. 'And for goodness' sake – sit down. I purposely sent Thea on a mission that will take a few minutes because I don't want her to hear what I have to say,' Sara added as he lowered himself down into his chair.

'I've hardly slept all night, worrying myself sick about

your intentions,' she continued. 'I'm being as civilised as I can about the whole business. Only because, for some crazy reason, I happen to believe that you mean us no harm. Although for the life of me I can't think why – when I clearly have every reason to mistrust you.'

'You have nothing to fear from me,' he assured her.

And, strangely enough, she was quite sure that she hadn't.

Call it a gut feeling – or whatever – but right from the onset of their brief acquaintance she had been far more curious than fearful. Perhaps that was due to the fact that she'd lived for some time on the Greek islands, and had always found she could trust the people she'd met and worked with. Or maybe it was because he was obviously such a respectable citizen and she had never heard anything bad said about him. Besides, Alexander was also the father of a child. Which must mean that he was unlikely to harm her daughter. All the same...he was far too attractive...

'But how can I really *know* that I have nothing to fear from you?' Sara persisted. 'Ever since I arrived on this island you've been behaving in a most peculiar way. As for last night...well, your conduct can only be described as bizarre! And yet here you are again, forcing yourself on both myself and my daughter, and further encroaching into our lives.'

'It is necessary,' he said quietly.

'No, it isn't,' Sara insisted, shaking her head. 'Nothing is "necessary", unless and until you tell me what this is all about. What *is* the point of bringing us both here and then not saying what you want from us?'

When he didn't reply to her outburst, Sara found herself struggling to control her temper.

'Quite frankly, I'm not prepared to stand another day of this nonsense. I shall just pack up and leave.'

He smiled thinly and toyed with the edge of Thea's discarded napkin.

'Yes, I do believe you would,' he said. 'And I admire you for your caution where your daughter is concerned. You're clearly a devoted mother, and that is a great relief to me.'

Sara rolled her blue eyes up at the sky. 'Here we go again! The man who speaks in riddles! Why on earth should the fact that I'm a normal, caring mother be a great relief to you?' she asked impatiently.

'Because it shows that you have all the right attributes to be a successful wife.'

There was a sudden glint of humour in his dark, luminous eyes. But it was sadly wasted on Sara, who merely shook her head in exasperation.

'You know, I've tried to piece together the various weird remarks and statements you've made since we met – and for the life of me I still can't get the picture.'

'You will, when all is revealed,' he murmured enigmatically, before all trace of humour left his face and he leaned across the table, his tall figure rigid with tension.

'But for the present – will you trust me?' he demanded, his voice harsh and insistent. 'Forget that I am a stranger to you and Thea. Forget all that I have done to get you here. Believe me, I care what happens to you and your daughter,' he added, his voice throbbing with deep sincerity. 'I only have Thea's best interests at heart.'

'Well, *if* you care so much about Thea and myself – and I don't see how you can, since we've only just met – why can't you tell me what's going on? Why all the mystery? And if it's some sort of puzzle why not give me the rest of the pieces, so that I can solve it for myself? You're simply not being fair or reasonable.'

'No, I am not,' he agreed. 'Mainly because I have no wish to be cruel. Something you will only understand when we get to know each other better. However, it is necessary. It's the only way.'

Sara glared at him, inwardly counting the minutes or even seconds before Thea reappeared. She had wanted to get this sorted before her daughter came back, but Alexander was being his usual impossible self. Why wouldn't he tell her what was going on – *right now*! – and put an end to this secrecy once and for all?

'I want you to imagine that we met on the beach, just now,' he murmured softly, obviously equally aware that the little girl was likely to return to the terrace at any minute. 'A casual morning stroll. You've asked me back for coffee, and we will make arrangements to spend the day together. A very relaxed, happy day: swimming and laughing together, having fun…'

'My imagination isn't capable of being *that* wild!' she interjected sarcastically. 'Besides, how do I know that you're actually *capable* of having fun?'

There was no doubt about it – he really was the *most* peculiar man she'd ever met! Now it appeared that he wanted to act out some crazy drama with her – a bizarre sort of 'getting-to-know-you' scenario. And what was that supposed to lead to…?

Grimacing with impatience, Sara jumped to her feet. 'Get a life of your own, Alexander,' she advised him flatly. But before she was able to take more that a step towards the interior of the villa, he swiftly grasped her arm, pulling her roughly towards his tall figure.

'Until only a few months ago I was quite capable of having fun,' he told her in a deep, throbbing voice, his handsome features twisted with pain. 'Indeed, I lived a perfectly normal life. But all that changed when I discovered something that concerns not only myself but also you and your daughter. And now there will be no more fun, or joy, or happiness in my life. Not until the problem is resolved. I've tried to assure you that I mean you no harm, but still you will not trust me. I don't want to resort to forcing you to do anything against your will. But I may have to, if you won't give me a chance...'

As he suddenly let her go Sara heard a sound, and swung round to see Thea stepping over the threshold of the kitchen door, gingerly carrying a coffee cup and saucer. Alexander, who must have heard her approach, had quickly dropped his expression of grim determination – and was now all charm and warmth once again. But only for her daughter, Sara noted grimly.

'How kind of you, Thea. Strolling on the beach makes me thirsty,' he said, taking the cup and saucer from the little girl. 'It's nice to be invited to coffee,' he added, giving Sara a meaningful look, as if urging her to join in the game he had invented for them all.

Thea gazed up at him and smiled shyly. 'I'm not allowed coffee yet. Mama says I'm too young. I don't like it, anyway. It tastes bitter.'

Alexander nodded. 'She's right; you are too young. Now if Mama would like to pour me some coffee, we can plan what we will do with the day.' With a wide smile he swung the cup and saucer in Sara's direction.

Sara instinctively took it from his hands, before glaring angrily at him, only too well aware that her daughter was regarding Alexander with wide-eyed, childish awe.

'Would you like to see something of the island?' he was asking Thea. 'There are many coves to explore, and...'

'It's what I like doing best,' the little girl responded enthusiastically. 'Mama calls me a beachcomber, because I like to find crabs and shells. That's because my papa loved the sea, and Mama says that I'm just like him.'

Secretly wishing her lovely daughter wasn't quite so open, Sara was startled to see Alexander's dark eyes becoming clouded, a pulse beating wildly at his temple as he clenched his fist, the knuckles white with tension. And then, quite unexpectedly, she suddenly found herself instinctively wanting to comfort this man. To soothe away the sight of such distress and misery which tugged painfully at her heart.

'Will you allow me to show you both around the island?' he asked Sara. His voice was low and slightly cracked, and she wondered what could possibly be the cause of such deep unhappiness.

'Oh, please, Mama, let's go. I want to see the island. Stefios says there are caves and dragons...'

'No dragons, I promise you,' Alexander laughed.

Sara almost gasped out loud, her heart giving a sudden lurch at the unexpected tenderness and laughter in Alexander's face as he gazed down at Thea.

Damn the man! Not only was he clearly capable of turning his charm on and off, like a tap, but he was also far too sexually attractive for his own good – or hers. Already Thea was halfway to eating out of his hand. And as for herself...?

Sara gave a helpless sigh of resignation. She hadn't the heart to disappoint her daughter, who was clearly determined to accompany Alexander around the island. And she certainly wasn't prepared to let Thea go on her own. Not when this man was behaving in such an odd, unstable manner.

'Can we go, Mama? Please say yes!'

It seemed she had no choice. So Sara forced herself to smile and nodded her agreement. Thea jumped excitedly and ran back into the villa to get everything she needed for their day out.

Left alone on the terrace, the two adults gazed at each other. Alexander was the first to speak.

'This is the beginning,' he murmured softly.

The beginning of...*what*? she queried silently, knowing it was useless to continue asking questions which he had no intention of answering. Increasingly, this whole bizarre situation seemed to be taking on the character of quicksand, with herself in imminent danger of being sucked down into an unknown dangerous quagmire.

'OK – you've got your own way. We are going to spend this day with you. But I would like something from you in return,' she told him quietly but firmly.

He stared at her silently for a moment. 'I'm not used to striking bargains in my private life,' he said at last.

'Nor am I!' Sara retorted. 'But so far you have given very little. Surely a promise isn't too much to ask in return for satisfying your extraordinarily strange whims and fancies?'

'Be careful, Sara,' he warned. 'The problem I face is not a trivial one. Indeed, when you have to face the truth, you will regret treating it so lightly.'

'I have to treat it lightly because otherwise I'd be scared to death,' she told him bluntly. 'You've stated that you have no connection with Spiros's family and have no interest in claiming Thea,' Sara continued tersely, 'but your obvious preoccupation with both my daughter and myself is, quite frankly, something I find deeply disturbing. If it wasn't for the fact that you are a father yourself, I wouldn't even be standing on this terrace talking to you.'

'How did you know that I have a daughter?' he demanded, his expression suddenly tense and strained.

Sara gave a heavy sigh, heartily fed up with all this subterfuge.

'It came up in…er…my enquiries,' she told him evasively, not wishing to admit that she'd been given the information by Maria. The other woman had become a friend, and she didn't want to cause any trouble for someone who worked for Alexander. 'It's one of the reasons why I'm sure that you mean us no harm,' she continued quietly. 'But I need…I *have* to know the truth that lies behind all these mysterious statements of yours. So, that's what I want in return for this outing, Alexander. I want your promise to tell me everything, by the end of the day.'

He sighed, and shook his head. 'If I made that promise it would present me with an impossible task.'

Sara frowned. 'Why?'

'To have only just one day to convince you of the necessity…to make you realise that you have no choice but to commit yourself to me for the rest of your life…is impossible. I cannot do so in such a short space of time.'

Sara gazed at him in open-mouthed astonishment, before giving way to a ripple of slightly hysterical laughter.

'Oh, come on, Alexander – do me a favour! What are we talking about here? Some sort of crazy marriage proposal?' she grinned. 'I like to think that I've got a good sense of humour. But…but this is utterly ridiculous!'

He stiffened, his face frozen into a rigid mask of anger. 'I didn't realise that you would find the idea of marriage to me quite so amusing,' he ground out tersely.

Realising that he was deeply offended, Sara swallowed quickly, trying to control the bubbles of laughter threatening to break from her throat any minute.

To be fair to the man, she had to admit that most women would probably jump at an opportunity of marrying a gorgeous-looking, extremely wealthy Greek ship-owner. But she wasn't one of them. In fact, marriage was just about the *last* thing on her mind, she told herself wryly, still trying to suppress her laughter.

And then, quite suddenly, she found herself sobering up fast, her heart pounding like a sledgehammer. Surely he couldn't…he couldn't be *serious*? Was it possible that all those peculiar remarks and odd statements had *really* been leading up to a marriage proposal? No – of course not! For heaven's sake, she barely knew the man!

Sara shrugged, quickly deciding that she must have mistaken his meaning. So, obviously the best thing to do would be to keep on treating the whole subject as a huge joke.

'Not slipping on a banana skin sort of funny, Alexander.' She grinned. 'More funny *peculiar*. Because if I didn't get around to marrying the man I lived with, and whom I loved so much, I'm hardly likely to consider marrying a complete stranger!'

He smiled, and Sara was relieved to see that she'd been quite right. While it really wasn't all that funny, Alexander had obviously been only joking about the subject of marriage.

'These circumstances are dramatically different, as you will find out,' he informed her cryptically. 'Love may not be a consideration with us, but our marriage will happen because it is necessary.'

Sara's blue eyes widened and her heart was tumbling now. 'You *can't* be serious!' she exclaimed.

He remained silent, but his eyes said so much. They were dark and penetrating and very, *very* determined.

She could feel her heart beginning to thump in panic. *Oh God – he wasn't joking*! He really *did* mean it. For some completely unknown reason, he appeared grimly intent on marrying her!

But why on earth should he want to do so? Because he wanted Thea and it was the only way of getting her? But, no, that was absurd. In fact, this whole situation was becoming totally surreal!

'My answer is no. Emphatically no,' she ground out, her chin clenched with determination. 'If I ever marry, it will be for love. And, since I lost the only man I've ever loved, it's hardly likely that I would marry *you*!'

'Only *hardly* likely...?' he mocked, placing his hand beneath her chin and tilting her face up towards him.

Sara froze, recalling that the last time he'd done that his touch had been swiftly followed by a kiss.

'So, it seems that I will just have to make you love me. Because our marriage will definitely take place,' he told her softly, his words ringing in her ears with deadly intent.

As Thea ran out on to the terrace Alexander quickly let go of her chin, although still firmly holding Sara's wide-eyed, outraged gaze with a steely, determined glint in his dark eyes. Almost as if he was daring her to contradict him, she told herself incredulously.

'I'm ready,' Thea announced excitedly.

Sara spun around to her daughter, eager for the diversion and thankful that the little girl had appeared when she did. If he had emphasised his determination to marry her with a devastating kiss, then…then what…?

Thea had scrubbed her face until it shone, and changed into her very best floral print cotton dress, all blues and yellows, which were her favourite colours. She was clutching her plastic see-through rucksack, brimming with all her precious possessions – books, shells and coloured pencils – and grinning from ear to ear with excitement.

Knowing that she couldn't bear to disappoint her daughter, Sara gave a slight shrug of resignation. 'I'd better leave a note for Maria,' she muttered. 'She'll wonder where we are when she arrives to clean the villa.'

'When I passed through the village I had a word with Maria,' Alexander told her, a faint smile on his lips. 'She knows that you won't be here.'

Sara frowned. It obviously hadn't crossed his mind that she might refuse his invitation. Did he always get his own way?

'Thea, you can't possibly want to take all that stuff with you,' Sara told her daughter, who merely grinned, before turning her wide eyes on Alexander in mute appeal. 'You won't need books when you're beachcombing and…'

'There's plenty of room in the car. She can take anything she wants.'

Sara stiffened in response to the fact that Alexander was clearly overriding her authority with her daughter. Of course, he was only interested in Thea, she reminded herself grimly. Oh, God – why couldn't he have come out with the truth before they set out? And would he tell her what was going on at the end of the day? She doubted it. Because so far each and every one of her questions had been met with evasion. Well, he wasn't going to get away with it after this evening. Or certainly not if she could help it!

Touring the eastern coast of the island, they came across wonderful views that almost took her breath away, and Sara soon realised that it was far better to try and relax and enjoy herself – rather than brood over the problems and peculiarities of Alexander. Tourism hadn't yet begun to change the island, but there were signs of imminent invasion, with plots scoured out of the hillsides for villas and apartments. But mostly, however, it was as tranquil, hot and sleepy as it had been for centuries.

Alexander drove leisurely, pointing out places of historic interest and knowing instinctively when Thea was on the edge of boredom and doing something about it. Like just now, when he had pulled off the main road and taken a narrow winding track down to a small secluded, sandy cove, with rock pools beneath the cliffs.

The cove was completely deserted, and after insisting that Thea change into her swimsuit Sara sat on a rock in the shade of some prickly shrubbery. Pulling her light Indian cotton skirt up over her thighs, and resting her chin on her bare knees, she watched as Alexander and her daughter carefully examined the rock pools, stooping over them to stare down through the clear, still water at small sea creatures.

It was quite obvious that they were completely at ease with each other. Although Thea was growing up without a father figure, she seemed to be having no problems with Alexander. And he, maybe because he was a father himself, was clearly at ease with the little girl. Sara guessed he was probably a good father, caring and attentive. But his wife was dead. So, was he looking to somehow extend his family and provide a stepmother for his daughter? With herself and Thea as a ready-made family, with no other encumbrances? Was *that* the reason he had alluded to their future together?

Sara suddenly hugged her knees, almost laughing out loud at herself for even considering such a ridiculous idea. She must be out of her mind! This was everyday life – not some fantastically exotic soap opera!

'Hey, I'm getting hungry,' she shouted down the beach to them.

Alexander turned from his crouching position over a rippling pool and gave her an encouraging wave.

'Mama, come and look. Alex says it's something fantastic,' Thea called out, before putting her small hands over her mouth, trying to stifle her giggles.

'Oh, yes, very funny!' Sara said sarcastically a few moments later, leaning over the pool and peering into its depths. 'Goodness me! It must be a prehistoric beer can. And English, too. We'd better inform the British Museum!'

Alexander stood up and grinned at her. 'You never know, it might be worth a fortune in a few thousand years' time.'

'It must have come all the way down the River Thames, and under all the bridges, and into the English Channel,' Thea told them quickly, then fell silent as she tried to think which sea came next.

Alexander laughed and ruffled her glossy dark curls. 'Don't worry about it, Thea. I think that one came via the airways, not by sea.'

'Oh, yes,' Thea murmured, still bent over the pool.

Sara met Alexander's eyes over the top of her daughter's crouched form. He looked so relaxed, so different from the man who had studied them from the cliff top with such a brooding, menacing air for well over a week before finally breaking his silence. But she noted that, deep within his dark gleaming eyes, there still remained a trace of pain and sadness.

'If I don't eat soon, I shall faint away,' she joked lightly, deliberately breaking the eye contact between them. 'Thea, are you hungry?'

'Yes, I'd like fishes – just like the ones you told me about. The ones you and Papa used to cook on the beach,' Thea said, before looking up at Alexander. 'Have you ever cooked fishes on the beach?'

For a second, Alexander looked wistful. 'No...no, I haven't. But it sounds fun – and very romantic.' He was looking at Sara as he spoke, and she could feel a flush of hot colour flooding over her face.

'You keep Spiros alive for her, don't you?' he stated quietly as they strolled back across the beach to the car. Thea had run on ahead, bumping her rucksack filled with seashells over the sandy dunes and thick, stiff tussocks of grass.

'Of course,' Sara murmured. 'It's always seemed the natural thing to do. Most children have two parents, even if they're not living together. I have photos of Spiros, and Thea knows that he is her father. So, yes, I've done my best to keep him alive for her.'

'There has been no other man in your lives since his death...?'

'No, there hasn't been anyone else,' she admitted, her eyes slightly misty. 'There couldn't be,' she added sadly.

'He really did mean everything to you?'

'Yes, he did.'

Alexander shrugged. 'He was a very fortunate man,' he murmured under his breath as he stared straight ahead.

If Alexander regarded a man losing his life at twenty-five as 'fortunate' – what did he think of as misfortune? Sara asked herself grimly. However, she remained silent, because she knew what he meant. And it had been a compliment, in a way, although not one she found welcome.

'And what about you? Do you keep your wife alive for your daughter?' Sara asked as they reached the car, deliberately keeping her voice low because of Thea, who was busy loading her rucksack into the boot of his car.

About to open the driver's door, he suddenly swung round to face Sara. Gone were the relaxed features, and once again he was stiff and rigid with tension. Sara wished she hadn't asked. The death of his wife had obviously devastated him.

'If it hurts to talk about it, I will understand if you don't want to,' she assured him softly

'Eleni's mother died only two years ago,' he said tersely. 'My daughter remembers her, and a day doesn't pass without her asking for her mama – nor a night in which she doesn't pray for her return. Believe me, Sara, my daughter doesn't need *me* to keep her mother's memory alive for her.'

He turned back to the car and snatched open the door. Thea was already in the back, buckling up her seat belt and eager to go wherever this man was planning to take them.

Sara took a few seconds to bring herself under control, before sliding in the passenger seat next to Alexander, feeling as if her heart was about to cave in. She was beginning to understand that his present life held great sadness and sorrow. Although Thea had lost her father, she had never suffered the grief of loss, principally because she had never known him. But Eleni, Alexander's daughter, had known her mother, had suffered the tragedy of her death and clearly was still deeply mourning her loss.

'I'm very sorry,' she murmured softly. 'I really didn't mean to pry,' she added helplessly, knowing that her words were inadequate, but the best she could manage.

He said nothing, simply nodded his dark head in acceptance of her apology, and Sara didn't speak again till they

pulled up outside a beachside taverna, specialising in bar-
becued fish.

'You're spoiling Thea,' she told him as they all got out of
the car, with Thea running on ahead, ever eager to explore
new sights. 'However, I think you might live to regret it.'
Sara grinned, desperately wanting to lighten the atmosphere
between them.

'Meaning what?' Alexander asked. He had clearly relaxed during the short drive from the cove, and was once
again capable of responding to her light-hearted teasing.

'You'll soon find out,' she laughed, following her
daughter around the side of the taverna towards the beach.

There were a few Greek families there already, some
sitting at parasol-covered tables, others on beach rugs
sprawled on the hot sand. All turned and gazed in curiosity
at the new arrivals, before continuing their family gossip.

Alexander directed them to a canvas parasol-shaded
table, far enough way from the other diners not to be
overheard, but close enough to be a part of the gathering.

'Do you know anyone here?' Sara asked after the owner
had brought them a huge flagon of iced wine. Thea was
already fidgeting and looking longingly at the other children, who were playing with frisbees and beach balls.

Alexander looked around and shook his head. 'I move
around, so I'm not often here. My work is chiefly on the
mainland. And, of course, I own property on other islands.'

Sara smiled at her daughter. 'OK, Thea, you can go and
play with the other children. I'll call you when the lunch
comes,' she added as Thea jumped to her feet, calling out to
the children in Greek.

Alexander stared after her and then directed an astonished gaze at Sara. 'You are teaching her Greek?'

'Of course. She *is* half-Greek, after all,' Sara pointed out
as she poured the cold wine into their glasses. 'You said you
move around. With your daughter, Eleni?'

He stared at her, as if he had completely forgotten what they'd been talking about.

Sara grinned at him. 'You don't like it, do you? When *I* am the one to probe into your life, as you have done in mine.' She pushed a glass of wine towards him. 'I guess you won't approve of me pouring the wine, either!'

'It is usually the man's place to do such a thing,' he agreed stiffly. 'Especially on a first date. But then, Sara, you are not a very *usual* sort of woman!' He was smiling now, his dark eyes sparkling beguilingly as he lifted his glass.

'No, I'm not,' she told him lightly. 'And if you think engaging in a flirtation is the way to my heart – or likely to turn me into your *usual* type of woman – then I'm afraid you're sadly mistaken.'

Sipping the delicious wine, she held his gaze over the frosted rim of her glass. 'I've had to be strong since Thea was born,' she explained softly. 'I've had to make decisions for both of us – to take on the job of a father as well as a mother. When I returned to England it meant rebuilding my life without any help from my family. My parents are divorced and have new lives of their own,' she added with a shrug of her slim shoulders. 'But, in any case, I suspect that they would have disapproved of my relationship with Spiros.'

Sara paused for a moment, gazing down at her glass of wine. 'Just as Spiros's family would probably have disapproved of me, if they had known about our relationship,' she admitted with a heavy sigh. 'Anyway, I came back to England with a Greek baby. Definitely *not* what my parents had planned for my future.'

'Have they never accepted her?'

'I haven't exactly given them the opportunity to do so,' she admitted ruefully. 'I returned home mentally bruised and still in deep shock over the sudden loss of Spiros. So I just withdrew into a closed world with Thea. Caring for her and loving her, while weeping my heart out for our loss. And then I gradually came to my senses. I realised that there wasn't anyone else to lean on, and so it was up to me to bring up my daughter. I started working from home linked up by computer to my previous travel company. I've now got a nice, small terraced house on the outskirts of London, Thea is at school nearby, and perhaps when we get back home, I'll look my parents up and...'

She glanced up to see that he was regarding her with raised, quizzical dark eyebrows, a sardonic smile playing on his lips.

'Oh, dear – I seem to have forgotten that, according to *your* version of events, we're not going home!' Sara gave a gurgle of wry laughter. 'How did the story go...? We are staying, because you and I are going to be married? And with my daughter and your daughter – we are going to live happily ever after...?'

Sara suddenly glared down at her wine, wishing she hadn't sipped so much on an empty stomach. She looked up to see that he was watching her, his eyes dark and intense. Surprisingly, he didn't appear angry at her sarcastic jibe, merely pensive and thoughtful.

She shrugged and looked away, fixing her gaze on the blue horizon as it merged with the brighter blue of the sea. 'Sorry, I shouldn't have brought that up. Especially as it was such an utterly daft idea. We were having a nice time, and it looks as if I've gone and spoiled it.'

'There is no point in pushing the idea of our marriage under the carpet,' he said firmly. 'I can promise you that it *is* going to happen. So, perhaps it's best that we do discuss the subject. Because the sooner you realise that I'm *not* joking, the sooner you will accept that neither of us has any choice in the matter and come to understand – as I have done – that we have no alternative but to make the best of it.'

Sara gazed at him intently. Oh, my God! He really *hadn't*

been joking. In fact, he was deadly serious!

Realising that there was absolutely no point in arguing with the man, here on the beach and in full view of so many people, Sara decided to ignore the whole mad idea. Whatever *he* might say, *she* had absolutely no intention of marrying him – or anyone else for that matter. So, why get upset and spoil the day for Thea?

However, despite her best intentions, she found herself idly wondering what it would be like to be married to Alexander Karakou. Living with him, sleeping with him, making love with him…? Quickly pulling herself together, Sara couldn't seem to prevent a deep tide of crimson flooding over her cheeks; her thick lashes fluttered in embarrassment as she hoped and prayed that he wasn't able to read her mind.

'What were you thinking about?' he murmured, his voice low and husky, as if he knew *exactly* what she had been thinking.

'Oh – nothing very important,' she answered swiftly, making a determined effort to think about something else.

Looking across the beach, Sara watched as the owner of the taverna lowered a grill of sardines over the hot, burning olive wood on the barbecue. Just as she and Spiros had sometimes built a fire on the sand at night, grilling sardines and watching the sunset as they sipped their wine together.

Quickly blinking away the weak tears welling up in her eyes, she saw that the children had gathered around to watch the fish being grilled, Thea amongst them. *Oh, no! Thea was far too near the hot grill, her hands raised towards the flames…*

Even as she was opening her mouth to scream a warning, Alexander was already on his feet and racing swiftly across the white sand, reaching the scene well before Sara had even risen from her chair. Running over to join them, she noticed that, so as not to alarm the child, he'd simply drawn Thea back from the cast-iron barbecue, just a few feet out of danger.

In a moment of utter relief and gratitude, Sara placed a trembling hand on his arm. The muscles were hard and knotted with tension, yet his hands resting on her daughter's shoulders appeared relaxed and reassuring. Standing silently beside Alexander and Thea as they watched the sardines sizzling on the fire, Sara was aware of a curious stirring inside her. She had no doubt that he would be a caring husband, a caring father…Quickly withdrawing her hand, she make a desperate effort to pull herself together, vowing not to drink any more wine.

A few minutes later Alexander burst out laughing at the sight of Thea's expression of outrage and disgust as she spluttered and rubbed at her mouth with a paper napkin.

'Oh, I hate sardines! They're horrible!' the little girl cried, reaching for a glass of water on the table.

Sara grinned, leaning across to wipe some drops of oil from her daughter's flushed cheek. 'You'll get to like them in time, darling. Sardines are a bit of an acquired taste.'

'They are horrid – all bony and fishy!'

'I thought you liked fish, Thea?' Alexander laughed, now clearly understanding Sara's amused warning on their arrival at the beach.

'I do. I like fish fingers. I thought the fish cooked on the beach would be the same,' Thea told him, giving one last shudder.

'Fish fingers?' Alexander queried.

'Covered in breadcrumbs, deep fried in oil or butter, and served with piles of chips and tomato ketchup, 'Sara laughed.

'Chips!' The bar owner grinned as he brought another plate of sizzling sardines to the table. 'The little princess shall have chips, *and* tomato ketchup!'

Five minutes later, a plate of chips with a huge fluffy

omelette was placed in front of a very hungry Thea. She
turned to the big man and thanked him in Greek and Sara
noticed how proud Alexander looked. Yes, he would be a
caring, loving father…but not to Thea.

Sara didn't live in a dream world. She never had done.
She might have been silly, and fantasised just now about
being married to Alexander Karakou, but she was only too
well aware that life wasn't a fairy tale. It just wasn't going
to happen. Without love it would be utterly impossible for
her to marry Alexander.

There was no denying that he was a highly attractive man,
whom she found highly disturbing. In fact, she was quite
prepared to admit, if only privately to herself, the devastating effect of his tall firm body pressed closely to her own
when he'd pulled her into his arms before kissing her so
soundly last night. And she was undoubtedly susceptible to
those dark gleaming eyes and his aura of vibrant sex appeal.

But that wasn't so strange. After all, Sara knew that she
wasn't a cold woman. She had more than enough warmth
and love in her. But since Spiros's death she'd allowed no
one to pierce her bruised heart. And if she was now presented with a highly charismatic, sensual man, capable of
causing her heart to flutter, that was hardly a good basis for
marriage!

'Have you enjoyed the day so far?' Alexander asked as
they sipped thick sweet Greek coffee. He was keeping a
watchful eye on Thea playing with the other children on the
beach. And, now Sara came to think of it, he'd clearly been
keeping a watchful eye on the little girl throughout the day.

'Yes, it's been very nice, and Thea has loved every
minute of it.' Sara told him, before being struck by a sudden
thought. 'Is…is your daughter with you on the island?'

'Yes. Why do you ask?'

This time Thea wasn't holding his attention. Sara had it
all. His dark eyes gazing at her intently.

'Well, why didn't you bring her with you? If she's a similar age to Thea, they could have played together,' Sara explained. 'And even if she's a bit younger, Thea would have loved to look after her. She responds well to older children too. So why did you decide to leave your daughter at home?'

His eyes flickered uneasily for a moment, as if he was deciding how to answer her question. But then he gave what appeared to be a small sigh of defeat, before muttering, 'She is very shy and doesn't mix well.'

Once again Sara found herself wishing that she'd kept her mouth shut. The child was obviously still not over her mother's death. And, as a mother herself, Sara felt a tug at her heart, wishing that she could help in some way.

'We'd better go now,' she murmured, setting her empty coffee cup down on the table. 'Thea will be getting tired and…'

'Ah, but the day isn't over yet,' he told her firmly as he rose to his feet. 'We have one last port of call. And then our lives together will begin in earnest.'

He left her standing under the canvas parasol, the shade darkening her face and masking the deep concern in her blue eyes. Why did he have to go and spoil everything with that final, stupid remark? They'd been having a nice time, and although she hadn't forgotten all his nonsensical ideas, they'd at least been able to enjoy each other's company,

With a heavy sigh, Sara turned to walk slowly across the sand to join Thea and Alexander, as he waited by the beach bar to pay the bill.

As she approached, he was chatting to the taverna owner, with Thea smiling up at the big Greek who had cheerfully provided the barbecue for everyone. The small girl had only a tiny grasp of the language, and clearly didn't understand what was being said over her head. But Sara had no such difficulty; her blood ran cold and her spine prickled with apprehension.

But she couldn't step forward and challenge Alexander. Not in front of the grinning taverna owner, nor in front of her daughter. But she definitely had no intention of letting it pass. *Absolutely not*!

As soon as the limousine was in motion on a smooth stretch of road, and Thea had fallen asleep in the back seat, Sara could contain herself no longer.

'I heard your exchange with the taverna owner,' she ground out, seething with anger and barely able to hang on to her temper as she twisted to face him. 'I am definitely *not* your wife and Thea is *not* your daughter. How *dare* you claim us in that way?'

He didn't reply, merely glancing in the rearview mirror as if checking that Thea was asleep. And then, with his eyes firmly fixed on the road ahead, he said quietly, 'The man complimented me on my beautiful wife and daughter. He clearly believed us to be a family…'

'Which we are *not*!' Sara said indignantly. 'So why didn't you correct him?'

'It seemed unnecessary.'

'To you, maybe – but not to me!'

'You are making too much of all this,' he ground out impatiently. 'It is nothing. Forget it.'

Sara glared at him fiercely. 'I am not making too much of it. This is serious, Alexander! You quite deliberately said and did nothing to correct the man's mistake. So, OK…that might be amusing, and I might have been making too much of a small incident. But I also happened to overhear the rest of your conversation. And that wasn't at all amusing.'

As Alexander remained silent, she forced herself to take a deep breath, desperately striving not to lose control. Clenching her fists tightly in her lap, she fought to prevent herself from grabbing hold of the steering wheel and insisting that he stop and let them out.

'For your information,' Sara continued grimly, 'I heard

the owner of the taverna say that your daughter must follow your side of the family, because…because of my blue eyes. And…and you didn't deny it. In fact,' she added angrily, 'you had the cheek to say that Thea was like *your* mother…and took after *her* side of the family!'

Still he said nothing. There was no response from him at her angry protest, only the whitening of his knuckles as they gripped the leather steering wheel, and…and the sight of that damned emotional pulse, once again throbbing at his temple.

Sara leaned back in her seat and closed her eyes tightly. This strange man was driving her crazy! And yet the day had been a happy one. In fact, if she hadn't overheard Alexander's bizarre conversation with the owner of the taverna, she might by now be glowing with a sort of contentment. Because she had to admit that she'd enjoyed their day out together. There had been no male company in her life for so long and…and, yes, she had to admit that she was becoming more and more attracted to him. Strange? Yes, he most certainly was! An enigma? Definitely. Charismatic…? More than any man she'd ever met.

Sara bit her lower lip fiercely. She needed to think of Spiros – right now! She needed to concentrate her thoughts, and…

Her eyes suddenly snapped open, her head jerking round to stare at his hard profile as she felt a strong, warm hand closing firmly over her own, squeezing it gently. She didn't understand and parted her lips to speak, but he gently shushed her.

'Don't wake Thea,' he whispered. 'Not till we are home.'

'Home?' Sara croaked, her heart and pulse-rate beginning to gather pace. She gazed out of the windows to see lush green landscape whizzing by. They were on a part of the island she wasn't familiar with, inland, towards the hills, further and further away from the beachside villa.

'My home…your home…Thea's home,' he muttered under his breath, before letting go of her hand.

Staring blindly down at her fingers, which seemed to still burn from his touch, Sara desperately tried to get some sort of grip on the situation. But the only thought in her mind was that somehow she and Thea were being kidnapped, and…

And then, quite suddenly, a mirage appeared before her eyes. A stunning white palace surrounded by lush green gardens, terraces dripping purple bougainvillaea and tall, swaying palms.

'Mama, where are we?' Thea asked sleepily, unclipping her seat belt to lean forward as Alexander drove slowly up the long drive to the Moorish arches of his palatial home.

'We're home, Thea. This is where you are going to live from now on,' he told her.

As soon as the vehicle came to a halt at the foot of a column of marble steps Sara leaped out of the car and snatched open the rear door. Reaching in and grabbing hold of Thea, she pulled her roughly out, clinging protectively to the little girl.

'Mama!' Thea cried out in bewilderment.

Sara clung tightly on to her, glaring at Alexander in fury and confusion.

'You can't *do* this!' she ground out angrily. 'You have no right. This is *not* our home and…and we are *not* going to live here!'

'You are frightening Thea,' Alexander warned her sternly.

'Mama! Look – there's Maria,' the little girl cried, suddenly twisting out of her mother's grasp and running across to the side of the villa, to where Maria had appeared on their arrival.

Deeply shocked at the sudden appearance of the maid, Sara could only stare at her in stunned confusion. What on earth was Maria doing here? None of this made *any* sense, she told herself, as she turned to follow her daughter.

Alexander stepped quickly forward to catch hold of her arm, swiftly pulling her back – and into his arms. Finding herself held firmly against his tall figure, and utterly bemused and bewildered by the speed of events, it was some moments before Sara slowly began to comprehend the full extent of Alexander's devilish scheme.

With his arms tightening about her like bands of steel, he lowered his dark head, his breath hot and harsh against her face. 'Maria was instructed to pack up all your stuff and bring it here. She believes us to be in the throes of a whirlwind romance, and —'

'*No!*' Sara gasped, suddenly realising that anyone watching them would think they were a loving couple in a romantic embrace. Jerking her head away, she stared up at him, her blue eyes glinting with baffled rage and fury.

'Maria believes nothing of the sort!' she cried. 'We are friends. I was with her yesterday, and she *knows* that I would have told her if there was any romance between us.'

But he ignored both her words and the helpless efforts she was making to twist free of his hard embrace, merely continuing to smile lovingly down at the angry woman in his arms. Clearly this whole nonsense was nothing but an act put on for Maria, who had squatted down to talk to Thea, occasionally throwing inquisitive glances in their direction.

'Love flowers quickly in the heat.' Alexander murmured softly, his arms tightening as he pulled her closer to his hard body. 'It would not have come as a surprise to Maria to know that we are now lovers.'

'*Lovers*…? You must be out of your mind! Why bother to try and fool a maid? And why…*why* try to fool my daughter into thinking that she is going to be living here, in your house? '

He lifted her chin and she knew what he was going to do…but only for Maria's benefit, of course. Thank God her daughter had her back to them and couldn't see what was happening to her mother.

As his mouth came heatedly down on hers, to prevent any further protests with a devastating kiss, she finally realised just what power this man had over her.

She should have listened to her first instincts. Because she now knew just how dangerous he was. He'd said that he wanted her and Thea. And, having tricked and virtually kidnapped them, he now had them trapped here at his home, miles away from any hope of rescue!

She tore her mouth from his, hating the things it did to her body. She was fire inside, her legs weak and trembling, her heart in her mouth and…and almost out of her mind with rage.

'You'd better let us both go – right this minute!' she hissed. 'You and I are not lovers, and we *never* will be. You've no right to make us stay. You have no claim on us, and…'

'You are quite right. I have no claim on you,' he agreed, his deep voice sounding taut and strained, his hands sliding down from her narrow waist to her hips and holding her possessively against his hard body, as if they were truly lovers. 'But as you will discover,' he added grimly, 'I have every right to claim Thea.'

'No! I won't let you take her!' Sara gasped, almost fainting at the thought of losing her beloved child, fiercely drumming her fists on his broad chest and violently twisting as she fought to escape from his firm embrace. But it seemed that her efforts were all in vain, as he quickly gripped hold of her wrists, forcing her at last to give up the unequal struggle.

'It *has* to be this way,' he ground out through harsh, twisted lips. 'We have no choice. Because Thea is *my* daughter, my own blood…'

Sara froze. Her body suddenly rigid and stiff, as if she had been turned to ice. Her eyes widened painfully. Never would she have thought that anyone could be so horribly wicked and cruel, she told herself, before suddenly finding herself released from his embrace.

'What I say *is* the truth,' he whispered huskily, taking a step backwards and staring down at her, a strange mixture of grim determination and pity etched on his austere features.

And then, there was silence…complete and utter silence, as if she had become totally encased in a huge, thick blanket of cotton wool.

Alexander was totally insane, of course. He'd obviously been badly affected by his wife's death, and he was clearly still traumatised – even after all these years…

But through the deep silence surrounding her, Sara suddenly heard the sound of her daughter's laughter – and the real world came crashing back to life. Noise and more noise: cicadas buzzing, birds singing, the whisper of wind through the cypresses up on the mountain beyond the white villa.

Slowly turning to gaze at Alexander, she saw that he looked completely and utterly drained, as if some alien force had sucked the lifeblood and all energy from him.

Continuing to stare silently at him, Sara desperately tried to pull herself together. But her brain seemed filled with a mass of jumbled thoughts and emotions, swinging violently between horror, and anger, and even…yes…even pity. Pity for this poor, deluded man, who had somehow convinced himself that he was the father of *her* daughter, Thea. An utterly tragic and totally mistaken belief, which now left her feeling nothing but deep sorrow for a man who was clearly insane.

'I…er…I need to speak with Maria,' she whispered faintly, her legs trembling as she turned to walk slowly towards the villa, leaving Alexander Karakou standing motionless on his own driveway.

chapter three

'Mama, my room is so pretty. I love it. Next door is another pretty room. And we have the same balcony, and I can see the sea a long way away. Maria says it must be Eleni's room. Who is Eleni?'

Numbly, Sara turned away from the long windows, with their white louvred panels to keep out the sun, and faced her daughter. She had been standing in this room, which was apparently her bedroom, for what seemed like an age, and was now beginning to recover from the feelings of fear and panic which had almost overwhelmed her when Alexander had claimed that Thea was his own child.

It was all complete and utter nonsense, of course. Especially since she knew that he couldn't *possibly* be the little girl's father. Which could only mean that poor Alexander had lost his wits – and was obviously still suffering from grief at the loss of his wife. Which didn't make the current situation any easier, she told herself grimly, making a determined effort to calm down, if only for the sake of her daughter.

She smiled and held out her arms, so that Thea would run to her. She needed to hug her daughter; she needed to feel her heat and her firmness and, above all, Sara desperately needed confirmation that she and Thea were still their normal selves – and nothing to do with Alexander's nightmare.

But Thea was too excited for hugs, running across the golden wood floor to the double doors between the windows. The doors were open wide, a fine white voile curtain over the opening wafting gently in the breeze. Beyond was a long tiled terrace with a white stone balustrade which overlooked the twin swimming pools below, and the exquisite Mediterranean gardens beyond.

'Mama, look, isn't it lovely? Are we really going to live here?'

Sara followed her out onto the terrace, standing behind her daughter as she leaned over the balustrade to look down at the swimming pools.

What could she possibly tell her daughter? That Alexander Karakou was out of his mind? Fortunately she didn't have to say anything, as Maria hurried into the room behind them, carrying a pile of fresh springy towels for the luxurious white and gold *ensuite* bedroom. Singing happily to herself, Maria placed the towels on the king sized bed, before joining them out on the wide terrace.

There had been no opportunity for her to have a private word with Maria. From the moment of their arrival Sara had been surrounded by the many members of staff serving the large, sprawling villa, all clearly anxious to make the new visitors feel welcome. Still shattered by the scene between Alexander and herself, outside in the driveway, Sara had found herself being escorted up a sweeping, Hollywood-style curving staircase to a palatial suite of rooms. There was a spacious bedroom, a dressing room furnished with white louvred wardrobes and a grey silk-covered *chaise longue,* a stunning bathroom with two washbasins nestling in white marble – plus a huge bubble-jet bath set into the marble floor which seemed to have enough room inside it for a small army.

It was all amazingly grand and luxurious. But unfortunately Sara wasn't in the right frame of mind to appreciate it. She was far too busy attempting to suppress her own worries and fears in order to appear cool, calm and collected in front of her daughter. And she knew that she must continue to remain as calm as possible – until she had an opportunity to get Alexander Karakou on his own, and find out the answers to some pressing questions. The most important being: *Where on earth had he got hold of the completely crazy, bizarre idea that Thea was his daughter?*

'It's all so beautiful, isn't it?' Maria breathed excitedly. 'I am so happy for you and...'

Sara frowned a warning, and Maria grinned, nodding her understanding of the need for discretion in front of the little girl.

'Come and see my room, Mama,' Thea urged. 'It has everything. Dolls and toys and *so* many books!'

Sara's stomach clenched, and she suddenly felt sick. Oh, God – this crazy situation seemed to be getting worse by the minute. Because it was beginning to look as if their arrival at this villa had been planned well in advance, and not just a matter of calling by on their trip around the island, as she'd hoped.

'I'll come in a minute, darling, I just want to have a word with Maria.'

As Thea skipped happily off, Maria suddenly frowned at Sara. 'Something is wrong?'

Everything was wrong, but Sara knew she couldn't burden Maria with her troubles. To tell the other woman that her employer was quite, *quite* mad would probably come as a shock to her – especially when she clearly believed that he was bathed in eternal sunlight!

Sara forced herself to smile weakly at Maria. 'Oh, no, nothing is wrong.' She spread her hands. 'How could there be anything wrong with all this?'

If she'd had a mercenary turn of mind, she might be able to appreciate that 'all this' was a definite improvement on the rather basic, simple beachside villa which they'd called home for the past week. But Sara was far more interested in discovering what Alexander had in mind for Thea and herself. And how to find a way of escaping from this island – as soon as possible.

Maria nodded happily, sharing in Sara's supposed happiness. 'I think it so wonderful, so romantic. Oh, Sara, I hope this doesn't affect us? Our friendship, I mean.' She giggled. 'When you marry you will be my mistress and...'

'For heaven's sake, Maria!' Sara spluttered. 'I have no intention of being anyone's mistress!' *Or wife, come to that!* she added to herself grimly. Damn Alexander for weaving this web of lies around them.

'You're *his* mistress now,' Maria teased.

Though Sara tried to smile, there was no way she could appreciate the joke. Did all the staff believe her to be Alexander's new mistress?

'Maria,' Sara murmured pensively as they turned back into the bedroom, 'Alexander's daughter, Eleni, is...er...is she here?'

Maria shook her head. 'No, the housekeeper told me she is out for the day.'

Sara frowned. What an earth was going on? If Alexander had a child of his own, why would he want to claim that Thea was also his daughter? It just didn't make sense.

'How old is she?' Sara asked. 'Have you met her?'

Maria shook her head. 'No, I've never seen her,' she said as she scooped up the towels from the bed and took them through to the bathroom. 'In fact, this is the first time I have ever been here, in the master's house!'

Maria was still smiling as she came out of the bathroom. 'Oh, Sara – I was so excited when he called early this morning and said to pack up all your belongings, that he would send a car to bring me and your luggage here, to his home. And to unpack and make sure everything was in order for you both.' Suddenly the smile slid from her pretty face. 'It is a pity that I'm only here just for the day. I have to go soon. You won't forget us, will you? You will come down to the village to see us?'

Sara flew to her and hugged her tightly. 'Don't be silly, Maria, we are friends!'

What else could she say? That nothing had changed, even though she was now ensconced in Alexander's villa – with all his servants clearly convinced that she was his mistress? Or, even more nonsensical, believing that she was about to become Alexander's bride. So how could she tell Maria that they were unlikely to meet again? Because there was no way she was going to be forced into a marriage with someone she didn't love. Which meant that she must find a way to escape from this huge mansion.

There was no way she was going to be browbeaten into agreeing that Alexander was the father of her daughter – however unhappy or grief-stricken he might be, Sara told herself grimly. Besides, it was all stuff and nonsense. And, while she felt very sorry for the poor unhappy man, he had no right to drag her and Thea into this stupid, dangerous charade. Damn it! As far as she was concerned they were going home to England, as soon as possible.

'Haven't you more duties before you leave, Maria?' Alexander's deep, authoritative voice startled Sara, who spun around to find him standing behind her.

Maria drew back from Sara and coloured deeply. She humbly whispered her apologies to her employer, before quickly leaving the room.

Alexander stood feet apart, golden arms folded firmly across his chest: a stance leaving Sara in no doubt that he considered himself Lord and Master in his own home. His words confirmed it.

'Don't be so intimate with the staff in future,' he told her flatly.

'Maria is a friend, not my servant,' Sara retorted, refusing to be intimidated.

'I don't employ servants; I employ *staff*. And becoming

over-friendly puts *them* at an embarrassing disadvantage. For the sake of dignity for all concerned in my household, I do not encourage intimacy.'

'But *you* are allowed to lie to *them*,' Sara bit back at him. 'You told Maria we are lovers, and...'

'She believes us to be lovers simply because she *wants* to believe it,' Alexander drawled coolly. 'Surely you must know that we Greeks are deeply romantic? And I do not lie, nor have I ever lied to my staff,' he added firmly.

'But you *have* lied to me!' she snapped, before taking a deep breath and striving to remain calm. 'How can I believe *anything* you say, when you're trying to pretend...when you're claiming that you're the father of my child? You *must* know that it's simply not possible!'

When he remained silent, merely staring at her with that deep, intense gleam in his dark eyes, Sara found herself struggling against an almost overwhelming urge to scream out loud with frustration.

'For heaven's sake, Alexander! Don't you think I would remember you if we'd ever made love to each other in the past?' she ground out through clenched teeth. 'Or do you *really* believe that I'm the sort of woman who spends her life having one-night stands with strange men?' she added scathingly. 'The truth is that I conceived my daughter with my lover, Spiros – not with you!'

His hands dropped wearily to his sides as he stepped towards her, his face grave and drawn. 'I have never claimed to have conceived Thea with you...'

'Damn right, you didn't!' Sara gave a shrill, high-pitched laugh. 'All the same, that's precisely how babies are made, Alexander. A man and a woman make love, and then...'

'Dear Lord – please stop this!' he suddenly pleaded, with such a deep throbbing note of emotion in his voice that Sara's heart nearly cracked in two. He buried his face in his hands as if in dreadful pain, pierced by some deep agony which was clearly tearing him apart.

Bemused, she could only stand motionless, staring at him in bewilderment. She didn't know what to say or do in this sort of situation, which was completely outside anything she'd ever experienced. While she was now convinced that he must be suffering from some sort of mental illness, she didn't really believe that he was dangerous. It was simply that she had no idea of how she was supposed to cope with the situation.

'I... er... I think I'd better go and see what Thea is up to,' she muttered, suddenly feeling totally drained, and so exhausted that she'd have given anything to be able to lie down. But she was afraid to let her guard down. She needed to stay alert, if only to protect Thea.

'Please forgive me,' he muttered thickly as she moved to walk past him. Reaching out, he caught her hand, holding it lightly and gently in his. 'I don't want you to be afraid of me, Sara. I only want to do what is best for us all. Please keep that in mind, always.'

Suddenly he lifted his other hand, trailing his fingers softly down over her cheek. The gentle touch seemed to set skin on fire and she found herself trembling. What was happening to her? She wanted to spit fire at him in anger one minute – and yet... somehow he seemed to have the power to melt her bones the next.

'Ah... I see that you *are* capable of responding to my touch, after all!' he murmured softly.

Sara stiffened, the arrogant note in his voice setting her teeth on edge. The very *last* thing she wanted, at this moment, was for him to get the idea that he was capable of affecting her emotionally.

'No, as far as you are concerned I'm still as cold as ice,' she told him frostily. 'You are a complex man, Alexander. Far too complex for me. In fact, being with you has re-minded me of why I was so attracted to Spiros – a supposedly *simple* fisherman. It was because he had a heart!'

'Ah, yes, Spiros – a man who lied to you about his family,' he drawled sardonically. 'Then, if what you believe of me is true, I should be everything *your* heart desires.'

Sara's breath caught in her throat. 'That was below the belt!' she seethed.

He nodded in agreement. 'It was indeed, and I apologise for it. Are you woman enough to apologise to me, for doubting my sincerity?'

'Until I know the truth I have no way of knowing whether you are sincere or not,' she responded quickly. 'Until then you won't get subservience or any apologies from me, Alexander. You appear to have temporarily kidnapped my daughter and myself – for some crazy reason which you are still refusing to explain. You are apparently content to have your servants believe that we are lovers, and are making veiled allusions to a marriage between us. All of which is, as you must know, complete nonsense!'

When he remained silent, Sara gave a heavy sigh. 'It's nearly teatime, and it looks as though Thea and I are probably trapped here, in this house miles from anywhere, until I can make arrangements to leave tomorrow morning. But if you think that there's any chance that I'm likely to agree to becoming your mistress – you can forget it! As for that stupid marriage business…' She gave a determined shake of her head. 'I can think of *no* reason in the world to marry you. *Not one*!'

His eyes glinted with anger and she flinched, expecting a verbal backlash. But he said nothing, simply gazing intently at her for some moments before slowly nodding his dark head.

She gave him one last glacial look of determination, before spinning around on her heels and hurrying off in search of Thea.

Alexander's home was beautiful. Spacious, cool, fresh and elegant. If she had thought about his home environment before, Sara would have imagined it sombre and heavily furnished with priceless antiques. But of course she'd never imagined that she would ever see his home.

Thea's room was across a cool tiled landing, facing the drive and the beautiful gardens at the entrance to the villa. The little girl was out on her shaded balcony, lining up dolls against the white wall and humming to herself, completely oblivious of anything out of the ordinary. She had apparently happily accepted the fact that they were going to be staying here tonight. A fact for which Sara was grateful. If Thea had shown any signs of distress at this sudden shift of accommodation, she would have been forced to take drastic action of some kind. Although, to be honest, she couldn't think what – especially as Alexander owned this small island.

Thea looked up at her mother and smiled. 'I'm making a family, Mama. All the dolls will be a big family, with lots of brothers and sisters.'

Sara simply smiled and nodded, before returning to Thea's bedroom. Back home, Thea had often played this game, creating a make-believe family. It saddened Sara to think she was compensating in fantasy for not having real brothers and sisters.

While Thea played out on the balcony, she wandered around the bedroom which the little girl would be occupying. But only for tonight, Sara reminded herself forcefully. First thing in the morning they would be off – running away from all this madness to the safety and security of their life in England.

Everything in the room seemed to be new, she noticed with a frown. The bed, the crisp linen, the toys and books and the ivory-coloured wood furniture – everything appeared to be brand-new. Sara's frown of concern deepened when she opened a connecting door into a room that was almost identical. Only the colours were different. Thea's room was predominantly ivory and pale yellow, while the second bedroom had been decorated in shades of ivory and pale pink.

There was another difference, of course. Because this room had obviously been in daily use for some time, both the toys and books appeared slightly frayed and worn. Was this Eleni's room? Sara felt a small shiver of fear down her spine. It looked as if Alexander had deliberately recreated *his own* daughter's bedroom, for *her* daughter Thea! It was distinctly creepy...

'Would you like tea for your little girl up here or downstairs?'

Sara spun around to face the woman who had spoken to her in Greek, taking it for granted that she would understand. She was small, grey-haired, middle-aged, and wore a light grey dress with a white apron over the top. She looked every inch the housekeeper.

The woman smiled at Sara. 'I am Anna, and I look after the house. If you need anything I will provide it for you. Tomorrow, you can give me your full instructions.'

'I... er... yes, tea downstairs would be fine,' Sara muttered helplessly.

Anna nodded, and left the room as silently as she had appeared.

Sara shivered nervously, trying to conquer her increasing feelings of alarm and apprehension. Along with all her other problems, the idea of Alexander's staff creeping around the house, ready to jump at her every command, was enough to give her a bad case of the jitters.

'There is tea downstairs for you, Thea,' Sara said as cheerfully as she could, as she poked her head around the door on to the terrace. 'And after tea it will be time for a bath and an early night.'

At which point, Sara promised herself grimly, she would tackle Alexander in earnest – and find out what the hell was going on! If it wasn't for Thea she'd have persisted earlier. But the last thing she wanted was for her darling daughter to overhear anything that might upset her.

'That must be Alex's little girl,' Thea said. She was leaning over the balustrade and looking over to the drive below. 'They've just come home. She's very pretty.'

Sara was at her side in a second, curious to see the child who seemed as mysterious as her father. It was a relief that she was here, because Sara had begun to wonder if she actually existed.

Gazing down, Sara saw a woman and a small child getting out of a car, and the tall figure of Alexander bounding down the marble steps of the villa to greet them. A moment later the little girl had thrown her arms around her father, and was hugging him as if she had been away forever, not just the day.

Alexander's daughter looked very sweet and pretty, immaculately dressed in a white dress and white shoes. Sara found herself watching the touching scene taking place between father and daughter with some interest. Because Eleni – if this was Eleni – seemed to be about the same age as Thea, but more petite in stature, with long dark hair caught into bunches and tied with pink ribbon. Although Sara couldn't help thinking that if Thea had been out all day she definitely wouldn't have arrived home looking as tidy and pristine as Alexander's daughter! Thea's hair would be a mess, with the ribbons long since discarded, and the white shoes would be scuffed beyond repair. But then her daughter lived a boisterous life to the full, whereas the little girl on the driveway below looked as if her life was one of immaculate, ladylike decorum.

Gazing down over the balcony, Sara found her attention slowly drawn to the woman standing beside the child. She looked beautiful, with dark hair hanging in deep waves to her shoulders, and her make-up was perfect – in spite of the dragging heat of late afternoon. Her clothes were well cut and expensive, and Sara had no problem in imagining the other woman wiping a manicured finger over a polished surface and then examining its tip with disdain.

Was this woman Alexander's mistress? And, if so, Sara could only agree with Maria's opinion, that she *looked* like a mistress – and she certainly *wasn't* his mother!

She couldn't hear what was being said as Alexander and the lovely woman spoke softly to one another. But she noticed that the little girl still clung tightly to Alexander's hand, although she appeared to be saying nothing. And then, after kissing the beautiful woman on both cheeks, Alexander turned to lead the small girl back into the house. As he did so, the woman glanced up quickly, meeting Sara's eyes very briefly before returning to her white car and accelerating away down the drive, leaving a cloud of burnt rubber and dust in her trail.

It had only been a fleeting glance between them. But it had been long enough for Sara to get the message. In fact she had no doubt that if she'd been down there at the front entrance the woman might well have metaphorically wiped a finger over *her*, before examining the result with disdain!

Dismayed, and disconcerted to find that she was trembling slightly, Sara quickly pulled herself together as Thea excitedly caught hold of her hand.

'I have someone to play with now,' the little girl announced happily, grinning from ear to ear. 'It's going to be wonderful here, isn't it?'

'Hmm,' Sara murmured, tightening her grip on Thea's hand as they went back into the bedroom, knowing that she hadn't the heart to burst the bubble of her daughter's obvious happiness. In her innocence, Thea had totally accepted the fact that she would be staying here, in this large house, and that Alexander's daughter was going to be her new playmate. It would be both far too unkind and even cruel if she attempted to explain that, far from being honoured guests, she and Thea had been virtually kidnapped by Alexander. Especially when she *still* didn't know why.

'I think you'd better get changed before we go down and meet your new friend,' she told Thea. 'You still smell of the beach and the sea.'

Thea giggled as they went into the bathroom. 'I hope Eleni likes the beach. We can go tomorrow and…'

And as Sara washed and changed her, teasing her black curls into some sort of order, Thea was busy planning everything she and Eleni were going to do with their time together.

Sara was only half listening. She was wondering why the lovely mistress had not stayed. Particularly as, according to Maria, she lived here in this house. But she soon came to the conclusion that wondering what Alexander was up to, was a complete waste of time. With a rueful sigh, she realised that ever since arriving here on this tiny island she'd been presented with one mystery after another. So one more wasn't likely to make any difference!

In the spacious entrance hall Anna told them tea was being served outside. And as she and Thea stepped out onto the large terrace, where Alexander and Eleni were standing beneath the shade of vines and scarlet bougainvillea, Sara noted that the little girl quickly shrank back behind the tall figure of her father.

Thea, normally so forward, and at times downright pushy, seemed equally overcome by shyness. The girls eyed each other warily. Alexander laughed under his breath and Sara wondered how he had explained their presence in the villa to the little girl.

Watching as Alexander tried to coax his daughter out

from behind him, and herself encouraging Thea to step forward and say hello, it seemed to Sara as if the situation was becoming increasingly fraught. There seemed no sane, sensible reason why Alexander should have brought her to the island and then manipulated events so that she and Thea were now staying here, in his house. But now – what? He had managed to get everyone dancing to his tune, but had no more idea of what he wanted than she'd had on first landing on this island. Surely he couldn't *really* believe that she would agree to marry him? Surely Alexander – even if he *was* suffering from some temporary mental affliction – couldn't believe that they were actually going to play happy families for evermore? No one could be *that* daft!

Unfortunately, even as she tried to see the amusing side of the situation, Sara realised that somewhere along the line she seemed to have completely lost her sense of humour. Gazing at Alexander, she saw that his face had grown pale and strained, the pulse beating wildly at his temple. Both sure signs, as she had learned during their short acquaintance, that he was suffering from extreme stress and tension.

Eleni needed a lot of coaxing to come out from behind her father's tall figure. But when she did appear, Sara could feel her heart-strings being painfully tugged. The little girl was obviously crippled with shyness and embarrassment; her cheeks were flushed, her blue eyes wide and fearful as a young doe's as she tightly gripped hold of her father's hand.

While Alexander was speaking softly to his daughter in Greek, Sara found herself thinking that it was highly unlikely the two children would manage to become friends. Apart from the language problem, they appeared to be as different as chalk and cheese: with Eleni so timid, and Thea so bold and confident,

At last the little girl spoke. 'Hello, Thea. I am very pl... pleased to meet you,' Eleni said in a small tremulous voice.

Her English was excellent, obviously practised and not completely natural, but an overwhelming relief to Thea, who immediately responded with a wide grin. And suddenly Alexander was grinning too.

'Eleni has been having English lessons,' he explained quickly.

'And I have been having Greek lessons!' Thea laughed, not shy any more as she stepped forward towards the other little girl. But Eleni immediately retreated, shrinking back behind her father. Thea stopped, looking hurt and upset that the other girl didn't appear to want to be friends.

Sara quickly decided that it was time she sorted out this difficult situation. Giving Alexander a scathing glance, as if to say, *I'm doing this for these girls – and I'll deal you with later*! she came forward, smiling warmly down at Eleni.

Speaking to her in Greek, Sara told her how pleased she and Thea were to be invited to tea, and what a lovely home she lived in with her father. But, try as she might, there was little or no response from the small girl. Her painful shyness almost broke Sara's heart. In any other circumstances she would have wanted to stay and help the child, since it was quite obvious that Eleni had a problem in meeting and socialising with people. Had Alexander over-protected the girl since her mother's death? Even as Sara told herself that it was none of her business, her heart ached for both father and daughter.

Anna arrived with tea for them all, and Alexander urged everyone to sit down at the table, which was now spread with small sandwiches and light pastries.

When they were all finally seated around the table the two children remained dumb as Sara and Alexander both tried to break the strained silence, with remarks about the weather, and the bright flowers in the garden. This *has* to be the tea party from hell, Sara told herself grimly, feeling increasingly embarrassed and ill at ease.

A phone rang in the distance and Alexander, looking highly relieved, quickly excused himself before jumping up from the table. It's all right for some! Sara thought glumly, offering the plate of sandwiches to Eleni, who took one before glaring down at it as it lay harmlessly on her plate. Thea gave her mother a look of confusion, clearly wondering what she was supposed to do about Eleni, and Sara could only respond with a helpless shrug of her shoulders.

The tense situation was interrupted as Anna arrived with a pot of tea for the grown-ups and two tall glasses of fresh orange juice for the girls. As Eleni reached for her juice Sara was just wondering how to break the increasingly strained atmosphere, when the little girl's nervous fingers slipped from the glass and sent it flying down on to the marble floor of the terrace.

Anna cried out in dismay, waving her hands theatrically in the air. While Sara, who'd expected Eleni either to burst into tears of embarrassment or rush from the table in a storm of weeping, was astonished to see the child gurgling with laughter.

A few seconds later Sara discovered the reason for such unexpected mirth – and it had nothing to do with the spilt juice. It was thanks to Thea who, behind Anna's back, was waving her hands in the air in accurate mimicry of the housekeeper's dismay. With Anna continuing to protest at the sight of the broken glass, the two girls began giggling helplessly.

'Honestly, Thea, that was very naughty of you,' Sara reprimanded her daughter after the housekeeper had hurried back inside the house for a dustpan and brush. 'I'm just glad that Anna didn't see you.'

'Thea is funny,' Eleni giggled, and then bit deeply into her sandwich.

Sara smiled at her. Well, at least Thea had broken the ice

between them. The girls started talking to one another over their tea, and Sara couldn't help thinking that adults could learn a lot from children. Here were two small girls, who knew nothing about each other and barely spoke each other's language, and yet they were now laughing together as if they'd been friends all their lives.

Just as she was wishing that she and Alexander could be so open and natural with each other, Sara was startled to hear his deep voice.

'You are not drinking your tea, Sara.'

Raising her head, she saw him surveying the children at the tea table, his normally austere features now bearing an expression of relief and pleasure.

Before she could say anything, Eleni was laughing and telling her father all about Thea's talent for mimicry. And Sara realised that there was a very strong bond between father and daughter. Similar to that between Thea and herself, of course – although possibly more intense because of the loss of Alexander's wife.

There was no doubt that Eleni was a beautiful child, Sara thought as she gazed at the little girl. More petite than Thea, but not as dark. Her blue eyes were a surprise, because Alexander's were so very dark. And, she found herself wondering about the child's mother. She must have been very lovely. They must have been a strikingly beautiful couple, with a lovely child and a gracious home. They'd clearly possessed everything to make them happy – and then they'd been struck down by tragedy. But, at least they had been married. Sara was surprised to find herself envying Alexander, who had at least known the happiness of being legally wed to his wife. If only she and Spiros had got married. They would have done so eventually, of course. But, alas, 'eventually' had proved to be too late for them.

'What are you thinking?'

Sara, deep in thought, looked up at Alexander in surprise.

She shrugged, picking up her cup of tea and moving away from the table where the girls were now giggling over something else. Standing by the white stone balustrade, she gazed blindly out at the two swimming pools connected by a low slung, Japanese-style wooden bridge.

'I was just wishing that I'd married Spiros,' she told Alexander as he came and stood beside her. 'Eleni is a lovely little girl, and you were obviously a very happy family. It must be a great comfort to you, now you and Eleni are alone, to know that you were legitimately married to her mother.' She sighed. 'I know it sounds weak, and probably pathetic in this modern day and age, but I can't help wishing that Spiros had been my husband. I wish I had that little piece of paper that said I was legally his.'

Alexander took the cup and saucer from her hand, placing them on the table before returning to take hold of her hands.

'What's in a piece of paper?' he murmured as Sara gazed up at him in surprise. 'Surely it's what's in the heart that matters?'

Sara nodded and slowly withdrew her hands from his. She took a deep breath and murmured softly and earnestly, 'Alexander, if you *do* have a heart, won't you *please* free myself and Thea? We don't belong in your life, although I know you seem to think that we do. I have no idea of your reasons for what appears to be totally inexplicable behaviour. But you have a lovely daughter of your own. And so why you feel it necessary to try and claim Thea as well is… is quite absurd,' she finished lamely.

To her surprise he nodded. 'Yes, but then life is absurd at times.' He sighed deeply and turned round to sit on the wall, stretching his long legs out in front of him. 'Look at the girls,' he told her, his voice low and throaty. 'What do you see, Sara?'

Sara gave a heavy sigh of deep frustration. 'I see two little girls eating their tea and enjoying each other's company,' she told him bluntly. 'Which, you must admit, is more than we've been doing!' she added with grim irony. 'So, what am I supposed to be looking for, Alexander? If there's a hidden agenda in your question, I'm afraid that it's escaped me.'

He looked up at her, that damned pulse throbbing at his temple, once again, his eyes so darkly intense and full of pain that Sara felt her own heart tightening with fear.

'I realise that I am expecting too much.' He sighed. 'I had hoped that you would understand. But of course I now see that it is impossible. However, they are more than two little girls, Sara,' he added, his deep voice thick with emotion. *'They are our bond*! A bond which will bind us together for the rest of our lives. They are our future, and we are theirs. And there is nothing either of us can do to change that.'

Slowly he stood up and turned to face her. Sara, her pulses racing, thought he was going to say more. But before he could add to that strangely emotional and determined statement about the future Eleni had appeared at his side and was sliding her hand into his. His strained features softened at the sight of his daughter's beaming face as she gazed up at him.

'Papa, we have finished tea. Can we go and play upstairs? I want to show Thea the dolls I chose for her.'

'Yes, of course you can.' Alexander smiled. 'Don't forget to thank Anna for your tea on the way upstairs.'

'Of course I will, Papa,' Eleni said, quickly kissing her father's hand before running away to join Thea.

'Eleni chose all those dolls for... for Thea?' Sara gasped in astonishment. 'What in the hell is going on? I can hardly believe that you've involved your small daughter in this... this sick, crazy fantasy of yours. That she knew you were bringing us here and is expecting us to stay! It...well, it's simply *unbelievable*!'

Sara waved her hands helplessly in the air. 'I'm sorry, but I... I really can't take any more of this nonsense. Your behaviour isn't just strange – it's now verging on the totally paranoid! You're not only claiming that Thea is your own child, but you've furnished a bedroom for her in *exactly* the same style as that of your own daughter. Quite frankly, Alexander, I'm beginning to think that what you *really* need is a good psychiatrist!'

He merely stared down at her in silence, not even offering one word in his own defence, leaving Sara to struggle against an almost uncontrollable urge to lash out at the damned man, to somehow force him to explain what lay behind his increasingly strange behaviour.

As he turned and strode away from her, her simmering rage and fury grew too much to bear. A red mist seemed to be filling her brain, and she ran swiftly after him, grabbing hold of his arm as he was about to leave the terrace.

'I demand to know what's going on!' she cried, her fingers biting painfully into his bare flesh. 'You *must* tell me the truth!'

'Yes, I see that I must,' he agreed quietly, carefully removing her tightly clenched fingers from his arm. And, although she'd expected to be rejected yet again, maybe even thrust aside, she was surprised when he placed a gentle arm tenderly about her shoulders. Leading her into the villa and across a large hallway, he opened the door of a long cool room which appeared to be a study, with large floor-to-ceiling windows shaded by slatted blinds, the only sound to disturb the silence being the faint hum of an air conditioner.

Sara hardly had time to take in her surroundings. She had only a brief impression of pale leather chairs, glass bookshelves and soft white rugs underfoot before she found a glass of pale liquid being thrust into her hands. And the tall figure of Alexander was standing in front of her, all dark predatory maleness, his voice seeming to come from a far distance as he urged her to drink the brandy.

Her eyes widened fearfully. Oh, my God! Was he trying

to make her drunk?

'Sara, please take a mouthful,' he urged. 'You clearly need it.'

She shook her head, glaring fiercely up at him. 'I *don't* need it. I...'

'Oh, yes, you do!' he growled, lifting the glass to her lips and forcing her to swallow a mouthful of the fiery liquid. And then her heart seemed to miss a beat as she stared up into his handsome, tanned face – and saw that his eyes were filled with tears.

'*Alexander*!' she cried huskily.

With a great effort he appeared to pull himself together and turned away from her, but his back was nevertheless stiff and rigid with tension. Walking over to pick up a file on the table across the room, he muttered something, but Sara didn't quite catch what he'd said.

Her fingers tightened about the glass of brandy as she suddenly realised that, whatever he wanted to say to her, he was completely unable to say the words to her face.

'I... er... I didn't hear you,' she told him tremulously.

And then he repeated it. And although Sara heard every word this time, what he'd said made no sense at all. How could it?

As if from a far distance she heard the sound of her own voice, screaming in total disbelief, fervently denying everything he'd said. The brandy glass slipped from her fingers, its fall absorbed by the thick white rug at her feet as his arms closed tightly about her, holding her possessively by the shoulders to steady her almost hysterical, swaying figure; her stricken eyes fused to the movement of his lips as he formed the words that echoed and echoed in her ears.

'Thea is my daughter. Eleni is yours,' he was saying again. 'They were born within three minutes of each other in the small hospital on Zanos, and a terrible mistake was made...'

'*No! No! No!*' Sara screamed, and then suddenly she was fighting for breath, a thick mist clouding her brain, and she would have fallen to the floor if she hadn't been supported by Alexander's strong arms.

No matter how hard she had tried, she had never been able to forget the night of the storm, on which her child had been born and when Spiros had lost his life, the panic on discovering that her baby was arriving before it was due, the pain and the emergency Caesarean operation. And all the while so many people rushing around the small hospital, the news of boats capsizing…the casualties…

'You really *are* crazy!' she cried fiercely. 'You're completely out of your mind!'

'Dear heaven – I only wish that I were!' Alexander groaned.

And then she was lashing out at him, hands, fists, clawing at him in an effort to punish him for telling her such lies, before he managed to catch hold of her wrists and she slowly calmed down, before opening her eyes to see that his face was streaked with tears.

She was living a nightmare. He *was* her nightmare! None of this was real – *none of it*!

'I could have left things as they were, and no one would have been the wiser,' he told her, his voice cracking beneath the weight of his emotion. 'But once I'd discovered the truth I found that I couldn't ignore it. I *had* to see her! I had to see Thea – *my own flesh and blood*! It changes nothing, of course, and yet it changes everything. There is no question of you giving up Thea or me giving up Eleni. I can promise you that never entered my head. But —'

'Stop it!' Sara cried, covering her face with her hands and sobbing as if her heart would break, so deeply that her breath rasped harshly in the still air of the silent room. 'It *can't* be true. It *isn't* true. Oh, God – please tell me that this isn't happening!'

Thea and Eleni were lost in a world of their own making. They sat cross legged on cushions out on the balcony that linked their bedrooms, surrounded by a pile of books and toys and happily unaware that they were being watched.

Sara stared at the two girls through the voile curtains that covered the open door. Alexander's strong arms were holding her upright, because she was temporarily incapable of supporting herself. Indeed, it felt as if she'd been injected with some strong drug which had left her mind and body completely numb.

She had no clear recollection of what she'd said to Alexander in the last hour or so. Mostly abuse, she supposed weakly. And he had taken it all. She didn't yet know the precise details of what had happened in the hospital at Zanos the night that Thea and Eleni had been born, but she had wanted to see the girls. Perhaps it would help her to understand the reasons why Alexander had chosen to smash her previously happy world to pieces: a world which could never be the same again.

She could hardly see Thea for the tears that filled her eyes. She shook her head. No, it couldn't be true. Thea was *her* daughter! And Eleni? The little girl looked up, gazing at a moth fluttering over the light on the balcony. Her eyes were so blue…! Sara's heart turned over and over. Eleni had *her* blue eyes, not Alexander's dark liquid pools, in which a woman could drown…

An agonising sob caught in Sara's throat, and she was aware of Alexander's arms tightening reassuringly about her frail body. And yet, as he raised a hand to gently brush a lock of hair from her brow, she could feel his hands trembling slightly.

She suddenly realised that over the past months he must have been facing the same pain and agony. So excruciatingly painful that it was almost unbearable. Without conscious thought she turned and buried her face in the

curve of Alexander's broad, powerful shoulder, before he
slowly he led her away.

Through the numbness which seemed to have her in
thrall, Sara knew that she no longer had the strength to fight
him. A terrible mistake had forced them together, and she
was incapable of any further rational thought. Her life had
been devastated.

chapter four

'I was not with Celeste, my wife, when our daughter was born. I was called away on urgent business. I did not see the baby till several days later.'

'But Celeste gave birth to her,' Sara argued vehemently. 'She *must* have held Eleni in her arms only seconds after she had been delivered. So how *could* the babies have been switched? It just doesn't make sense!'

Sara was coming out of her dreamlike state of shock. Hours could have drifted into days for all she knew. Anna had prepared the girls for bed, bringing them both downstairs to say goodnight to their parents. Sara had held Thea so tightly against her breast that her daughter had giggled and pulled away. And then, through misty eyes, she had simply stared at Eleni, not knowing how to feel. The little girl was a stranger – and yet she was apparently her daughter. Sara had been so choked up inside she hadn't been able to do anything other than bid the child a polite goodnight.

And now the demons were driving her insane. No mother could be expected to cope with this, the shock statement that the little girl she had thought to be her very own daughter wasn't genetically linked to her in any way. That, in fact, Alexander Karakou was Thea's *true* father. And Eleni, whom he had always believed to be his own child, belonged to neither his dead wife or himself – but was the daughter of Sara and Spiros.

'Sara, I know you are trying to look for every reason for this not to be so, but I can assure you that it is the truth,' Alexander told her softly. He leaned forward and poured

more coffee, his face pale and anguished after a long,
fraught night of tears and recriminations.

Sara was awash with coffee, and brandy, and yet more
coffee. It was getting light outside. All night they had talked,
and she had cried and wept bitter tears, before erupting into
anger and then finally descending into a stupor of grief.
Again and again they had gone over the same ground, Sara
looking for something…anything…that would prove him
wrong.

'I have to keep repeating it,' she murmured, rubbing her
forehead fretfully. 'I will never cope otherwise. Thea is mine
and…'

'Thea was born to my wife Celeste at three-thirty in the
morning. She had breathing difficulties and was not handed
to her mother. She was rushed out of the room for treatment.
Along the corridor you were having an emergency
Caesarean operation under general anaesthetic, and Eleni
was delivered. A storm was raging, casualties and dead
bodies were being brought in, and the small hospital
couldn't cope with the disaster. Somehow, completely by
mistake, the babies were switched. Hours later, when you
came round from the anaesthetic, you were handed my
daughter. There were no other witnesses to those little girls'
births. No one who could point out that you and Celeste had
been given the wrong babies. Only a doctor and nurse, under
extreme pressure and stress, doing what they could, trying to
save so many other people's lives.'

Sara nodded and a sob caught in her throat. The night
would forever be with her. The night when her world had
fallen apart. But she had coped, holding her daughter close
to her heart when they'd come to tell her that Spiros had
died. Somehow, through Thea, she had found the strength to
survive the disaster and make a life for both herself and her
precious daughter.

'If Eleni hadn't fallen sick a few months back you would

never have found out,' Sara whispered hoarsely. She raised her weary head to look at him. What anguish and torture the man had been through – anguish and torture which *she*, too, was now having to face.

'Eleni needed a blood transfusion after a small operation, and mine didn't match.' He shrugged. 'And then we discovered that Eleni's blood group didn't match with Celeste's either. The surgeon is an old family friend, and he remembered that Celeste had a rare blood group.'

'Does…does he know…know that…?' Sara could hardly utter the question.

Alexander slowly nodded his dark head. 'Yes. He was the one who gave me the devastating news. The information that Eleni couldn't be the child of either myself or my wife.'

'And then the torment started,' Sara muttered helplessly.

'I couldn't let it rest.' He gave a deep sigh. 'I didn't…I couldn't bring myself to believe it – not at first. Indeed, I am ashamed to say that at one stage I even found myself questioning Celeste's faithfulness. That was unforgivable, of course, but…'

'But understandable in the circumstances,' Sara interjected softly, perfectly comprehending what he had been through. After all, she was still in the midst of trying to cope with all the doubts and terrors of the disastrous situation.

Alexander gave another long, shuddering and weary sigh. 'It's all in the file. All the confirmation that is needed to prove that I've told you the truth. Because you were operated on, the hospital had a record of your blood group. And, of course, it exactly matches the blood group of Eleni. The hospital were helpful with the records of all that went on that fateful night. The staff concerned at the time have now moved on, but they could be traced and called as witnesses…'

'Witnesses…?' She stared at him in confusion, her sky-blue eyes clouded with exhaustion and grief.

Alexander nodded. 'We can sue. After all, we have every right. The law is on our side.'

'*Sue…?*' Sara exclaimed, jumping to her feet from the pale leather sofa on which she'd been huddled. 'Do you *seriously* think I'd want to gain any money from this ghastly situation? Do you *really* think that…?'

'I think you are as appalled as I am by the very idea, Sara,' he told her quietly. 'I'm merely pointing out the options available to you, making sure that you have all the information you need to come to terms with this tragedy.'

Sara waved a dismissive hand as she began pacing up and down over the floor, as if seeking some relief in action. 'This isn't about apportioning blame, Alexander. This is about two little girls' lives. This is bloody hell!'

She covered her face with her hands and sobbed relentlessly. And he was there for her once more, placing his strong arms about her as he'd done time and again through the long night. Gently soothing and comforting her fears…offering so much support and understanding.

'Sara, listen – this is about us, too. We have to do the best we can for our children,' he murmured huskily in her ear, his arms tightening about her trembling figure. 'I'm not the biological father of Eleni. But I cannot ignore the last five years,' he continued. 'After all, how do you define father-hood? Not by blood, but by feelings and emotions. And I love her as if she *was* my own flesh and blood. I'm *always* going to be her father. '

'And I love Thea as if she was *my* own flesh and blood,' Sara sobbed. 'I'm *always* going to be her mother!' she added, twisting herself from his embrace and glaring up at his tanned, handsome face.

'Oh, God, *how* I wish I'd never come to this island,' she breathed fervently. 'I wish I didn't know. Why didn't you keep your terrible secret to yourself, Alexander? You should have buried it deep inside you. For all our sakes, you should have kept quiet. Because it's going to mean nothing but heartache, sorrow and grief – and damned, *damned* purgatory for evermore,' she added, her voice cracking as she gave a shuddering sob of pain and agony.

Spinning around on her heels, she rushed towards the door, but he caught her before she could wrench it open. She had angered him now, and she didn't care. All through the night her emotions had swung violently back and forth – from sadness and understanding to anger and bitterness.

'How *could* I have kept silent once I'd discovered what had happened, Sara?' he grated fiercely at her. 'How *can* you bury something like that and expect to live a normal life? Believe me – you damned well can't! Once you've opened Pandora's box, there is no way of closing it again.'

'You didn't have to share it with me, though,' she accused bitterly, her eyes shooting him daggers of pure hatred for the burden he had placed on her slim shoulders. 'I needn't have known. I was quite happy with my life. Ignorance is bliss, Alexander. You should have left me and Thea alone. But oh, no – you selfishly wanted her, as well. And as for this marriage business – it's obvious that all you want is a wife to share your burden, a mother to care for the child who isn't your own, enabling you to form a bond with your own flesh and blood. All nothing but selfish, *selfish* reasons for bringing me here!'

She bit her lower lip fiercely as every spiteful accusing word ricocheted around the room. How could she be saying such awful things to him? She tried to force herself to mumble some sort of an apology, but his evident anger forced the words to die in her throat.

'You talk of *my* selfishness, but all *you* can think of is your own pitiful state,' he accused scathingly. 'That *you* should be burdened with such a disclosure, that *you* should have to endure the pain of what I have told you this night. Well, you can forget your own damned hurt and start thinking about the two small girls who are innocent in all this mess. They have the right to know the truth…'

'And just *who* is going to tell them?' she demanded angrily. 'There's no way I can possibly tell my darling Thea that I'm *not* her mother. Can't you see how it would leave her completely and utterly devastated?'

'Yes, of course I can,' he retorted firmly. 'And that is precisely *why* we are going to be married.'

The flat statement came without emotion. It was delivered so coldly, it chilled Sara to the bone; she was shivering with fear as she wrapped her arms around herself for warmth and comfort. Alexander was looking at her as coldly as the tone in which his words had been spoken. A glacial, icy-cold gaze of ruthless, grim determination.

'We must marry because I *cannot* allow you to take Thea away from here,' he told her, his voice harsh and implacable. 'I am her true father. She is my own flesh and blood. And I will *not* allow another man to have charge of my daughter's upbringing!'

'But…'

'However, I am not prepared to give up Eleni either,' he continued. 'I love her as my own, and, though you are clearly appalled at the thought of being her mother, I can only pray that you will grow to love her in time.'

Sara's hand came up to her mouth to stem a further sob. That was so cruel! How *could* she be expected to feel, after the devastating blow he had just dealt her? Had he expected her to throw herself on the strange child, and hug her to her heart immediately? Life wasn't that simple, and love could not be produced to order.

'It is the only answer to the problem,' he went on. 'You and I will be married as soon as possible. We will raise our daughters together, as sisters. And when the bonds of our family are firmly sealed, they will be told of their birthrights.'

Sara stared at him helplessly. Was that really the only way for them all to come out of this with their sanity intact? But...but how could she force herself to face marriage without love...? The thought was unbearable.

'N...no,' she stuttered in despair. 'I can't...I won't marry you. It...it's all horribly wrong. I'm going back to England, with Thea. She's my daughter, and...'

'She is *my* daughter,' he corrected her sternly. He placed his hand beneath her chin, and his fingers felt cold as ice as he tilted her face up towards him.

'You do, of course, have a choice, Sara,' he continued, staring grimly down at her. 'You can stay here. Or you can go. However, if you go – you go alone. Because you will have left me no choice but to apply for custody of Thea.'

She gasped with shock. Her eyes filled again, this time with tears of fear and alarm. 'You can't do that! You wouldn't...you couldn't...!'

He lifted a dark, quizzical eyebrow. 'Surely I do not have to remind you, Sara, that you are not Greek? You were never married to a Greek. The brutal facts of life are quite clear. You have no rights in my country. You have no money to challenge me in the courts. You have no influence. You have *nothing*!'

'And you, of course, are someone who has *everything*,' she ground out bitterly, knowing that she was powerless against his grim determination to claim Thea.

Staring up at him, she felt totally exhausted, her head swimming with weariness as she tried to force herself to continue the unequal fight.

'There has to be another way,' she muttered helplessly.

'Believe me, there isn't another way. It must be marriage. We must both make a sacrifice, for the sake of our daughters.'

Marriage as a sacrifice? She had never heard of it described as such. She gave him one last look of despair. But of course *he* was making the sacrifice. Once married, he would have to give up his mistress. Or would he?

Sara shuddered, her head and heart despairing. The last thing she wanted in the world was to be forced into marriage with Alexander, a man about whom she knew virtually nothing. And yet the thought of him continuing to maintain his mistress filled her with a peculiar dread. Which was nonsense, of course. Why should she care one way or another about his mistress? The fact of the woman's existence meant nothing – not when compared to what she'd been through during this dreadful night, which had left her feeling as though a thousand daggers were firmly embedded in her heart.

'I…I need to sleep,' she muttered faintly, unable to take any more.

He nodded, stepping aside and opening the door for her. But as she slowly made her way up the stairs to her bedroom, all she heard was the sound of the door being closed firmly behind her: the resounding echo of a prison cell door.

Sara nervously twirled the gold band on the third finger of her left hand, starring blindly ahead at the clusters of white houses, with their terracotta-tiled roofs, lining the shoreline. As Alexander's yacht was slowly manoeuvred into its mooring, harbour workers caught hold of the ropes thrown to them by the crew, the jerk as the yacht finally settled into its berth causing her to grasp at the mahogany rail to steady her trembling figure.

They had been married three hours ago, in the Mayor's office on another island. An impersonal service, merely a formality to precede the handing over of a piece of white parchment that stated they were man and wife. It had meant absolutely nothing, of course. Sara had no problem recalling her new husband's words: 'What's a piece of paper? It's what's in the heart that matters'. But there was nothing in her heart – and, she suspected, even less in Alexander's.

Her wedding ring was too big. When Alexander had measured her finger, three weeks ago, it would have fitted. The off-white silk dress that he had insisted on buying for her at the same time had needed to be taken at the waist yesterday, because she had lost so much weight.

Today had been her wedding day and she felt nothing, only exhausted and drained of all emotion, a mere ghost of her former self. Which was hardly surprising when she had been forced into marriage with a man who didn't love her.

Alexander had been very clever, using every emotional trick in the book to get her to agree to wed him – and now he was her husband. But the wedding had been a foregone conclusion, of course. Right from the moment she'd discovered the truth about her beloved Thea, and Alexander's Eleni.

But, in all honesty, she had no choice. There was no way she had the resources to fight Alexander in the Greek courts. And he had the all wealth and influence necessary to make sure that she didn't leave the island with her daughter. Nor could she have packed her bags and returned to England. Not when it would have meant leaving Thea all alone, here in Greece. On top of which, how could she have abandoned poor, sweet little Eleni – the daughter she hardly knew?

Sara blinked the tears back from her eyes as she heard shrieks of laughter from the girls below deck. Turning, she discovered Alexander standing close behind her. His un-expected presence caused her to jump, her nerves so badly on edge that the slightest thing seemed to have her twitch-ing like a nervous rabbit.

'We're home,' he murmured.

Sara lifted her chin to look at him. If the last few weeks had slimmed her down to a shadow of herself, he hadn't changed one iota. He was clothed today in a pale silver-grey suit, and his handsome tanned features and black hair contrasted sharply to the crisp whiteness of his shirt. Unburdening himself of the dreadful truth about their daughters had obviously benefited him, while she had gone steadily gone downhill, she told herself glumly, deeply resenting the fact that he appeared to be rising above all their problems, not suffering as she was.

'Your home, my prison,' she said curtly, turning her attention to the girls, who were racing towards them along the deck, eager to get ashore and return home.

'A prison without bars,' he grated under his breath. 'You are free to leave whenever you like.'

'But, as we both know, I cannot leave with my daughters,' she retorted, and her icy blue eyes shot daggers at him. 'Not now that we are married. Not when you'll enjoy reminding me of your legal rights…'

'You are a cold, heartless woman, Sara,' he told her thickly. 'How could you even *think* I would do or say such a thing, on our wedding day…?'

'A wedding day I'd rather forget!' she said under her breath, before quickly widening her lips into a smile for Thea and Eleni as the girls joined them.

While Alexander remained on board, to give his crew instructions, Sara led the girls ashore and into the car that was waiting for them. Sitting in the passenger seat, she listened to Thea and Eleni's excitedly chattering in a mixture of Greek and English. Both girls had made enormous strides in each others' language during these past weeks, and they seemed to have no problem in under-standing one another. Their relationship had developed too, with Thea emerging as the stronger and more independent one, while Eleni was clearly more clingy and vulnerable.

Ever since that dreadful night, when Alexander had revealed all, it had been as if Sara was elevated to a different astral plane from anyone else. She was there, of course…living with them…but somehow not *with* them.

It had been a terribly confusing time for her. The presence of the two little girls had filled her head, and her heart. Her feelings of deep love for Thea were without question. She still thought of her as *her* daughter, and always would. But as for Eleni…Eleni had thrown her heart into chaos.

Sara wanted to pinch herself every time she looked at the little girl to whom she'd given birth. Because she still had great difficulty in accepting that it *was* Eleni, and *not* Thea, to whom she'd given birth all those years ago.

Eleni had her blue eyes – there was no disputing that fact. But, search as she might, there seemed little else that she'd inherited from her mother. There was nothing in her character that Sara could connect with. Thea had it all: Sara's confidence, her openness, the fun-loving side of her, which contrasted so sharply to the sombre darkness of Alexander. Although, to be honest, she told herself with a heavy sigh, her 'fun-loving side' had been virtually non-existent ever since her first meeting with Alexander Karakou!

The very worst thing of all, which caused her great agony, was that, try as she might, she could find nothing in the pretty, shy little girl that seemed to connect with Spiros either. Frequently gazing at his photograph, which she always carried everywhere with her, she could find no resemblance…no part of his character which he might have passed on to the fragile little girl. Although maybe she had inherited his sensitivity…? Spiros had always been a very caring person. But then, Thea was also a kind and thoughtful little girl.

I must try harder, Sara had vowed every night of the past three weeks, when she'd tossed and turned, restless in her bed. I must try harder to accept that Eleni is my daughter; I must try to *love* the little girl. But she'd been so shocked over the whole affair it was proving very difficult to find the right emotions, which she knew she ought to have for her true daughter. And then she had woken one morning, heavy-lidded and still emotionally exhausted, to find Eleni standing by her bed and gazing at her with the eyes that stared back at Sara every time she looked in a mirror.

'My doll's arm is broken,' she'd murmured sadly in Greek and lifted the doll for Sara to see.

Silently Sara had mended the arm that had slipped out of its socket, her fingers nervous and trembling, her heart pumping. For the first time Eleni had come to her and not her father.

'There, it's all right now,' she'd told her as she handed the doll back. Eleni had hesitated, biting her lip, lowering her lashes and eventually turning away, mumbling her thanks as she hurried from the room.

In that moment Sara had wanted to stop her, to reach out and gather the little girl into her arms, holding her tightly and telling her that she loved her very dearly.

Instead, she had buried her face in her pillow, crying tears of relief that at last she had found the feelings she'd been so terrified didn't exist. Those feelings and emotions *were* there. They had just been swamped beneath all the turmoil she was having to cope with. And now it seemed as if she had given birth once again, and had another daughter to love. The sobs of relief had been cathartic, cleansing and purifying. She now knew that she was capable of loving little Eleni as a mother should. Why had she ever imagined it would be so difficult?

'I hope you will make an effort when we get home,' Alexander muttered under his breath, as he slipped into the driving seat beside her and started the car.

She turned to look at him as they drove out of the marina, his dark brooding gaze firmly fixed on the road ahead.

'We are man and wife now,' he added in a low, stern voice. 'And the staff will expect to see us enjoying a happy family life – not the sight of you glaring at me as if I had removed the batteries that control your sense of humour.'

Sara bit her lower lip and said nothing. True, she had been acting like a battery-driven automaton lately, but that was hardly surprising. The staff knew nothing of the disaster she'd faced. They had no idea that this was a marriage of convenience, precious little to do with love or romance. It was the only thing she and Alexander had agreed on in this charade – a total silence as far as the girls were concerned. No one was ever to know the secret of their births.

So, it looked as if she had no choice but to start living a lie. To pretend to be Alexander's adoring wife. And the only consolation she could find in the whole, horrible situation was that *he* was going to find it equally painful to have to act the adoring husband!

'Papa,' Eleni said in a small voice. 'Is Sara my mama now you are married?'

Sara stiffened. Perhaps it hadn't been wise to include the girls in the wedding ceremony? They were only five, heading for six, still just small children. However, Alexander had thought them old enough. He had wanted them to be there.

'Thea said not,' Eleni was going on. 'She said Sara is her mama and not mine. She said Alex is my papa and not hers…'

'Hey, hold on!' Sara laughed, quickly swivelling around to face the two little girls in the back seat of the car. 'Now, listen, you two. It's been a lovely day, but perhaps a bit confusing for you both. So, after your baths, we'll have a long talk about the day and…'

'It was a lovely day,' Thea agreed, before adding wistfully, 'But I want a wedding in a church, with a long dress and bridesmaids.'

'What is a bridesmaid?' Eleni asked.

Alexander started to laugh softly as Thea struggled to explain, while Sara bit her lip and stared blindly ahead, the girls' conversation fading into the back of her mind.

A church wedding. It was something she and Spiros had talked about…But now she was married to Alexander, and the cold, clinical ceremony had left her feeling cheated, as if she'd somehow missed out on something important and meaningful.

Anna was waiting to greet them in the cool spacious hallway of the villa. The girls ran up and hugged her, talking excitedly about the boat trip and the wedding – and the funny Mayor with metal glasses on the very tip of his long nose.

As Anna laughed and ushered them away, Alexander tossed his leather briefcase containing their wedding certificate on to a chair in the hall. 'We'll have to do something about a proper nanny to care for the girls,' he announced.

Sara stared sorrowfully at the briefcase. Such a dismissive gesture, as if now they were married nothing mattered. Not that anything had mattered *before* the ceremony, of course. Alexander had been attentive towards her since telling her the terrible news, but that had only been a façade, to make it easier for them all to go through with it. Now he had what he wanted – or he would have soon enough, when he legally adopted Thea and his name was on her revised birth certificate.

'I'll be caring for the children now. After all, I'm their mother. I don't need anyone to help look after my own children,' she told him fiercely as she moved towards the staircase. She would now have to adopt Eleni, of course, and then they would be a legally correct family. But a family without any real values, she thought miserably. A real family was composed of two people who'd married because they loved and cared for one another. Not this cold bargain which had been struck between herself and Alexander.

'Where are you going?' he demanded angrily.

Sara turned to face him, her eyes brimming with tears. 'I'm going upstairs to my room. To change my clothes,' she told him flatly.

Alexander loosened the tie at his throat. His eyes were dark and penetrating.

'You can't wait to get out of your wedding dress, can you?' he grated.

Sara took it the wrong way, knew it immediately as she said the words, 'I'm not *that* eager to leap into your bed!' Her hand tightened on the banister as she lifted her head and gave him a cold smile. 'But you didn't mean that, did you? And you're quite right. I can't wait to be out of it. It means nothing to me. Nor does this,' she added, raising her hand to display her wedding ring.

'And what *does* mean something to you, Sara?' he asked wearily.

'You know very well that I care about my two daughters.'

'No, your *only* daughter. Thea,' he retorted grimly. 'Eleni is nothing to you. I've seen you with her, the way you look at her. You are incapable of loving her…'

Oh, please stop, Sara pleaded inwardly. She didn't want to be hurt any more. She'd been through too much. Slowly, wearily, she started to mount the stairs, cold inside, hurting, aching with fatigue, and now to be accused of not having a heart…

She stopped dead in the doorway of her bedroom. It looked different. Impersonal. Slowly she stepped into the room. It *was* impersonal, stripped of all her few belongings. The dressing table was bare, with no sign of her few cosmetics, or her hairbrush and comb. It was all neat and pristine. Unoccupied.

She heard a step behind her and swung to face Alexander. He stood leaning in the doorway, cold and impersonal as this room.

'Did you really expect to go on as before? With you sleeping alone in this room and not sharing my bedroom?' he drawled sardonically.

'Yes…yes, of course I did!' she blurted out, although, to be truthful, she hadn't given it any thought until this moment. There had been too much turmoil in her head and heart to think of anything else, such as the sharing of a bed with him. But now they were man and wife, even if the arrangement had been entered into solely for the sake of two little girls. And the fact that she might be expected to lead a normal married life with Alexander simply hadn't occurred to her.

She had considered it once, of course. On the beach, that first full day they had spent together, which now seemed so long ago. The thought of sleeping with him, making love with him…Yes, the thought had filled her mind, causing her heart and pulse to race with excitement. But now…?

She gazed up at him intently. There was no doubt that Alexander had everything that a woman would physically desire in a husband. The good looks, the physique to melt bones, the power and charisma he exuded. Yes, he had it all – and yet it meant nothing without a heart. And Alexander had no heart. Or, if he did, it was not one that cared for her, and her alone.

Once…twice, he had kissed her with a passion that had rocked her. But he had kept his distance ever since the night he had told her about Thea and Eleni and demanded marriage as his price for allowing Sara to keep her daughter. Verbal comfort and support – but no physical contact. In fact, it had seemed as though he couldn't bear to touch her.

Her eyes narrowed. 'We are married, but that doesn't mean —'

He laughed, a cruel laugh that cut through her like a knife. 'If you imagine for one minute that I'm going to accept half measures in this marriage, Sara, you are very much mistaken! This will be a full marriage, in every sense of the word. So, from now on we will sleep, eat and make love together, and bring our daughters up in a caring environment. In time, of course, there will be more children, and…'

Sara suddenly felt faint, blindly shaking her head in disbelief at his preposterous blueprint concerning their future lives together.

'Don't you think two little girls in our lives is enough to cope with? Do you honestly believe I can forget everything that's happened and somehow force myself to enjoy a sexual relationship with you?' she demanded incredulously.

'So you have no intention of consummating this marriage?' he drawled coolly, although they both knew that he wouldn't take any notice of anything she said. Alexander was totally master in his own house, and if he insisted on consummating their marriage there was very little she could do about it.

'Not with any *pleasure*,' she muttered tersely.

She thought he would be angry, though she quickly re-minded herself that to arouse any emotion in him he would have to care. And he didn't care about her. He would demand and take just what he was entitled to. Which would result in a physical release and nothing more.

There was a long silence as he stared grimly and coldly down at her. 'Nor will I have any pleasure,' he said at last. 'I doubt the earth will move for either of us this wedding night. But that will hardly be a surprise. My expectations of your warmth, or of you being able to give anything in the act of lovemaking, are not very high. So I am unlikely to be too disappointed.'

'How gallant!' Sara murmured, determined not to let him guess how wounding she had found his remarks. And then, determined to give as good as she got, she forced herself to give him a wide, mocking smile. 'Maybe it will help you to bear any disappointment if I tell you that I intend to close my eyes – and think of England!'

He raised a dark brow, and she was surprised to see a small twitch of amusement at the corner of his mouth. But he said nothing, which was far more effective than if he had replied with an insult of his own.

'I…I want to get changed,' she told him in a small voice.

He lifted himself away from the door-frame, waving a sweeping hand to usher her out of the bare room. 'I'll show you where your things are and we'll both change,' he said, with a light lilt to his tone.

Sara followed him in silence, nerves braced, her skin taut with tension. She could hardly bear to look around the suite of rooms he occupied, and she defiantly averted her gaze from the huge white-canopied bed.

'You have your own dressing room,' he told her, nodding across the room. 'The cupboards are well stocked, though I doubt much will fit you now that you have grown so thin.'

Sara's heart nearly stopped. Was he expecting her to wear his dead wife's clothes? Surely he couldn't think that…?

'I ordered new clothes for you some weeks ago,' he said, prompting Sara to take a deep breath of relief. 'You only had enough for a vacation, and I didn't think you would be interested in clothes after what I had to tell you. They arrived from Athens this morning.'

She looked at him and nodded. 'That was thoughtful of you,' she said softly as she left him to cross the room.

When she opened the cupboards in the dressing room, and found dresses with labels she had only read about in glossy magazines, Sara found herself suddenly standing paralysed, overcome by a weird sensation that she was, somehow, losing touch with her own identity. Not only had she been emotionally blackmailed into marrying him, but now he was dressing her in what *he* had chosen! He owned her!

Defiantly she snatched at a dress of her own, which was

bunched up at the end of the rail: a skimpy, pale lavender-coloured cotton dress that was light and cool. She pulled off the suffocating silk wedding dress, which she hadn't wanted to wear, but, though desperately in need of a shower to wash away the events of the day, she knew that it would mean stripping completely, and she could already hear him moving about in the main bedroom.

Sara was slipping the thin dress down over her shoulders when she felt something pull on it. A moment later she found herself being spun around as Alexander roughly stripped the garment away from her and flung it across the room. Her hands instinctively crossing over her breasts, to cover her white lacy bra, she stood facing him: half-naked, her skin tingling with fear, her eyes wide and appalled.

His dark eyes swept over her, cruel in their disparaging disapproval.

'Will you stop this?' he grated at her angrily. 'I'm doing my best for you. I'm sorry if I'm making mistakes. But this is a situation that is as alien to me as it is to you. I bought what I thought you would like. Damn it, Sara! Can't I make anything right for you? Can't I please you in *any* way?'

Her mouth dropped open at this angry outburst, and then she was swept by a tide of guilt. Alexander was right. At least he was trying to please her – and she wasn't making any effort at all. She hadn't even looked at the clothes to see if she liked them. She'd merely read the labels and felt cheapened and disgusted that he should have such power over her.

Suddenly her eyes filled with tears. 'I…I'm really sorry, Alexander. I just…I just wanted something of my own,' she pleaded in a hoarse whisper. 'I don't suppose you can under-stand, but I feel as if I…I've lost everything. I don't seem to know who I am any more…'

'You are my *wife*,' he told her sternly, snatching her hands from her breasts and firmly holding her wrists in his strong hands. 'And don't *ever* hide yourself from me again!'

Sara stared up at him, aware of his dark eyes gazing down at her breasts, almost devouring them with the intensity of his gaze. Sara shivered, feeling as though a liquid stream of fire was rushing through her trembling body. How was it that he had only to look at her to set her senses whirling…?

He touched her, a small light brush of his fingers across the swelling curves of her breasts above her bra. Her knees nearly gave way, the hot rush of sensuality and an awareness of his ability to stir her emotions shaking her to the very roots of her being.

Mesmerised, she couldn't seem to tear her eyes away from his. This was her husband. The man to whom she was now married – for life. Someone she hardly knew because so much else had occupied her mind ever since she had found out the truth of why he had brought her and Thea to this Greek island. And suddenly she wanted her marriage to become what it should have been if they had met and married without constraint: a bonding of mind and spirit, love and caring. She wanted him to love her, to make it easy for her to help and comfort him. Which meant…which must mean…that her feelings for him had somehow transcended all their mutual unhappiness, seeping unbidden into her soul without her realising what had happened.

All the time she had been coming to terms with the devastating fact of Thea and Eleni's birth something else had clearly been going on inside her. Was this strange, quivering sensation under her skin the first acknowledgement that Alexander meant something real to her?

Her whole body stiffened as the light brush of his fingers across her skin somehow turned into a burning, searing sensation that left her feeling terrified. He felt her reaction, and let her go as if she was on fire.

And she was suddenly burning as if in the throes of a fever. Hot and weightless and …

'Feeling better now?'

Cool water cascading down on the top of her head rapidly brought Sara back to her senses. She had no recollection of him lifting her into the shower. But here they were, standing under the jets of water, but while she was naked – he wasn't. His soaking wet shirt and jeans were moulded to his tall, athletic body, and it was all she could do to tear her eyes away from his magnificent physique.

Sara lifted her face to the cool spray and swallowed hard. What had happened just now? Had she fainted at the damning realisation that this man could sexually arouse her? Had five years of not having a man in her life culminated in a swooning fit when he had touched her so intimately? Was she going crazy?

She nodded. 'Yes…er…I feel much better. You…you must have taken the rest of my clothes off.'

'There wasn't much to remove.' He laughed softly. 'Will you be all right now?'

She nodded and murmured, 'I'm sorry. I didn't mean to be so silly. It's been a long day, a very strange day….' Her voice faded as she felt him move away, and she squeezed her eyes tightly shut and bit her lip. He hadn't taken his clothes off, so he clearly hadn't wanted to put himself in a compromising situation with her. No feelings for her had crept into his soul in the build up to their wedding day, and no feelings ever would, because all he had ever wanted from her was the total possession of his true daughter.

And, although it was quite ridiculous, she was stung by the thought that he had absolutely no feelings for her. None at all.

Sara eventually stepped out of the shower and wrapped a towel around her body before wandering out onto the balcony. It had been the longest day of her life, and although it was dark now, hot and dry, it still wasn't over. She breathed the fragrant air, listening to the girls having supper on the terrace with Anna, and heard the low, deep tones of Alexander's voice as he chatted to the children and the housekeeper.

She felt a dreadful loneliness wash over her, as if she wasn't a part of them. But gradually she began to regain some of her old spirit. Sara knew that she had been in far worse situations in her life – such as the death of Spiros – and had still managed to survive with her spirit unbroken. And if she made the effort she could survive this loveless marriage to Alexander, too. In fact, she now saw that she had no alternative. If she didn't, she was in danger of losing one or both of her daughters.

Maybe he did care for her, in his own way, she thought, trying to convince herself that there was some hope for the future. He had, after all, done his best for her and Thea in a material way, and perhaps that was as good as it was going to get. Whatever, there was no escape. It was done, and she must just try and make the best of it.

Opening the wardrobe again, she gazed at its contents. The designer dresses were expensive and tasteful; the blouses were pretty and cool; the long floaty skirts and exquisite silk underwear – everything he had ordered for her – was beautiful. She'd never had such lovely things. As she ran her fingers over the rails, touching the fine fabrics, she found herself wondering if these were the sort of clothes he had bought for his wife, Celeste…

She sighed, wondering which outfit to wear this evening. At least she was thankful that she wasn't living in the shadow of his wife…his first wife, she corrected herself quickly. Alexander had told her that this villa had been little more than a holiday home while his wife had been alive. Apparently Celeste hadn't cared for the small island, seldom visiting it since she'd preferred the hustle and bustle of life in Athens.

'Oh, Mama, you look lovely,' Thea cried as Sara stepped

out onto the softly lit terrace. She rushed to her mother and flung her arms around her waist. Sara had finally settled for a shimmering silver dress that skimmed her knees. It was a soft fabric that draped rather than clung and didn't accentuate her weight loss.

And it really had been some weight loss, Sara had realised for the first time as she had tried on outfit after outfit in despair. But not surprising; she'd hardly had any appetite lately. But she was going to put that to rights now. It would give her an aim in life, to regain her weight.

'I…I didn't know what to wear,' Sara told Alexander over her daughter's head. He had dressed in black trousers with a grey silk short-sleeved shirt and was looking casually elegant. Sara could see that Anna had taken the trouble to decorate the table on the terrace, which was set for two, the white tablecloth seemingly covered with flowers, sparkling crystal and gleaming silver. Sara was thankful that she'd decided to make a special effort to look nice this evening…their wedding night.

'Thea is right. You look very lovely, Sara,' Alexander acknowledged with a small nod of his head. 'Don't you think so, Eleni?'

The little girl, clinging to her father's hand, simply nodded and then quickly hid her face against her father.

Sara felt a curious pain inside her at the little girl's shyness, and the realisation that the child still wasn't sure of her. In her heart, she clearly still carried a picture of Celeste, and it would be a long time before she would think of Sara as her mother.

Oh, what a dreadful situation this was, she thought with heartfelt compassion as she held Thea against her, gazing across the terrace at Eleni clinging to Alexander. Alexander was right in accusing her of only thinking of herself. How were these two girls going to cope when they found out the truth of their heritages? Thea believing her father to be a hero, dying before she was born, and believing that Sara was her real mother. Eleni still grieving for a woman who hadn't been her mother, and believing that the tall handsome man to whom she was clinging was her father – when in reality she was the daughter of a poor fisherman.

It was a real-life Greek tragedy which no one could have contemplated five years ago, when an unexpected raging storm had changed so many people's lives.

Sara smiled warmly at Anna. 'Thank you for this, Anna,' she breathed softly, gazing at the beautifully set table.

Anna nodded, colouring slightly as she smiled, her black eyes twinkling as she glanced back and forth at the newly-wed couple. 'I wish you both every happiness,' she murmured, and Sara was touched at the genuine note in the housekeeper's voice.

'And now,' Anna continued, 'it's time the girls were in bed. They are both exhausted. So, I will wish you a very special night – the beginning of your lives together.'

Alexander held Sara's eyes, and if she hadn't known the truth she might have thought that Alexander was moved by Anna's good wishes for their future. But then he was hardly going to laugh cynically in front of his housekeeper, was he?

'Thank you, Anna,' he replied gruffly. 'No need for you to come back to serve us. We can manage.'

'Yes…yes, we can,' Sara added quickly. It would be embarrassing to have Anna watching their every movement tonight. She was already feeling bone-weary, and the thought of having to act out the opening sequence of this artificial marriage in front of a member of the staff was almost more than she could bear.

Thea hugged and kissed her goodnight, and then ran to Alexander and did likewise, a gesture that always appeared to leave him deeply moved. Thea had a very open and loving nature, and right from the start she had taken to him.

Eleni was far more reserved. She'd never hugged Sara. A formal handshake was all she could manage.

Alexander opened champagne once they were alone. It didn't pop, it sort of fizzed dully as he poured the sparkling wine into tall crystal flutes.

'I guess that says it all,' Sara stated flatly as she slid into her seat at the beautifully set table. 'Starting married life with a muted fizz rather than a bang!'

He said nothing, as always, totally ignoring her sarcastic remark.

'I'm sorry,' she muttered with a slight shake of her head. 'I guess I'm going to do a lot of apologising until all this sinks in.'

He passed her a glass of champagne, gazing intently into her eyes. 'Don't expect any apologies from me, Sara. I still believe that I made the right decision for everyone concerned.'

She nodded, holding up her glass up to his. 'So what shall we toast? Our future? Our marriage? Or our…our children?'

He held her eyes, those dark, dark pools she had once wanted to drown in.

'All three,' she murmured hastily as she clinked his glass. And then she gulped down the whole glassful of sparkling wine. She wanted to weep for them, because what an earth could lie ahead of Alexander and herself but deep unhappiness? He was convinced they had done the right thing, but she had severe doubts. One day those little girls would see what Sara already knew, that Alexander Karakou didn't…couldn't…love his wife. And, they would also see that she, too, had been living a lie.

Silently Alexander refilled her glass. Sara stared at it, and then lifted her eyes to meet his apprehensive gaze.

In a blinding flash she suddenly realised that he was finding the situation every bit as scary as she did! He had wanted…needed his biological daughter so much that he'd forced himself to go through with this marriage. And he loved her daughter, Eleni, so much, that he was willing to suffer this barren, loveless charade for the sake of both children. And Sara knew that she had no choice but to go along with it. It looked as if they were both trapped in the quicksands of this arranged marriage.

'Oh, God, what a mess,' she whispered desperately.

And, because he made no reply, didn't deny it, didn't promise to make it as easy for them both as he could, she couldn't control her despair. Slowly tears trickled down her cheeks.

She felt him lift her away from the table, aware of his arms closing about her trembling body, his lips pressed against the side of her head, his fingers splaying into the silky mass of her hair.

Still he said nothing. He just held her, as if mere words couldn't help either of them any more.

She made a huge effort to pull herself together, slowly twisting out from his embrace.

'I…I'm sorry, but I'm really not hungry,' she muttered helplessly. 'I…er…I think it's time I went to bed.'

Alexander didn't argue. He didn't try to stop her. The last thing she heard as she slipped upstairs was the clink of the champagne bottle against his glass as he refilled it.

Hours later she heard him coming into the room. Lying under a sheet on the canopied bed, she hadn't managed to seek oblivion in sleep, although tiredness had dragged at her till she ached. Now her body stiffened and she bit her lip.

She realised she had been waiting for him. It was shocking to realise that her toes were tingling, excitement sweeping through her veins and reaching every part of her body.

She was wearing a sensual slip of a satin nightie, white with tiny embroidered flowers at the rolled hem. She had picked it because it was beautiful and had slipped it on over her head, knowing that she had to face facts. This was their wedding night.

She wanted it to be over quickly – a release from the agony she had suffered recently – perhaps a little bit of comfort, if she thought about it objectively. She knew that people did that at times of stress…made love for release…a sexual act to liberate the mind and body of tension. And if she could think of it that way she might be able to survive this marriage.

Sara felt the weight of his body on the mattress next to her. She tensed, waiting for him to reach out to touch her. And then the bitterly cold realisation that he had *no* such intention hit her like whiplash some moments later

His breathing was deep and even. He was asleep, distanced from her by at least two feet in the huge wide bed.

Sara lay stunned, hardly able to breathe. She didn't know whether to be angry, hurt, or…relieved. But relief wasn't the feeling that took precedence, and she wished with all her heart that it did. She felt horribly rejected and painfully hurt.

Pounding her pillow to try and make herself more comfortable, Sara squeezed her eyes tightly shut. What had she expected? she asked herself roughly. In truth, she had expected him to carry out his earlier threats – that there would be no halfway measures in this marriage. And, if she was honest, one small corner of her being would have welcomed his strong, muscular body. But it was becoming crystal-clear that he couldn't bear to touch her. He didn't want her. He didn't even find her desirable. The stark truth was that he couldn't even bring himself to consummate this marriage.

And it didn't take her long to realise why. Because he already had someone to satisfy his sexual needs. He had a mistress – and a wife clearly wasn't going to make any difference to his love-life!

chapter five

Sara was up first, showering and dressing quickly before he awoke. It had been a long night, hot and restless, and she didn't feel in the least refreshed. She wondered how she would be feeling this morning if Alexander had made love to her last night. Would the physical union have changed anything between them? Broken down some of the barriers between them?

As she slid into a pair of her old shorts, a vest style T-shirt and espadrilles, and raked a hand through her tousled dark hair, she dismissed all such thoughts and concentrated on the order of the day. Start how you mean to go on, she told herself firmly.

'I don't expect Anna to attend to Thea and Eleni all the time,' Sara began as Alexander joined her on the terrace for breakfast. His hair was damp from his shower and he wore an aubergine-coloured silk shirt and thin off-white linen chinos. He looked fresh and handsome, and Sara wished she hadn't dressed so hastily in her old clothes.

She had waited for him, though, sipping some orange juice and not starting on the fresh, crisply baked rolls and honey and coffee. 'Anna was up before everyone this morning, and has made their breakfasts and got them sorted out for the day,' Sara said. 'She has enough to do, and...'

'I don't expect my wife to take the full responsibility for two children,' Alexander told her as he poured coffee into her cup.

Sara gripped her hands tightly beneath he table. 'I have nothing else to do, Alexander. I thought you wanted me to be a mother to the girls...?'

He poured coffee for himself, a measured action that had Sara watching with irritation. He did everything so precisely, exactly as *he* wanted it.

'In England, you successfully combined motherhood and a career. I see no reason to change that now that you are living in Greece.'

Sara's mouth dropped open. 'Are you saying you expect me to resume my career now that we are married?'

'I'd rather you didn't. But if it makes you happy, I'll swallow hard and put up with it.' He gave her a small smile before lifting the coffee cup to his lips. He held her gaze over the rim of the white gold-rimmed porcelain for a moment, before Sara looked away.

She tore a roll to pieces, not quite sure that she'd heard him correctly. He didn't mind her having a career? She was astonished.

'The thought hadn't crossed my mind,' she mused thoughtfully. 'I...I suppose I can work from here. As you know, I'm a freelance travel consultant now, and if I had the right computer equipment...'

'Find out and I'll get what you need,' Alexander said shortly. 'Meanwhile, if you are not happy with Anna I will bring Irena back. Eleni has been asking about her anyway.'

'Irena? Who's she?' Sara asked with a frown of puzzlement.

'Where are the girls?' Alexander asked suddenly, looking around the terrace and to the gardens beyond.

'Swimming in the small pool,' Sara told him, reaching for more coffee.

Alexander shot to his feet, growling furiously, 'Eleni can't swim, and they shouldn't be allowed near that pool alone.' He threw down his napkin, quickly scraping his chair back from the table to head off towards the pool area, when Sara stopped him short.

'Anna is with them and Eleni *can* swim, actually,' Sara

told him, feeling guilty now for not having told him sooner. 'Thea and I have been teaching her. She can only manage a few short breast strokes, of course, but it's a start.'

Alexander glowered at her, fists clenched at his side. 'My daughter has learned to swim – and no one has thought to tell me?' he exclaimed in an outraged tone of voice.

'You were too busy arranging our damned wedding!' Sara snapped back. And before she could stop, heard herself adding heatedly, 'And she's *our* daughter – not exclusively yours!'

He leaned across the table, glaring at her. 'Oh, she's *our* daughter now, is she? And what brought about this sudden change in your feelings towards the child? The realisation that this marriage has really happened? That you'd better make the best of it, because there is no other way?'

Sara shot to her feet, slamming her hands down on the table and leaning furiously towards him. 'Let me remind you, Alexander, that Eleni is in fact *my* daughter. And if you think I have no feelings for her, then you must have lost the sense you were born with.'

'I know what I see…that you hold back from her,' he blazed.

'No!' Sara gave a vehement shake of her head. 'No – Eleni holds back from *me*. Which is perfectly natural. And if I suddenly swamped her with suffocating motherly love I could easily do more harm than good. I do care for her, very deeply. But I can't treat her the same way I do Thea, because…'

'Because you don't love her! You don't love your own daughter,' he seethed.

'I was going to say because they are very *different*, Alexander,' Sara pointed out as reasonably as she could, trying to keep her cool. 'Thea is a warm, giving person who responds well to affection. She's open and up-front, which Eleni isn't.'

Alexander looked so angry Sara thought he might explode. 'Eleni *is* affectionate,' he argued hotly. 'She is also a warm, giving child – and how dare you suggest otherwise?'

'I have every right to suggest anything I damned well please!' Sara yelled at him. 'She's *my* daughter, after all. But I haven't had a hand in her upbringing, and…'

'And Eleni's shyness, which you interpret as a lack of warmth and affection, is apparently all *my* fault?' he roared, his dark eyes glinting with fury.

'I didn't say that!' Sara snapped. 'What I'm *trying* to say – if only you'd listen! – is that Thea has had an easy life with me. Just the two of us, in a safe and loving world of our own,' she added, as calmly as she could. 'Thea never knew her father, and so has never suffered his loss. She doesn't miss him, Alexander, because she never knew him. Whereas Eleni was old enough to be affected by Celeste's loss. Which is why I know that I can't expect love and devotion from her yet, because Celeste is still in her heart. And she isn't as tough as Thea; that's why I'm taking it carefully, one step at a time.'

As Alexander remained staring at her in silence Sara gave a heavy sigh. 'I do care about Eleni,' she assured him in a softer tone. 'So please stop accusing me of being heartless, because I'm not. Only a few weeks ago you sprang on me one of the most devastating shocks of my life. I've had a lot to cope with – something that you have managed to come to terms with because you've had longer to accept it. But you must see that the whole situation is deeply complex and it could take years to resolve.'

She sighed deeply once again, brushing the hair back from her forehead with a tired, weary hand. 'Alexander, please don't expect so much of me,' she pleaded.

Suddenly he slumped back into his chair and held his head in his hands. ''You're right. I am expecting too much,' he murmured thickly.

Sara gave a helpless shrug. 'We are scarcely twenty-four hours into this marriage and already we're at each other's throats. Quite frankly, I don't think I can bear another twenty-four years of it!'

She was surprised to hear him give a low laugh. She looked up and her heart seemed to flip over in her chest. He was looking at her almost warmly. It could all be so different if he cared…Sara thought dismally. Unfortunately, they seemed to be totally incompatible. And without love and consideration for one another, these inevitable rows were likely to make their lives a torment.

As they both avoided each other's eyes Sara sipped her coffee, feeling the heat of another Greek day on her back and wondering if she could survive it all. Leaving the girls aside, she didn't see how she and Alexander had a chance of making this marriage work. But because of their daughters they were inextricably bound up with one another.

Glancing through her eyelashes at him as he sat staring down at his coffee cup, she realised that he'd probably come to precisely her own conclusion. That the situation between them was unbearable on one hand, but inevitable on the other.

However, Sara's thoughts went beyond their daughters' care and well being. She saw Alexander for what he was: a very charismatic and attractive man, a man any woman would desire. And, yes, she was prepared to admit, if only to herself, that she found him desirable. In fact, just looking at him was enough to set her heart thudding. But he'd made it plain that he didn't desire her. Last night was clear proof of that. He had cold-shouldered her on their wedding night. So how could she let her heart reach out to him when he felt nothing for her?

'Are you listening?' he asked.

'Hmm…?' Sara's eyes had been transfixed on his mouth, watching him forming the words on his full, well-defined

lips, lips that had once touched her so persuasively. But she
had heard nothing.

'Er, yes…well, no, I'm afraid I wasn't listening.'

He smiled, faintly amused. Had he guessed what she had
been thinking?

'I was saying that I have decided to bring Irena back,'
Alexander told her. 'It will be good for Eleni; she was
getting closer to her and she has asked about her. I'm sure
that Thea will get on with her, too. She isn't a nanny, of
course, but she was Celeste's best friend.'

A cool breeze fluttered across Sara's brow. She frowned.
There were no cool breezes in Greece at this time of the
year.

'Irena…?'

'She was living here with us, this summer,' Alexander explained. 'Running the holiday villas and looking after Eleni.'

Sara suddenly realised that he was talking about his
mistress! She of the poised index finger, waiting in the
wings of Alexander's life, ready to re-enter on cue, just
when he was ready for her.

'And…and you want her back?' Sara uttered in a faint
voice.

'Yes, I want her back,' he said decisively. He held her
eyes and Sara felt the chill of rejection so deeply she almost
winced with pain.

So, she had been right in her assumptions last night. He
hadn't made love to her because he could get his
pleasures elsewhere. Well! If Alexander thought she was
going to put up with such nonsense – he had another thought
coming!

She crumpled her napkin, tossing it down on the table as
she rose to her feet.

'You bring her back to this house over my dead body,
Alexander,' she told him fiercely. 'Like it or not, we are man
and wife now. So I have a say in who comes into this

household, and I don't want her here.'

'You haven't met her yet,' he drawled smoothly, a glint of laughter in his dark eyes.

'I have seen her, and heard about her,' Sara told him, remembering that glance of icy disdain and disapproval his mistress had thrown up to her on the balcony, when delivering Eleni back to the villa.

'She's beautiful, isn't she? And she *is* my mistress, of course,' Alexander stated firmly, as if challenging her to make something of it.

She could hardly bear the look of wicked mischief in his eyes, but somehow she managed to hold his gaze. Sara knew he was doing this on purpose, although she had no idea why he was enjoying teasing and goading her. Was he trying to make her jealous?

'Yes, she is very beautiful,' Sara agreed with a saccharine-sweet smile. 'And, yes – I can well believe that she is your mistress. But I am your wife.'

He smiled thinly. 'Suddenly you want to be my wife? Well, perhaps you had better start acting like one.'

Sara narrowed her eyes at him. 'It's not difficult to see what you mean by that snide remark,' she retorted grimly. 'However, it takes two to tango, you know. When you start acting like a husband, we might start getting somewhere!'

He stood up, walked slowly around the table towards her, his eyes sweeping derisively over the woman standing defiantly in front of him.

'You dress like a holidaymaker,' he told her contemptuously, gesturing scornfully at her worn shorts, the downtrodden espadrilles and her tousled hair. 'The first morning of our marriage – and you can't even be bothered to make an effort!'

'I might have done, if *you* had bothered to make an effort last night,' she snapped, secretly stung by his criticism, but not prepared to admit it. So…OK, she should have made an effort. But she was damned if she was going to apologise.

He grinned down at her, and Sara's palms itched to slap that supercilious expression off his face. 'You wanted me to make love to you?' he drawled sardonically.

'Well…I *expected* that you would,' she retorted evasively, hands on her hips, her chin jutting defiantly up at him.

'And you were disappointed?'

'Who…me? Hardly! Actually, I was relieved that you didn't,' she added, well aware that she was lying through her teeth.

He laughed. 'And yet you object to me having a mistress?'

She shook her head. 'No, Alexander, I don't object to you having a mistress. But I do object to *your* mistress looking after *my* children!' she flung back at him. 'This isn't about jealousy. So there's no point in thinking that you can make me feel jealous.'

'Can't I?' he murmured, reaching for her so speedily that he took her completely by surprise. His strong arms snaked around her small waist, and suddenly she found herself clasped tightly up against his warm, muscular chest. His breath, his lips so close to her own…

'So…you feel nothing at the thought of me kissing my mistress?' he muttered thickly, his breath fanning her cheek. And then he was trailing his lips across her face as his arms tightened, pressing her fiercely up against the length of his hard body.

His arousal shocked her, her breath catching in her throat as she found herself responding to a tremor of sensual excitement at the touch of his mouth brushing across hers, seeking, finding, and persuading her soft lips apart, possessing her so completely that his kiss was almost as powerful as sex itself.

Suddenly Sara knew what jealousy was all about, as her

mind filled with images of this man, her husband, claiming another woman in such a way. The prelude to their making love, their kisses and their mutual arousal, the tender touches with the underlying fire of possession…There seemed nothing she could do to banish the erotic, deeply sensual images which filled her head, leaving her feeling sick with heart-burning fear and…and jealousy.

Sara was totally stunned to realise that she *did* want him. And that, despite all her protestations, she was more than capable of becoming a thoroughly jealous woman – which left her feeling totally shattered.

He released her at last, but didn't cast her aside carelessly. His eyes were darkly hooded, his mouth drawn into a tight line as he gazed down at her.

'So, you *were* disappointed last night,' he breathed softly.

Sara licked her moist lips. Damn him!

'Ah – so now I know that I've managed to scare the life out of you, with threats of bringing my mistress back into this house, I shall expect more from you tonight!' he drawled, before plundering her mouth once again, in a scorching kiss that burned her lips. 'Or perhaps now would be more fitting, while you still have the heat of arousal in your blood,' he murmured softly, as his lips eased their pressure to a gentle tenderness.

Yes – now! was Sara's first bemused thought. *Now…* on impulse…with no time for her to think about it. Now, in the heat of the moment. Because then she wouldn't have to remember that his feelings for her were only physical.

But she had to face the painful truth that, as far as he was concerned, this was only about sex. Perhaps her feelings went deeper because she was a woman? Women were supposed to be on a different wavelength from men. But only marginally. How could she come to *love* an arrogant man like this?

The thought that he was only playing with her gave Sara the strength to break out of his embrace, quickly pulling her top down over the waistband of her shorts.

'I have better things to do this morning than consummate our marriage,' she told him haughtily.

To her surprise, he laughed out loud, throwing back his dark head in a roar of genuine amusement which said far more than words ever could.

Well, she'd guessed that he didn't take any of this seriously. And why should he, when their marriage meant nothing more than the opportunity to gain hold of Thea? She, herself, meant nothing to him, and she could well believe that his feelings for his mistress were of little consequence either.

On the other hand, she had to concede that Alexander really did care about both his daughters. So at least he had *one* good point.

'I need a car and some money,' she told him firmly. 'And at some time we ought to take stock of our future. For instance, I'll have to return to England to sort out my affairs. We also should begin to make plans for the girls' education. And we need to decide where we're going to live. And...' Her voice trailed off.

He had turned from her and was walking away, still chuckling to himself. She called after him, 'Alexander! There are things we need to be discuss.'

But he made no response. She watched him jog down the steps of the terrace, hands plunged deeply into the pockets of his chinos. No doubt to seek out the company of Thea and Eleni, she told herself glumly. After all, they gave him far more pleasure than she ever could.

With a heavy sigh, Sara started to gather up the dirty breakfast things, before shaking her head at her own folly. There were members of staff willing and able to do this job. Lunch would be taken care of, the bedrooms would be cleaned, and the rest of the house and gardens given their daily once-over. So what was *her* function in this new life of hers? As far as she could see – precious little!

Sara stretched her bare sun-tanned legs out under the metal table on the cobbled pavement and sipped the iced lemon and lime drink Maria had prepared for her. Maria was inside the taverna helping Forte prepare a meal for a crowd of English youths on holiday, who'd just ordered pizza and chips. They were sitting waiting at another table out on the street, drinking imported beer straight from the bottle and talking and laughing noisily.

Maria and Sara had exchanged glances, grinning when the English boys had ordered the sort of food that was obviously familiar to them. It was clearly pointless telling the holiday-makers that Forte's *kleftiko* was out of this world, his *houmus* and *tsatziki* to die for; his salads and the local feta cheese mouthwatering. They wanted pizza and chips!

Sara had brought Thea and Eleni with her, and they were playing across the road with Stefios and Chloe, beside a water pump where the locals drew water twice a day. Earlier she had demanded the freedom to go out, and Alexander had tossed her the keys of a white Peugeot which he had apparently bought for her. She was rather ashamed that she hadn't even known that it had been delivered. But that was mostly because her mind seemed crammed to the hilt lately.

Alexander had asked where she was going. And when she had asked, 'Does it matter?' he had merely shrugged his broad shoulders and returned to his study, slamming the door after him – and that had been that.

And now they were here, on the other side of the island, visiting Maria and her family. And for the first time in a long while, Sara didn't feel so terribly alone.

Maria came out into the street with a tray piled high and the boys cheered and flirted with her as she served them.

'My husband, he say try the *dolmades*. You enjoy!' She grinned at them.

'*Dolmades*, what are they?' one of the youths asked, peering at them suspiciously.

'Meatballs,' Maria said sweetly, and winked at Sara over the boys' heads.

Maria sighed wearily as five minutes later she slumped into the metal chair next to Sara. 'Now they are settled,' she said under her breath.

'And enjoying their meatballs,' Sara laughed.

'So, what are you doing down here in the village, when you should be on your honeymoon?' Maria asked bluntly.

Sara waved a dismissive hand. 'Oh, we are taking it later,' she told her friend airily. 'Alexander has some work to clear up before he can take time out, and there is much to do with the girls. We have to sort out their education, and all sorts of other things.'

It had been Alexander's suggestion that they delayed their honeymoon, and Sara had agreed. Thea and Eleni had a lot to cope with – the marriage and new parents to come to terms with – and to leave them alone with Anna for a couple of weeks didn't seem a good idea.

Maria eyed her suspiciously. 'So, why the haste to be married? I help move you into his villa to be his mistress, and the next I hear is that you are married! The whole island knows. Rumour says that you are pregnant, but I don't believe that. You have only been on the island five minutes. I've heard of whirlwind romances – but a whirlwind pregnancy…?' Maria went into fits of laughter.

Sara tried to laugh with her, but it was hard when you couldn't see the joke. It was on the tip of her tongue to spill it all out to Maria – the awful, agonising truth of everything that had happened to her ever since she'd arrived here in Greece. But already the small island's gossip network was in full flow. And to expect Maria to keep quiet about the reasons for her swift marriage to Alexander Karakou would be too much to expect of her friend.

'No, I'm not pregnant.' She smiled. 'But, well…when love…er…hits you, what's the point of waiting…?'

'Stefios! Stefios!' Maria suddenly screamed, leaping to her feet and dashing across the quiet cobbled road. 'You must not splash Eleni…Thea, no!'

Too late. In a fury with Stefios for splashing Eleni, and soaking the front of her pretty cotton sundress, Thea had drawn her hand back and lashed out at Stefios, catching him across the nose. Discovering that his nose was bleeding, the little boy let out a howl. Sara rushed across the road to join Maria, dodging around the rear of a white car that had slowed to a halt in the narrow roadway, its driver obviously curious to see what was going on.

Eleni sobbed and flung herself into Sara's arms. Thea stood rigid against a white wall, shocked that her protection of Eleni had resulted in a mini-bloodbath. Chloe burst into fits of giggles and Stefios, clutching his nose, kicked out at his elder sister.

'That's enough!' Maria bellowed at all of them.

'Anything I can do? I'm a medical student.'

Sara, clutching a damp, tearful Eleni tightly to her waist, turned to one of the youths from the taverna, who had sprinted across the road. She smiled gratefully. 'It seems the children have fallen out with each other,' she told him with a laugh, nodding towards Stefios. 'And I'm afraid the result, is one bloody nose!'

'I didn't mean it,' Thea cried, and went to Maria, who gave her a hug and assured her it was an accident and that no one was cross.

The young man grinned at Sara and stepped towards Stefios. 'Here, young man, put your head down.' With finger and thumb he pinched the bridge of the small boy's nose and, while holding it, turned back to Sara. 'You're English?

On holiday?'

'Er…no, I live here,' Sara told him.

'Nanny to this lot?' He grinned, eyes sweeping over Thea, Stefios and Eleni, who still had her face pressed hard against Sara's waist. He took a white handkerchief from the back pocket of his cut-off jeans, and wiped Stefios's nose clean, to see if the bleeding had stopped. He looked at Sara quizzically when she didn't reply.

Just then Eleni lifted her face away from Sara's waist to look at the stranger.

'Oh, I see that one is your daughter,' he laughed, nodding at Eleni. 'I guess that means dinner is out tonight? Unless of course there *isn't* a husband in loving attendance.'

Sara's felt colour rush to her cheeks, glancing quickly at Maria to see if there was any reaction to what this stranger had instinctively recognised: the physical resemblance between mother and daughter. But mercifully Maria's English hadn't been good enough to pick up on the young man's meaning. Besides, she was far more concerned about Stefios's injury and the need to comfort Thea.

'*Is* there a loving husband in attendance?' the stranger enquired, clearly intent on flirting with Sara.

Sara felt Thea's hand creep into hers and grip it tightly. Eleni was still at her side and Sara held the two girls close to her. Oh, sure there was a husband in attendance – but it wasn't loving attendance. And then, as she took a good look at the handsome young man, registering his good looks but knowing that she had absolutely no interest in him, she found herself wishing with all her heart that her husband *did* love her.

Sara summoned a smile. 'Yes, there is a loving husband in attendance,' she told the young man softly.

'Some men have all the luck,' he muttered in resignation, and then gave Stefios his full attention. 'Hey, young man, no damage. You'll be just fine in a few moments.'

Maria was thanking him profusely, and Stefios was grinning now and the stranger's companions across the road
were giving their friend a rousing cheer and the inquisitive
driver of the white car, curiosity satisfied, accelerated away
with a screech of rubber on cobbles. While Sara, clutching
hold of Thea and Eleni, only wanted to be home with her
husband. Even when she was well aware of his lack of
feeling for her.

'But I must feed you all before you return home,' Maria
insisted, after Sara said that they ought to be making a move.
Maria ushered the now giggling children inside the taverna,
and with a shrug of resignation Sara followed. What had she
to go home for, anyway?

It was late afternoon, extremely hot with little moving air.
The palm trees were motionless, and Sara was tired as she
drew up outside the villa and switched off the engine. But
not too tired to avoid the bat out of hell who'd just pulled out
of the drive without a thought for any traffic that might be
approaching.

Not that there was much traffic in this part of the island.
Sara excused the driver. He or she, whoever they were, had
obviously not been expecting anyone else to be on the road.

Anna came out onto the front terrace on hearing them
approach, followed by an irate Alexander who looked as if
he had spent the afternoon raking his hands through his
badly tousled hair.

He scooped Eleni up into his arms for a hug, although for
some reason Thea held back. Alexander, putting on a smile
for the girls, held out a hand to Thea. It was only then Thea
ran to him for her usual hug.

Sara stood watching the touching scene, emotion tugging
at her heart.

'Oh, Papa – there was a fight!' Eleni told him excitedly as
he put her down on the tiles. 'Stefios threw water at me, and

then Thea hit him, and there was blood everywhere. A nice man made Stefios better, and…'

'Yes, I know,' Alexander told her, glowering at Sara across the top of the children's heads. Sara felt her heart beginning to thud as he added, 'Anna, please take them inside and put them straight into a bath. They're both filthy!'

And filthy they were, Sara noticed for the first time, as Anna took two grubby hands and led the girls away. Thea was often a bit of a mess at the end of the day. She threw herself so tomboyishly into everything she undertook that it was inevitable she didn't stay tidy for long. But not Eleni. Eleni had a very feminine disposition. She hated a hair out of place, a crease in her dress, or a scuff on her expensive shoes. But not today. Her hair was as tousled as Alexander's, while her dress was creased and spotted with blood from Stefios's nose, and her knees were black where she'd been kneeling in the dust in Maria's back yard.

Sara folded her hands across her chest, waiting for the verbal dressing down which, from the look of Alexander's grimly set features, was about to break out over her head any minute.

'And you can get upstairs and wash that smirk from your face, too,' he growled at her. 'After which I will expect a full explanation as to why you allowed my daughters to wallow in filth and dirt all day. Not only that, but I understand they have been involved in a street fight, and have been frequenting downmarket tavernas in the company of drunken foreigners!' he added, almost shaking with anger and fury.

Sara held her ground, staring back at him with cold defiance. 'Just *who* in the hell do you think you are talking to, in that tone of voice, Alexander?' she demanded icily. 'Some new member of staff who isn't coming up to scratch and needs fifty lashes? How did you know where we have been all day? Or what we have been doing? Have you been following us?'

'Irena witnessed the whole sordid scene outside the taverna. She saw you openly flirting with a drunken tourist and...'

Sara's mouth dropped open with shock, and then tightly clamped shut. Irena had been spying on them – and then reporting back to her husband?

Propelled by sheer outrage, she suddenly flew up the marble steps towards him, giving him the blackest of looks as she swept past his tall, angry figure. Head held high, she raced up the curving stairway, before attempting to slam the bedroom door behind her. But it seemed that Alexander was capable of moving just as swiftly, quickly entering the room after her. She spun round to face him, her face pinched with rage.

In her rapid flight from him, and before she did something physical she might regret, she had scanned through her memory, coming up with the image of the white car that had pulled up in the road by the taverna before screeching off in a hurry.

It must have been Irena! Clearly, in a hurry to report back to lover-boy! Sara told herself with mounting fury. But, not content with that, it had also been Irena who'd almost driven herself and the girls off the road on their return to the villa just now. Sara hadn't noticed the driver on either occasion – she'd had no reason to do so.

'How *dare* you arrange to have me followed by your lover?' Sara cried. 'It's outrageous!'

'She was in the area, just passing by, and thank goodness she was – because now I know you are not to be trusted with my daughters!' he thundered at her.

Sara stared at him, eyes wide and incredulous. 'I don't believe I'm hearing this!' she ground out. 'Whose daughters? *Your* daughters?' she mocked. 'No, Alexander, we're talking about *our* daughters. For your information, I took them across the island to visit Maria. As their mother,

I feel perfectly entitled to take them out,' she added coldly. 'But your damned mistress isn't entitled to do *anything* – least of all to spy on me, and then come running back to you with highly exaggerated tales of drunken debauchery, child negligence, and God knows what!'

'Where the hell are you going now?' he roared at her as she turned her back to him and headed for the bathroom.

Without a glance back, she threw over her shoulder, 'To wipe the smirk from my face, before it becomes a permanent fixture!'

He caught her before she reached the bathroom door, swinging her back against it, the force knocking the air from her lungs before she knew what was happening to her.

His eyes were black with rage. 'A Greek wife doesn't argue with her husband, and –'

'I'm *not* a Greek wife!' Sara flung back at him, before he could finish. 'I'm your *English* wife – and don't you dare to throw that "Greek-women-know-their-place" rubbish in my face. I never got it from Spiros, and I'm sure as hell not taking it from you!'

'He wasn't your husband,' he reminded her cruelly.

'That's a real pity!' Sara yelled back at him. 'Because Spiros wouldn't have wrapped his daughter in cotton wool as you and Celeste obviously did. Today, for the first time in her life, *my* daughter Eleni has seen some street life, and –'

His grip on her shoulders tightened; his face twisted with rage. 'I don't want *my* daughter experiencing the seedy side of life.'

'The seedy side of life?' Sara laughed cynically. 'Stefios playfully splashed Eleni with water. So Thea hit him – not meaning to hurt the little boy, but purely in defence of her new sister. Unfortunately, she made his nose bleed. His sister Chloe laughed, and then Stefios kicked her. Would any normal person call that "seedy"? No, Alexander – they wouldn't. It's merely childhood – growing up, living and learning. It's what children *do*. It's life, and it's what Eleni has been lacking, and probably one of the reasons why she is so shy and withdrawn.'

'And you know all about the art of bringing children up, don't you?' he accused sarcastically. 'If Thea did punch the boy on the nose, it's because you have never taught her right from wrong!'

'Oh, no, Alexander, you're not landing me with that one! This is genetic. She carries *your* genes, right? The ones that are pinning me to this door. The bloody arrogant, *pushy* genes! And now, if you have quite finished wiping the floor with me for allowing the girls to gain access to their childhoods, I'd like to take a shower.'

'You will shower when this conversation is terminated – by me!'

Sara was verging on hysteria. She felt as if she had left the villa this morning in the modern era, only to return in the eighteenth century.

'So, you have something more to say to me, O Lord and Master?' she ground out sarcastically. 'If so – kindly get on with it. I'm bored to death with all this nonsense!'

He nearly shook her with rage. 'This is no laughing matter. No wife of mine flirts with tourists outside tavernas!'

'So, it's OK to do it *inside*, is it?' she couldn't resist.

Sara really thought she had gone too far this time, tipping him over the edge of his rage and into some dark pit of apoplexy. He was shaking with anger, gripping her shoulders so tightly that she winced with the pain.

'For goodness' sake, Alexander, lighten up!' she cried, squirming under his grasp. 'I can't be what you want me to be! Some simpering little wife who buttons her lip when you make mad accusations. I was *not* flirting in the street!'

'You smiled, you blushed, you laughed softly…'

'My God! Is your damned mistress, also your private

detective?' Sara blazed, furious that the awful woman hadn't missed even the flutter of an eyelash. 'I merely smiled at the boy in gratitude, because he'd managed to stop Stefios's nosebleed. I blushed because he commented on Eleni being my daughter, and I was worried Maria might discover our secret. And, and if I laughed softly, it was in relief that he took my refusal to have dinner with him in a good spirit!'

Did he believe her? Did she care if he didn't? Oh, yes, with all her heart. She didn't want him to believe that she'd done something of which she was innocent. But he'd been only too eager to believe the worst; he'd already taken his mistress's word – and not hers.

'So, there you have it, Alexander,' she breathed raggedly. 'It's a case of my word against Irena's, isn't it? So who are you going to believe? Your mistress – or your wife?'

She held his gaze, blue eyes challenging him, defying him to back up his mistress's lies and distortions of the truth.

'And now you give me the choice,' he grated through thinned white lips. 'To believe my wife, whom I scarcely know – or my *mistress*, who is well known to me?'

Sara ran her tongue across her lips. 'I already know the truth, so I don't give a damn *who* you believe,' she whispered hoarsely. 'But *I'm* not the mistress whose lover has just taken a new wife. Has it occurred to you that maybe Irena isn't *too* happy about that?' Sara added quietly. 'That she might have been expecting you to marry *her*, and not some English woman, whom you hardly know?'

Her voice trailed away. What an earth had she been saying? Sara asked herself, ashamed to have given voice to such spiteful, shrewish comments about another woman, who clearly should be more pitied than anything else. To have told such outrageous lies Irena must be almost consumed with jealousy. For all Sara knew the other woman might have been in love with Alexander for years. And, as his late wife's best friend, she must have confidently expected him to marry her once he'd recovered from his tragic loss.

'Let me go, Alexander,' she pleaded wearily. 'I really don't care *what* you believe of me.'

His eyes narrowed suspiciously. 'So, if you don't care what I think, why did you refuse the dinner invitation from a good looking compatriot who…?'

'Because I am married to you – you idiot!' Sara yelled, finally losing her temper, and wishing he would release her so she could pummel him wildly for being so damned infuriating! She hadn't asked for all this nonsense, and had done nothing to deserve it. It just wasn't fair!

'Is that the only reason?' he questioned harshly.

'Do I *need* another?'

'Yes, you do! You need to come up with the answer I want to hear. I'm not interested in some nonsense about the fact that you're my wife. You'll have to do better than that, Sara. A whole lot better!'

Sara, her head aching now from this interminable argument, didn't have a clue what he was talking about.

'I'm not a mind-reader,' she protested. 'How should I know what you want to hear?'

'Try it. Go for it! Start with any damned reason you can think of for refusing a dinner date – other than the fact of being married to me.'

'You're mad…utterly crazy!' she yelled angrily, twisting and turning in an effort to escape him, but it was impossible. 'There *is* no other reason. I didn't even look at him properly,' she added helplessly. 'I couldn't tell you if he had green or brown eyes, or one of each. He was faceless. He didn't exist for me. I don't want anyone else but…' She quickly swallowed the rest of the sentence.

Her gaze widened as she saw his eyes suddenly glittering with triumph. It was only then that Sara realised she had been led like a lamb to the slaughter. And so skilfully that she hadn't realised what was happening. She had given herself away. Now he knew what she had only fully realised this afternoon when another man had flirted with her: that there was no one else for her but Alexander.

And how happy she would be if she could have read relief instead of triumph in his eyes. But now he had it all. A complete hold over her, as if the marriage alone hadn't been enough for him.

'You didn't finish,' he murmured softly, lowering his dark head and pressing his mouth dangerously close to hers.

'I don't have to, do I? You have it all now,' she whispered, trembling helplessly as if in the grip of a raging fever. 'Total possession.'

'Not "total" possession – not yet...' he breathed thickly.

And then it began...starting with a kiss, deep, hard and purposeful, daring her to object. Stiffly, she stood with her back hard against the door, inwardly fighting him, not wanting him to have the full satisfaction of knowing that he was getting to her. It was useless to deny that she cared for him; he would merely laugh in her face. But to deny him with her body, to stay stiff and unyielding, would prove to him he that was wrong, that she still had some spirit left and that she didn't want him this way – only interested in sex, and with no feelings of love or even affection.

Unfortunately, her firm intention of being 'stiff and unyielding' was proving to be extraordinarily difficult to maintain. Her skin seemed to be on fire, her pulse and heartbeat almost racing out of control, while the ache in her loins was burning for him. She was slipping away, melting under the pressure of his mouth on hers, and if he hadn't been firmly pinning her to the door she would be sliding down into oblivion.

His hard, muscular body was pressed closely to hers, his arousal, his heat, his mouth and his tongue, all combining to produce a nuclear force, against which she had no defence.

Sara suddenly found herself being swept up in his arms, and in a daze she felt herself being lowered carefully down on to the soft bed. Slowly opening her eyes, she gazed up at the man leaning over her.

Her heart slowed. She saw no love, no caring emotion in his dark hooded eyes. She saw nothing but lust, and the need to possess, own and control. She saw only negative emotions, nothing positive; nothing to give her any hope that their marriage had a real chance of survival.

She drew in her upper lip and turned her head away as he reached down and moved her vest top aside. She felt the pressure of him on the bed next to her, his hand on her breast, and she stiffened.

'Just try,' his voice grated in her ear. 'Just try and show some damned emotion!'

And then he twisted her face towards him, pressing his mouth firmly against her lips. And his insistence angered her. He wanted it all – but wasn't willing to give anything. And she was entitled to more consideration than this rough demand for her to surrender to his possession. She wanted him to care about her – and he damned well didn't!

She struggled then, fought him blindly, not really knowing what she was doing and unable to admit – even to herself – that she was fighting her own desire, a deep and almost overwhelming longing to submit to his possession. And then Alexander was suddenly astride her, pinning her down, holding her wrists away from his face. She blinked open her eyes and saw a scratch mark on his neck. Appalled at what she must have done in her despair, she started to sob quietly, thrashing her head from side to side.

'I didn't mean to do it…. I didn't mean it…' she cried helplessly.

'Oh, yes, you did – and this is the only answer, Sara,' he breathed thickly. 'It seems that there is some damned barrier which has to be broken down between us. Until this is over and done with we can't get on with our lives.'

Maybe he was right. Because her body, as his mouth plundered hers, was rapidly succumbing to the rising heat of passion and desire, her breasts swelling beneath his touch, her flesh on fire for his possession, the blood singing in her ears. But the spiritual part of her was in despair. He might possess her, but it would be coldly clinical, without feeling, without any emotion other than the urgency for release.

And she tried to steel her whole body against him, determined not to give him anything other than what he was offering her: a quick, explosive consummation of their marriage. Grimly she reminded herself, if she needed such a reminder, that it was just another formality to go through.

chapter six

As an increasing soft submission replaced her steely determination to control her feelings, Sara realised that it was
useless to try to act coldly and detached when you had no
bones, no muscles to stiffen in rejection. Now there was no
thought but to let go, to indulge in this sweetest of all
pleasures.

She lay naked and tremulous against his hot body. He had
languorously removed her clothes, his eyes devouring every
inch of golden flesh he exposed. She saw only hunger in the
drowning pools of his eyes and wished for more, but knew
he wasn't capable of giving it.

He covered her in soft exploratory kisses, her throat,
her shoulders, the curve of her breasts. But it all lacked
depth of emotion, as if he was just doing what was expected
of him and nothing more. His breathing might be slightly
laboured, and his arousal was evident, but it meant nothing.

How could this mean anything to him? He hadn't chosen
her to be his wife. His child, her child, two beautiful babies
switched at birth had brought it all about. In a twist of fate
destiny had triggered the coming together of two people
who would never otherwise have met, let alone married.

Sara twisted her face into the crook of his neck and
wanted to cry with the agony of it all. She wanted it to be so
different, not to have the past hanging over them for
evermore. She wanted what she couldn't have: his love,
unconditional, without the encumbrance of the dreadful
mix-up that had brought them together.

Suddenly her whole body stiffened. The backs of his

fingers tenderly brushed over the slash of the Caesarean scar, above her pubic bone. His soft touch brought it all back…that stormy night, her pain and fear. If it had been a normal birth…if, maybe…

'I should have been there,' she heard him murmur. 'It should have been our child.'

Her head swam sickeningly. What did he mean? That if he had been with his wife that tragic night of the births none of this would have happened? That if he had been there he would have possessed his own child, and wouldn't now be married to a woman he didn't love?

Sara wanted to scream, but she bit hard on her lower lip as he lowered his mouth to the raised scar. His tender soft kisses were a balm to her distressed and painful thoughts. Small, butterfly kisses, backwards and forwards, soothing her, and yet raising her blood pressure until she ached for more.

And then he was pressing kisses over the mound of soft, coiled hair that covered the very core of her femininity. With a sob she reached down to stop him, but it was too late…deliciously too late. Her whole body arched against him urgently as he drew deeply on her, lapped her, sent her crazy with longing for his complete and utter possession.

She was at breaking point, on the edge of ecstatic, re-lease when he raised himself and looked down on her. As he had moved, so had she, clasping her hands around him, fingers kneading into his back, drawing her knees up and apart. Her face was already lifted towards his, eager to give and receive the bittersweet torment of his kisses; her hips were arched, eager to feel the hard pressure of his penetration…

'Alexander…!' she breathed faintly, wondering why he was holding back; why wasn't he triumphantly thrusting into her?

'Don't say anything,' he ground out between bared teeth.

'Not one word!'

She could feel the heat of his arms as he supported himself over her, his muscles bunched with tension. His whole body was so stiff and hard with fiercely controlled passion that Sara's heart floundered for a moment. She could feel rejection beginning to bite hard into her soul. He couldn't do this to her…punish her so…not now!

'I'm terrified of hurting you,' he muttered thickly. 'I can't stop. I need you, Sara, but…'

And then he was coming down on her, filling her, tentatively at first and then, as her silky moisture tempted him further, he let out a deep, low groan of despair and thrust into her deeply, knocking the breath from her lungs, releasing his tension into her, pulsing hard and fast into exquisite, fiery pleasure.

She grasped his hips and drew him ever deeper into her, drawing him down and down till they could hardly breathe. She moved with him, hard and fast and then slow and sensual, matching him, anticipating his needs and giving herself to him with complete abandon.

And when her climax claimed her, demanding release in an upsurge of molten heat, she cried out as his mouth clamped over hers, and he rode her higher and higher, knowing, feeling, giving her everything her body craved. And as she broke under the strain, finally letting go, all her feelings erupting in a wild frenzy of release, she felt his final swell, heard the muted roar of emotion catch in the back of his throat, and then he was pulsing hard inside her, flooding her in the last final thrust of sexual ecstasy.

Sara awoke in darkness and heat. Languid and sleepy, she reached out a hand and started to slowly and gently run her fingers down over Alexander's firmly muscled arm until she reached his hand. He was sensuously caressing her between her legs. She was moist and silky and the sensation was a catastrophic assault on her senses. She tried to entwine her fingers in his, to stop the excruciating pleasure of his touch, but she only succeeded in gripping his wrist and gasping, helpless with desire as his lips claimed hers.

She had never experienced such an orgasm, a soft, soft release of such exquisite intensity it made her want to cry. And she wasn't even properly awake.

Sara lay next to him, in the crook of his arm, listening to the slow, gentle rhythm of his breathing. She lay there with him till a creamy dawn broke into the room. Her husband was a wonderful lover and yet, instead of it delighting her, she found it deeply troubling. She was now enslaved. His lovemaking, in the middle of the night, was testament to the power he had over her. When he had woken her so erotically, had made love to her without demanding or needing anything for himself, he'd been demonstrating his complete mastery of her emotions. Her husband was a dangerous man.

'Well done, Eleni,' Alexander cried with enthusiasm as the little girl puffed and panted with exertion, so eager to please her father that she was nearly purple with the effort of swimming the length of the pool.

Alexander, in white swimming shorts that were a glaring contrast to the darkness of his tanned skin, reached down to the edge of the pool, grasping Eleni's hands and hauling her up out of the water and into his arms. She clung to him, laughing with delight as he swung her around in the air, spraying water everywhere.

Sara lay on a comfortable lounger several feet away and watched them both through the dark density of her sunglasses, an unread glossy magazine on her lap.

Eleni was blossoming, Alexander grew more devastatingly handsome by the day, Thea wasn't making a very good recovery from a virus and had been lacklustre and withdrawn over the past few days and…and Sara was pregnant!

Only a few weeks into this poor excuse for a marriage, and the very worst had happened.

At first she had put her feeling under the weather down to the same virus that had hit Thea, making her feel nauseous and lethargic. But whereas Thea was now making a slow recovery, Sara was gradually feeling worse.

Trying to hide it from everyone seemed to exacerbate her condition. Although the villa was luxurious and spacious, with Anna living in rooms of her own in a mezzanine floor at the side of the villa and the other staff living in nearby villages, Sara still felt as if she was living in a goldfish bowl – with herself as the prize exhibit.

Maria had said there had been rumours that Sara's swift and unexpected marriage to Alexander was due to the fact that she was pregnant. So Sara had no problem understanding why she was being peered at relentlessly. Anna, in particular, had been giving her some strange looks lately.

But Sara could hardly admit it to herself, let alone tell anyone else that she thought she was pregnant. She wanted to glow, as she had when she had found she was pregnant with Thea…Eleni. But how could she glow when a baby was just about the last thing she wanted or needed in this loveless marriage?

Wearily, Sara rubbed at her brow as she watched her husband laughing with Eleni. Thea…Eleni…There were times when she found herself swamped with emotions, and she became so confused that the two girls seemed to merge into each other. How could she have allowed herself to get pregnant so soon? Especially when she already had two daughters who needed all her care and devotion? There wasn't enough of her emotions left for another child…a baby that certainly hadn't been conceived in a warm loving relationship.

And Alexander was so distanced from her. Nights of passion had seemed to change nothing between them. After every exquisitely erotic sexual union Sara would bury her face in her pillow and mentally scream for a different sort of release. She would have traded every pleasurable, excitingly sensual moment for just one word of love. What was the point of driving each other to the threshold of madness with lust and passion if it meant nothing in the end? It was a crazy sort of torture.

'Alex doesn't love me as much as he loves Eleni!' Thea's plaintive voice broke into her dismal thoughts.

Sara snatched off her sunglasses and sat up, the shock of Thea's words sending her senses spinning. She hadn't heard Thea creeping up beside her, and what the child had just said tore painfully at her heartstrings.

But she couldn't show it. Instead, she forced herself to give a light laugh, grabbing Thea and pulling her gently down on to her lap. She sat with her between her bare legs, nuzzled her mouth into her hair and rocked her to and fro.

'Who told you that? The trouble fairy?' she teased softly. 'Every night Alexander comes to your and Eleni's bedroom when you are asleep. He stands at the foot of your beds and blows you kisses and says how much he loves you both.'

'Does he really?' Thea said with little enthusiasm, toying with the silk beach wrap which Sara was wearing over her bikini.

'Are you feeling better, Thea?' Alexander asked as he plumped down on a lounger next to them both, picking up a towel and wrapping it around Eleni and then hugging the little girl to him.

'No,' Thea pouted. 'I'm getting sick again.'

'I'm sick too,' Eleni cried, giving Thea an icy look. 'I'm sicker than you,' she added, turning to bury her face in Alexander's chest, her small hands clutching at his arms.

Alexander looked perplexed.

'Neither of you will want ice cream, then?' Anna said behind them.

Suddenly she had the attention of two pairs of interested eyes, one startling blue, the other a liquid brown.

'Hmm...I thought that might perk you up. Into the kitchen, at the table. I'm not clearing up dripping ice cream from these tiles any more.' She marched the pair of them off, Thea barefoot and in shorts and T-shirt, Eleni still wrapped in a towel but having insisted on slipping on her red sandals.

Sara lay back in her lounger and closed her eyes. Alexander cleared his throat.

'So, what is happening between those two?' he asked somberly. 'They are not exactly the best of friends lately.' He swung his legs up onto the lounger and leaned back, closing his eyes against the sun.

'You can't expect them to be,' Sara murmured. 'Children are always falling out with each other. It would be unnatural if they didn't.'

'But they were such good friends – '

'Well, they're not now!' Sara snapped.

There was suddenly a wall of silence between them, broken only by the sudden buzzing from an irate cicada. Sara sighed and sat up, pushing her hair behind her ears.

'I'm sorry that I snapped at you, Alexander. The fact is, Thea thinks you love Eleni more than you love her.'

Alexander sat up with a grunt of dismay. He looked totally appalled. 'Did she actually say that?'

Sara nodded. 'Just now. She saw you making a big fuss over Eleni after she swam her length in the pool. She must have felt jealous of the attention you were giving her.'

'But, I'm always praising Thea for her swimming,' Alexander protested. 'She's a brilliant swimmer, and making marvellous headway with her diving too. What...what's so funny?'

'Headway with her diving,' Sara repeated with a smile.

Alexander, elbows on knees, gazed out over the twin pools, clearly not amused. 'Thea is my very own daughter, so of course I love her deeply. I wouldn't be human if I didn't,' he murmured thickly. 'I can't stop loving Eleni. But how do I get the balance right?'

Sara brushed a weary hand through her hair. It was hardly a question she felt qualified to answer. Raising Thea for her first five years had been plain sailing compared to this. In fact, she was beginning to think that there was a lot to be said for single parenting. It wasn't ideal, of course, but it did have some compensations. Just one decision, one voice, and a singular route to take. So much easier all round.

If Alexander was experiencing difficulties, Sara's were equally perplexing. Only rarely did Eleni show any emotion where she was concerned. She worshipped her father, and that was understandable. But Sara wished with all her heart she could have some of that adoration. And now Thea was showing signs of rebellion after her initial easy adaptation to their new life.

'Have…have you thought of letting Thea call you Papa instead of Alexander?' Sara suggested, suddenly wondering if that was what had been bothering Thea. Hearing Eleni calling him Papa all the time.

'It's too soon to tell her the truth,' Alexander said gruffly.

'I wasn't saying that you should tell her the truth,' Sara said quietly. 'I'm just suggesting you could mention that, as we are now married, she is more or less your daughter and she can call you Papa.'

'And we say the same to Eleni about you? That instead of calling you Sara, she calls you Mama?' He gave a snort of derision. 'I don't think Eleni is ready for that yet. And *you* sure as hell aren't ready for it, either!'

Sara physically winced. Alexander rose to his feet and stood by the edge of the pool, so he was unable to see the mask of pain he had inflicted on her. She didn't need to be reminded that her very own daughter wasn't bonding with her as well as she had hoped.

'Thank you for that vote of confidence where my parenting skills are concerned,' she grated sarcastically. 'Pity we didn't know about each other's inadequacies before we embarked on this farce of a marriage!'

She got to her feet, gathering up her magazine and her sunglasses, and tightening the knot of her sarong at her breast as she began walking back to the villa.

He caught hold of her wrist, sending the magazine and her glasses flying to the ground. His eyes were darkly challenging.

'And it is a poor excuse for a marriage, isn't it?' he grated harshly. 'I can do nothing right for you. I've suggested a trip away from here – Athens, Crete, even London – and…'

'You know why I refuse to leave here,' she retorted angrily. 'The last time I left the villa a stranger recognised that Eleni was my daughter. I don't want to run the risk of that happening again.'

'Because you are ashamed of her!'

'No, damn you! Because of Eleni's feelings and because of Thea's feelings. They are both only five years old, far too young to understand what happened to them the night they were born. It's too soon!'

'So we imprison ourselves here till they are twenty-one and then tell them the truth?'

Sara stared at him blindly. Dear Lord, she didn't know the answer to that question. She only knew was that she wasn't coping with the situation. She'd thought she could, but every day dragged her down a little further. She could be strong if…if this marriage was all right, if Alexander loved her as deeply as she now loved him. And she did love him, although how and when she had come to that realisation she had no idea. But the depth of feeling was there – and unfortunately it appeared to be becoming stronger and deeper with every passing day. Which was obviously a disaster, because Alexander didn't love her. And it was becoming crystal-clear that, whatever she did or said, their relationship would never be anything other than a pale imitation of true, loving partnership.

'I always suspected this marriage would be a life sentence,' she grated bitterly, staring icily up at him. 'Every day is a punishment.'

A faintly sardonic smile creased the corner of his thin lips. 'And every night is a liberation, isn't it, Sara? A release from the purgatory of your life with me. How do you do it? Do you imagine someone else in my place when I am locked into your body? Do you close your eyes and think of your fisherman lover…?'

Instinctively, her hand flew up to slap his face, but he caught hold of her wrist before it struck home. She felt cheated. Horribly so. She had wanted to hurt him for that. She had only kept Spiros alive in her heart for Thea, and never *once* had she done what he had just so cruelly suggested: put her lover in the place of her husband, when they were making love.

'And who do you imagine in *my* place, Alexander?' she hissed venomously at him. 'Irena? Or perhaps you don't have to imagine her? Perhaps, in the small hours of the morning, you creep out of the house, and –'

'Don't be absurd!' he snapped, his dark eyes glittering dangerously down at her. 'I haven't left your side since the day we were married.'

'Huh, not bodily maybe, but there are other forms of unfaithfulness,' she argued relentlessly. 'In the mind. In the heart. You are only too eager to accuse me of disgustingly cruel behaviour, so don't expect me not to retaliate with some cruelty of my own!'

'Am I being cruel?' he drawled dangerously.

Sara's breath caught in her throat. Anger and jealousy had spurred her outburst. Had he recognised it? Was he painfully prodding her into some sort of confession of her true feelings for him? But for what reason? To have more power over her? She didn't know – and just at this minute she didn't care. Nausea was welling up inside her, and she urgently needed to seek refuge in her bedroom.

'No, only boring, Alexander. Mind-blowingly boring!' she answered grimly as she turned away.

'I guess I am,' he unexpectedly admitted, voice thick with weariness of it all. 'So perhaps it is time I did something about it. This marriage needs some livening up.'

How he was going to achieve that, Sara didn't ask. And it certainly didn't happen that night. Alexander didn't come to their bed at all. She waited and waited, and then dozed off – only waking with a jolt in the middle of the night to realise he wasn't with her and clearly had no intention of being with her. It hurt very much, the assumption that he couldn't even bear to sleep with her any more, that he was as bored with her, as she had pretended to be with him.

Late the next afternoon, when the cicadas were at the height of their mating call, Sara at last discovered how he intended bringing some sparkle into their marriage. A car throbbed up the long driveway. A white car that Sara knew only too well by now. And with a squeal of pleasure Eleni ran outside, throwing herself into Irena's arms.

Watching the arrival of Alexander's mistress as she leaned over the balcony of Thea's bedroom, Sara was comforted by the company of her daughter. Thea had been a lot more cheerful today, although there was clearly now a black cloud about to cast gloom on Sara's day.

'Eleni thought that lady was going to be her mama one day,' Thea told Sara. 'Has she come to take Eleni away?'

'Never in a million years,' Sara uttered with feeling. But unfortunately it looked as if Irena was coming to stay. Anna was helping the glamorous woman to remove some luggage from the boot of her car.

So, Eleni had expected Irena to be her new mother…? Well, no wonder the little girl was finding it difficult to bond with Sara. One minute Irena was the light of her father's life – and then another woman, a complete stranger, had suddenly married him. No wonder that poor little Eleni had become confused and withdrawn.

'Shall we go down?' Thea asked doubtfully.

Some time they would have to, but for the moment Sara needed to get her head together. Pride wouldn't allow her to appear in front of that woman looking as desperately unhappy as she was. And the last thing she wanted was to have Alexander see that she cared a brass farthing about Irena's presence in this villa. It might take her some time, but Sara definitely needed to get her adoring wife act together!

'We need to get changed first,' Sara said determinedly. 'We have a guest in the house and we want to look our best, don't we?'

'I like my shorts,' Thea protested. 'I don't like dresses like Eleni's.'

'You like your lovely blue sundress, though. It's not fussy like Eleni's clothes.'

'And what are you going to wear?'

'Something pretty,' Sara murmured thoughtfully.

Something sexy? Yes – definitely something positively dripping with sex appeal! She would never forgive Irena for telling tales on her the day that Thea had made Stefios's nose bleed. Sara wanted revenge! She was going to show Irena that Alexander had not married beneath him, as the other woman obviously believed.

Sara finally settled for understated elegance, after spending a fruitless ten minutes clawing through the racks of clothes looking for something that would have Irena

turning pea-green with jealousy and, with any luck, maybe
have Alexander look at her in a new light. To think of her as
his sexy wife – instead of the Wife from Hell! Unfortunately
there was nothing remotely sexy in the whole wretched
wardrobe. Alexander obviously hadn't seen her that way
when he'd chosen the outfits for her.

However, she finally decided to wear an exquisitely
cut Chanel dress in a light soft blue crêpe, the exact
colour of her eyes. It was simple, sleeveless and set off her
golden tan to perfection. Teamed with a pair of high-heeled,
thinly strapped white sandals, it looked cool and elegant.
Sara took care with her make-up, only needing a smidgen of
glossy lipstick and a few strokes of mascara to darken her
eyelashes. Her hair was as glossy as …as Eleni's.

Sara's heart nearly gave out as she took one last look at
herself in the mirror. Did Irena know why Alexander had
married her so hastily? Alexander had sworn to keep their
secret – but the woman was his mistress after all. But, no.
Sara realised that she couldn't know the truth. If Irena had
been aware of their secret she wouldn't have been so
vengeful, wanting to discredit Sara in her husband's eyes.
Surely no one was that cruel?

But might she guess now, seeing them all together? Did
Thea take after Celeste? Alexander had said not, that Thea
was more like his mother, but Irena had been Celeste's best
friend and women saw things differently from men. And
Eleni? A stranger had seen the likeness between the real
mother and daughter. Would Irena?

'Mama, are you all right?' Thea asked with concern.

Sara had slumped onto the edge of her bed, wondering
where her strength was going to come from. Already
debilitated by this unexpected pregnancy, she didn't know if
she had it in her to face her husband's mistress with a smile
and the look of a confident wife.

She lifted her head and grinned at Thea. 'These sandals

are killing me!' she laughed, rising to her feet and taking Thea's hand. As they went down the stairs Sara pretended she couldn't walk properly in her high-heeled sandals, staggering and grabbing at the banister to steady herself, with Thea in fits of laughter by the time they reached the bottom of the stairs.

Alexander looked haughty and disapproving, frowning as he waited for them in the hallway.

'Oops!' Sara giggled, and righted herself in front of her husband. Thea's eyes were watering with laughter.

'Irena is waiting to meet you both,' he said stiffly. His dark eyes shifted over them both and he nodded with approval. 'I'm glad to see you have made an effort with your appearance, Sara. You look lovely.'

Of course the comment was double-edged: it served as a compliment and a put-down at the same time. Sara smiled in acknowledgement of his compliment, but the put-down hit home, too – the implication clearly being that she really hadn't made much of an effort before. Lowering her lashes, so that he wouldn't see how he'd hurt her, Sara followed Alexander through the villa to the rear terrace.

'Well, Sara, you have certainly succeeded where I have failed,' Irena said enthusiastically, after the introductions had been made and they were all seated under a shady parasol by the poolside.

Sara steeled herself for the first of many caustic remarks which she was anticipating from this glamorous woman.

'I never did manage to teach Eleni to swim,' Irena added meaningfully, holding Sara's wary blue-eyed gaze and getting across the real message without anyone else noticing: that she had failed to get Alexander to the altar whereas Sara had succeeded.

Irena turned her attention back to Eleni, who was thrashing around in the water like a sea nymph. 'How did you do it, Sara?' she asked in a simpering voice. 'Throw her in at the deep end, and…?'

'Mama wouldn't do that!' Thea cried defensively.

'She didn't have to,' Alexander interjected, beckoning Anna out onto the terrace. 'It was all Thea's doing anyway. Eleni could see how much Thea enjoyed the water, and suddenly she got interested enough to want to try swimming for herself. Ah, Anna.' He turned to the housekeeper. 'I think we'll have drinks out here, before the girls' supper, and then you can take them off to bed. There will be three of us for dinner tonight, and I'm sorry about the short notice of Irena's arrival.'

Anna laughed and lifted a hand dismissively. 'No matter. It is always a pleasure to see her. Her room is ready. It's nice to see you Irena,' she added, as Irena gave her a wide, beaming smile.

Sara's heart sank. Irena probably had all the staff under her beautifully elegant spell.

'Can I swim with Eleni before supper?' Thea asked Sara, pulling at her sundress. She was obviously bored with grown-up formalities, particularly as Eleni was having fun and she wasn't. Sara was about to remind her to change into her swimsuit, which was over in the changing rooms, when Alexander beat her to it.

'A quick dip, Thea, but change into your swimsuit first,' he told the little girl.

'I swam nude yesterday. Why can't I today?' she protested defiantly.

'Because I said so,' Alexander said firmly.

'Why should one day be different from another?' Thea argued.

Sara's eyes widened. Thea was always quite pushy, but this was asking for trouble!

'Because today we have a visitor,' Alexander said, calmly but firmly. 'And you are old enough to realise that we act differently in company. Now, do as you are told and change into a swimsuit, because if you don't you won't get a swim at all.'

Thea parted her lips to protest further, but then thought better of it and sulkily turned away, running towards the changing rooms. Sara breathed a sigh of relief. Alexander unclenched his fists and Sara could almost swear that she heard Irena laughing softly under her breath.

'I had a call from Marios last week, Alexander. He sends his very best regards and said he'd be happy to hear from you some time,' Irena said to Alexander, as if Sara wasn't there and the little disagreement between Thea and Alexander hadn't happened. 'You know he's involved with the Rhodes deal? You should have been in on that instead of burying yourself down here. You really have been very negligent lately.'

Alexander laughed. 'You sound like Celeste. The Rhodes deal doesn't interest me, Irena. I have a wife and family now.'

Sara felt her stomach churn. She scraped her chair back and got to her feet. 'Excuse me,' she mumbled, 'I think I'll just go and help Anna with the drinks.'

Just before she was out of earshot, Sara heard Irena's mocking reply, 'Ah, Alexander – you had a wife and family before, but it didn't stop you…'

Stop him – what? Having an affair with that awful woman? Sara shuddered and gripped the edge of the wide stainless steel sink in the kitchen for support. She didn't want or need Irena's baleful presence. And Thea's behaviour to Alexander just now hadn't been helpful. What on earth would Alexander's mistress be thinking…?

Sara heard a step behind her, and swung round to see Anna coming out of the utility area with a bucket of ice from one of the freezers. She eyed Sara warily and then gave her a small smile.

'Sometimes you have to say things just for the sake of

saying them,' Anna said mysteriously.

'Wh…what do you mean?'

Anna shrugged and started to break the ice cubes up with a wooden spoon. 'You know, to be polite.' She laughed softly. 'She has a bad habit, you know,' Anna held up an index finger and waggled it. Then she ran it over the work surface next to her and peered at the tip of her finger disdainfully.

Sara felt a smile spread across her face. She knew exactly who Anna was talking about, and what she meant.

'It isn't a nice thing to do,' Anna said conspiratorially. 'Certainly not to a housekeeper of *my* experience.'

Sara nodded knowingly. Wishing to be polite, Anna had obviously lied about Irena always being welcome here – at least as far as she was concerned.

'She will go soon – maybe in a few days. And when she leaves *you* will still be here,' Anna said sagely, giving Sara a warm comforting smile.

Sara's eyes filled with tears. Out of loyalty to Alexander, Anna obviously couldn't say more. But what she had said, and implied, was enough to warm Sara's heart. How much Anna knew about Alexander and Irena's relationship she couldn't ask, and didn't want to. It was just such a relief to know that someone was rooting for her.

With a renewed spring in her step, Sara took the ice bucket out to the terrace, Anna saying she would follow with the drinks trolley. As she approached the table under the parasol, Sara could see that her husband and Irena were locked into a deep conversation. Somehow it didn't matter so much now. Because Anna was right. Irena would eventually leave, whenever, and she would still be here, married to Alexander. And in time, perhaps, his heart might melt towards her, and…

'Eleni, get off that end of the bridge!' Sara suddenly cried out in alarm.

The wooden Japanese-style bridge formed an arch between the two pools: the small pool being without a deep end, where the girls were allowed to swim, and the much larger pool for strong swimmers.

But now Eleni was crouched near the dangerously deep end of the adult pool. Sara had already expressed her concern about the dangers of the two pools being so close to each other. But Alexander had explained that they'd been designed by Celeste, in the early days of their marriage, before Eleni had arrived.

Sara ran towards the child, her unaccustomed high heels jarring under her as she reached the bridge.

'I'm not going to dive in, Sara.' Eleni giggled at her concern. 'But there's something funny here – a fat furry brown caterpillar.'

Sara, on the gentle downhill slope of the bridge, now couldn't control her momentum. Her sandal heels wobbled under her and suddenly she was flying forward. With a shriek Eleni went to grab at her. Sara instinctively reached for her too. Together, they plunged off the low bridge – and straight into the deep end of the adult pool.

Spluttering and shrieking with laughter they both bobbed to the surface, Eleni clinging to Sara's neck, her legs wrapped around her chest.

Thea, laughing so much that she was bent double with mirth, was standing beside Alexander, who was grinning widely as he reached out for Sara to grab his hand.

'Oh, Mama, you were *so* funny!' Thea cried when Alexander had hauled them both out of the pool. 'It was like when you were coming down the stairs, toppling all over in those silly shoes.'

'Those silly shoes are at the bottom of the pool now,' Alexander laughed.

'Oh, gosh, my dress,' Sara gulped, the laugh dying on her face. 'It's ruined!'

'It doesn't matter,' Alexander assured her quickly.

'Where's that fat caterpillar?' Eleni cried.

'There!' Thea shrieked, and spread-eagled herself on the edge of the pool. 'Floating in the water. Get it, Eleni, before it drowns.'

Still laughing and trying to catch her breath, Sara swept her sopping wet hair back from her face. Alexander was supporting her, his arm possessively clasped about her slim waist. She tilted her face up, and he was looking down at her with such deep emotion in his dark eyes that her heart suddenly began pounding.

Now he was going to berate her in front of his mistress for making a fool of herself – and indirectly a fool of him, for being married to such a clumsy idiot, Sara told herself glumly, stiffening in anticipation of his anger.

And then he pulled her hard against his chest, and held her so tightly that she could hardly draw breath.

'Don't scare me like that again. I nearly had a heart attack!' he rasped gruffly against her face, before raising his dark head and giving her a long, searching look that sent her senses spiralling almost out of control. She could only stare back at him with dazed eyes, but before she knew what was happening his mouth closed firmly over hers.

The kiss was so deeply emotional it shook Sara to the very core of her being. What sort of a man was this, to kiss his wife so passionately in front of his mistress? She couldn't respond to it. She couldn't let herself go and indulge herself, as she did in the heat of the night with him. This was cruel, uncaring to them both. Her heart went out to Irena. What must she be feeling?

She forced Alexander away from her, her whole wet body straining with the effort to separate them.

'Don't do that!' she said under her breath.

He let her go, so suddenly that she nearly fell back into the deep end of the pool. His eyes were now black with anger because she hadn't responded. But what had he expected her to do, in front of his mistress? And then her gaze swept past his broad shoulders and she saw that the terrace was now empty. How long Irena had been gone Sara had no way of knowing. Oddly, Sara found herself hoping that it was before that kiss, because she knew how *she* would feel if she'd witnessed Alexander kissing Irena that way. Absolute despair. And Sara wouldn't wish that feeling on her worst enemy.

But even if Irena had witnessed their kiss, the other woman needn't have worried, Sara reasoned quickly. Because it hadn't meant a thing. All it had done had been to prove was that Alexander got some sort of perverted pleasure out of winding women round his little finger. He was obviously playing the same games with his mistress as he was with his wife, playing one off against each other. As far as she could see, her husband got more dangerous by the minute.

So Sara decided to work on the knowledge that her husband was a cruel man, and try to convince herself that she couldn't possibly love him after all. The longer his mistress was under this roof, the more opportunity she'd have for racking up minus points where he was concerned.

'Quiet, you two,' Sara hushed the girls. They were both ready for bed, bathed, pink and shining in cotton nighties – and giggling for all they were worth.

Sara was the cause of their mirth, of course. Teetering down over the bridge, out of control in her high heels, and then plunging into the deep end of the swimming pool, was obviously going to keep them laughing for months.

'What an earth is all this commotion?'

'Oh, Papa,' Eleni giggled as her father stepped into her bedroom to say goodnight as he usually did. 'Sara is so funny. Just as funny as Thea!'

Sara shrugged helplessly. 'I only fell in the deep end of the pool.'

'With your clothes on!' the two girls shouted in unison, and fell against each other, laughing their heads off.

'I don't think Charlie Chaplin could have made them laugh much more,' Alexander said with a smile.

Sara grinned. 'I guess not. Perhaps my true vocation in life is slapstick comedy?'

'No, you have found your true vocation,' Alexander said softly, 'Motherhood,' he added sincerely, and caught her eyes and held them.

Embarrassed, Sara looked away. She wasn't sure how to take that.

'Come on Thea, back to your own bedroom. Anna is cooking and I have to get dressed.' She was still wearing the short light blue cotton robe she had changed into after her unceremonious dip. But she'd have to get a move on, because Alexander had already changed for dinner. He was all dreamy elegance, in a white evening jacket and narrow black trousers.

'I want my bed in here, with Eleni,' Thea cried, snuggling down under Eleni's bed sheet.

Eleni snuggled down next to her. 'Yes, we want to sleep in the same room. We can talk and laugh and–'

'And we'll talk about it tomorrow,' Alexander cut in.

'No, now!' Eleni insisted.

Sara and Alexander both stared at Eleni with surprise. Thea was usually the one who demanded attention – not this shy little girl.

'I want Thea in my room.' Eleni went on, a little more subdued. 'She's my sister now, and we have secrets.'

'What sort of secrets…?' Alexander demanded, before Sara quickly nudged his arm.

'Don't even ask!' she warned him with a grin.

'I suppose we ought to be glad they want to share a

room,' Alexander muttered under his breath.

He was looking a trifle perplexed, probably still shaken by Eleni's sudden display of strong willed tactics, Sara told herself. She had obviously picked up some confidence from Thea, and, though Sara could see the positive side of that, she wondered if Alexander was viewing the change in his daughter with approval.

'We could shift Thea's bed in here now,' Sara suggested thoughtfully.

'Yes! Yes! Yes!' the girls shrieked, suddenly jumping up and down on Eleni's bed, eager both to take advantage of Sara's suggestion and secure Alexander's as well.

With a sigh and a grin, Alexander shouldered his way out of his evening jacket. 'OK, but you girls will have to help. And, you can start by shifting all those dolls out of the way.'

With squeals of excitement, Thea and Eleni did as they were told, while Sara and Alexander went through into Thea's room to get her bed. Alexander manhandled the mattress off the wooden-framed bed, and carried it through into the other room. The floor was polished wood and the bed had castors, so Sara thought it would be easy enough to pull it across the room to the connecting door between the bedrooms.

For a blinding second of pain Sara let go of the bed and clutched at her stomach, placing a trembling hand over the scar left by her Caesarean operation. She gasped for breath, heard Alexander and the girls laughing in the distant background, and felt herself sway dizzily and sickeningly.

She knew then, in that split second of panic, that if it had been anything more serious than the mere pulling of the taut skin across the scar she would have wanted to die rather than lose the baby she was carrying.

She wasn't just pregnant. She was pregnant with Alexander's baby. The thought filled her, consumed her, wrapped around her till she could hardly catch her breath,

And she was glad. Overjoyed. Ecstatic! She clung on to the delicious feeling of surging relief for a few more luxurious seconds, before Alexander came back into the room. She wanted to relish the feeling. It was such a release not to feel bitter about the unwanted pregnancy. It *was* wanted. She wanted it, and Alexander had said there would be more children – so he would welcome it too. When she told him, he would surely be…

She heard Irena's voice coming from Eleni's bedroom, followed by then the soft tinkle of her laughter, and then Eleni's. *That was her daughter, laughing with her husband's mistress*!

Sara bit her lip and closed her eyes tightly. For a precious moment she laid her hands over her stomach, where her tiny, tiny baby lay softly and safely coiled.

'We're going to fight this!' she murmured fiercely to the little being inside her. 'Oh, yes, we are going to fight it – *and we're going to win!*'

'Darling,' she murmured smoothly from the doorway.

Alexander's head jerked up, as he wasn't quite sure if he had heard her correctly, while Irena gazed at her coldly and the girls carried on arguing over which doll should sit on whose bed.

Sara smiled beguilingly at Irena. 'Oh, Irena, thank goodness you are here.' She noticed that Irena was wearing the most beautiful cocktail dress of amethyst silk, fitting her glamorous figure like a glove! 'Do you think you could give Alexander a hand with the bedframe? It's much heavier than I thought. And I really need to get ready for dinner. You don't mind, do you? No, of course not. I knew you wouldn't.'

Sara smiled at them all, assured the girls she would be back to kiss them goodnight, and, pulling the robe over a shapely thigh that had been exposed for everyone to see, turned and spun confidently out of the girls' bedroom.

It had started. The fight back. And she was encouraged to know that she had won the first skirmish. Irena had looked appalled at the suggestion she should do something physical like moving a piece of furniture. As for Alexander… Her husband had looked totally bemused.

And the fight back had only just begun!

chapter seven

Forty-eight hours later, Sara was beginning to wonder if she had taken on one of Hercules's mythical twelve labours. Irena was proving to be a force to be reckoned with.

Sara had never realised just how deeply the other woman had been entrenched in Alexander's life, and Eleni's too. Not only had she been Alexander's first wife's best friend, but it appeared she had been deeply involved in some of Alexander's business ventures as well, particularly the tourism side of this island.

'You can't be serious about settling here for good, Alexander?' Sara overheard one morning.

Irena and Alexander were in the study together, and the long patio doors were fully open to let in the breeze as Sara passed by, on her way to the pool area. She was finding a good few lengths of the pool went a long way to easing her sickness.

'This was meant to be a temporary arrangement,' Irena was saying. 'I only agreed to stay here during the summer because I knew the stress you were under bringing Eleni up on your own. The villa rentals can be overseen from Athens, and it is where we both belong. We should be there, together – not here!'

'I belong here, Irena,' Alexander said curtly. 'The girls are happy here and Sara seems to have settled…'

'Pah, Sara! Some damned tourist you picked up and married without giving a thought to what you might be doing to yourself and dear Eleni. Celeste would turn in her grave if she…'

'That's enough, Irena!'

'The hell it is!' Irena retorted. 'Celeste would be *appalled* to see what is going on here. I imagine that you married that girl – I can hardly call her a woman! – to give Eleni some stability. But why marriage, Alexander? A fully trained nanny would have done the job far better. And what was wrong with *me*, for goodness' sake? You *know* how I feel about you, how close I was to Celeste, how involved I am in your work. It's not as if we don't have a history together, we were lovers…'

Sara couldn't bear to hear any more. Ears stinging as if they had been slapped, she slunk away, feeling guilty for being an eavesdropper, and feeling less important than a trained nanny. In fact, she felt totally undermined!

She abandoned her plan to for a swim. Instead she headed round the villa, straight into the kitchen. She stood there for a moment or two, clenching and unclenching her fists, and then, with a fierce determination to prove something to herself, she set about finding the ingredients she needed.

An hour later Sara stood back, proudly surveying twenty-four fairy cakes fresh from the oven, a huge slab of warm chocolate fudge brownie, and a rack piled high with Thea's favourite chocolate chip cookies.

Her face was flushed with the heat, there was flour in her hair, and a steady trickle of perspiration was running down her back under her short-sleeved blouse. Now she'd finished cooking she felt horribly nauseous, and couldn't have sampled any of her efforts if her life depended on it. And suddenly it all seemed so pathetic – just a weak, feeble attempt to prove that she was worth something. In fact, she felt like bursting into tears at her own stupidity.

'My, Anna's been busy,' Alexander commented as he came into the kitchen and strolled over to the fridge.

'No, Anna hasn't been busy. I have,' Sara told him heatedly as he pulled open the fridge door, taking out a carton of pineapple juice and shaking it vigorously.

He raised a surprised brow. 'You have hidden talents. They look delicious.'

'And there are a lot of other things I'm talented at,' she told him forcefully, and lifted her chin. 'I think it's about time I got back to my career!'

'And what has brought this about?' he asked darkly.

There seemed no reason to conceal the truth from him. 'Your mistress! You might as well know that I overheard you both talking, and I can tell you that she made me feel less than worthless.'

'What did you hear?'

'The content doesn't matter, but you thrusting her down my throat does. I've had enough of this nonsense, and…'

He gave her a sardonic smile. 'It didn't show before. In fact I thought you were rather a heroine. The last couple of days you have been all sweetness and light with me. Darling this, and darling that!'

'Well, it didn't come from the heart, I assure you. I wanted to drive it home to Irena that we are man and wife now, and it's time she began to live her own life!' Sara retorted hotly. 'But the damned woman's hide is thicker than an elephant's. Although if she isn't getting the message, I certainly am! You've spent all your time with her ever since she arrived to stay here. You have neglected me and the girls, allowing them go their own way and…'

'So, you are jealous.' He smiled knowingly.

Sara wanted to slap the tray of fudge brownies down his silk shirt.

'Yes, green with jealousy, Alexander. Not over you – but because Irena has a life and I haven't!'

'What on earth are you talking about?'

'Irena has a career. She is involved in your business life and…'

'And you are a wife and mother,' he pointed out icily. 'Isn't that enough for you?'

More than enough if the conditions were right, she wanted to throw back at him. Yes, more than enough if he loved and cherished her and it was a real marriage in every sense.

'No, it isn't enough. I want something just for me. Because this marriage is a hard struggle, and I need something I can escape into.'

He looked pained for a second, as if he was truly hurt that their efforts to make it work had failed. But she must have imagined it. The only thing that could ever get to him would be if something happened to the girls, or Irena.

'Why didn't you marry her?' Sara demanded huskily. 'I heard her say you had been lovers. Why didn't you do the decent thing by her and marry her once you were free to do so?'

He stood with the carton of juice still poised in his hand, staring at her as if she was out of her mind. Which, of course, she was, Sara had to admit to herself when he slammed the reason why he hadn't married Irena back in her face.

'Because I had to marry *you* to get my true daughter back,' he told her, his voice hard and cruel.

Sara's heart turned to ice, although she knew that she should have anticipated having to face up to the brutal truth. Brushing a weary hand through her hair, she muttered thickly, 'Yes, of course. That has to be the only reason for not marrying Irena,' and then took a shuddering sigh deep into her lungs. 'And I obviously have to put up with the harsh reality of our marriage because you have my daughter. But I also have to put up with your mistress under this roof – and that isn't fair, Alexander.'

'No, nothing is fair,' he agreed wearily. 'Irena will be leaving in a few more days. We have some more things to clear up and…'

'And that gives her a few more days to make my life hell,'

Sara protested. 'She wants you back, and so far she isn't winning. Or, more precisely, not what she wants. Because, while she might have you as her lover, I've got what she really hankers after – that stupid piece of paper that says we are locked together for life. She can't win. You and I know that, but she doesn't.'

'Are you suggesting I tell her the truth about why we married?'

'No, not that,' Sara insisted, her head dropping forward, appalled at the thought.

She heard the clatter of the carton of juice hitting the back of the sink and, as she jerked her head up she nearly bumped her nose on her husband's chin.

'So, you want me to tell her to leave because she is upsetting you?' he suggested, almost mocking her.

Sara stared at him coldly. And how he would enjoy doing that.

She drew a weary, exhausted breath. 'Do what you like. You've been lovers long enough. So, what do another couple of days matter?'

He grasped her chin and forced her to face him. His eyes were dark and hooded.

'Irena and I were lovers before I was married...'

Sara brought her hand up and sliced his from her chin. 'Yes, *and* during your marriage to Celeste. Her first day here, I heard you talking. You saying you had a wife and family now, and she sneeringly reminding you that it hadn't stopped you before. Celeste might have put up with it for a quiet life – but I'm not putting up with it during *my* life!' Sara ground out angrily.

This time he grasped her shoulders, his fingers so deeply punishing it brought tears to Sara's eyes. He almost shook her with anger.

'Irena wasn't talking about an affair – she meant work, because I was often away when I was married to Celeste. And, yes, Irena and I were lovers at university. But that was so many years ago it now seems as if it had never happened. She introduced me to Celeste – to whom I was *always* faithful!'

He drew a deep breath, glaring down at her. 'How very little you have learned about me during this brief painful marriage of ours. I've always considered myself an honourable person. I was faithful to my first wife and I have been faithful to you, my second wife. If that doesn't tell you something, Sara, you really must be as blind as Irena!'

His mouth swooped down on hers, and Sara's head spun at the hot force of his scorching lips on hers. She endured the pressure for, as long as it took for all that he'd said to sink in. And sink in it did, with heart-wrenching poignancy. Sara realised that he was an honourable man, and he had no reason to lie to her. Because what did it matter what *she* believed? She had no choice but to stay married to him, for the sake of her daughters, however badly he might behave. But, as for understanding *why* he should have been thrusting Irena's company on his new wife, it was entirely beyond her. Maybe when she wasn't feeling so tired and exhausted she might be able to look at the situation more clearly.

Her mouth burned painfully. Loving him was a worse agony than anything physical he could inflict on her. Sara tore her mouth from his, before she broke down and admitted that she couldn't bear it any longer. She loved him, and all she wanted was for him to love her. But that seemed as unlikely as ever.

She gave him a cold glance as he released her, and her heart bled as he returned the look with one equally as hostile.

Without a word he turned away from her, striding out of the kitchen door which led out on to the patio beyond.

'Very interesting,' Sara heard drawled behind her, and she swung round to see Irena leaning in the other doorway, the one that led to the interior of the villa.

Sara was acutely aware of her hotly flushed, frazzled appearance, after her marathon cook-in and after yet another row with her new husband. How much had the cool, sophisticated, interfering woman seen and heard?

Irena approached her, swaying her shapely hips, her thick glossy hair swinging as she moved, softly and silkily. Her dark eyes surveyed the cooling cakes and biscuits Sara had baked, and she twisted her lush lips into a mocking sneer. She made Sara feel small, helpless, and just about as interesting as a kitchen mouse.

'Yes, very interesting,' she repeated in honeyed tones. 'You'll have to do better than that, Sara. Celeste didn't know one end of this kitchen from the other. Come to think of it, I don't believe she ever ventured in here at all. That was one of the reasons why Alexander was so besotted with her. She was like an orchid, a hot-house flower, someone to be treasured and revered. And Eleni is just like her.'

Sara swallowed hard, the ever-present nausea just waiting to erupt. Little did this awful woman know that Eleni was nothing to do with Celeste!

'You and your arrogant daughter, Thea, can have no future with Alexander,' Irena drawled wickedly. 'It will never work. Alexander adores Eleni, and he could never feel the same way about your bastard daughter!'

Sara gasped, feeling as if she had just been punched in the stomach.

'He made a mistake in marrying you, but then you know that, don't you? When he kissed you just now, it wasn't the real Alexander Karakou. It was the man he has become recently, stressed out of his mind and struggling to bring up his adored daughter after the death of his adored wife. As for you…'

There were twin squeals of delight as the two small girls hurtled into the kitchen, skidding to a halt at the table where the cakes were laid out. Thea threw herself into Sara's arms.

'My favourites, Mama! Just like you used to make at home in England.'

'I'm impressed,' Anna enthused, bringing up the rear. 'That puts my cooking to shame.' She laughed at Thea as the little girl swelled with pride. 'Your mama is a wonderful cook, Thea.'

'She's my Mama too,' Eleni cried indignantly, wrapping her slim arms round the free half of Sara and hugging her tightly, her small face upturned excitedly as she pleaded, 'Can we eat some now, Sara? *Pleeese!* I can't wait till teatime!'

Sara nodded, her eyes stinging with tears and her throat so choked with emotion that she couldn't speak. 'She's my Mama, too' seemed to echo in her ears, over and over again, till it became a chanting mantra in her head.

Eleni was accepting her! Maybe, only just at the moment to feel equal to Thea – but it *was* a start.

Tears nearly blurring her vision, she looked across two bobbing dark heads as the girls reached out to try the cakes, while Anna was trying to get them to wait till she got plates and napkins. She saw Irena, stiff and unyielding, her eyes cold, and more than anything else, defeated.

Sara hadn't had to say a word. None had come to her lips, anyway. Seconds ago Irena had nearly defeated her, with her evil accusations and her cruel disclosure that Alexander had worshipped his first wife so very much. It hurt to know that. Just as it hurt desperately to have her beloved Thea described as arrogant, and a bastard daughter.

But Sara and Alexander knew the truth of Thea's birth and parentage. And suddenly she realised that what had once been a Greek tragedy was now a secure bond between herself and Alexander. A bond that couldn't be broken by a scorned woman. Alexander might not love her. But, as Sara now fully recognised, he needed her and the children – and he didn't need Irena.

She, Sara, had triumphed, and, in a way, the victory gave her some pleasure, because she hadn't deserved all that vengefulness from Irena. All the same, she couldn't help feeling sorry for the other woman.

She watched Irena leave the kitchen, her proud head held high, her shoulders stiff, the opposite to the arrogant way she'd entered the room only minutes ago.

Sara let out a long sigh of sorrow and Anna looked at her knowingly.

'You are too soft-hearted,' she muttered under her breath. 'Alexander too. He promised Celeste he would look after her and he has done so. Made sure she has work and money. Perhaps now it will end. It must,' she added firmly.

'Thank you, Anna,' Sara whispered emotionally, and wanted to hug the older woman, but she had no free hands. They were both occupied hugging two small girls with chocolate moustaches.

'Hey, you two, that's enough. You'll make yourselves sick!'

But even as she said the words Sara found herself dashing out of the room with her hand over her mouth, hoping that no one had noticed her sudden bout of nausea. No one noticed.

The heat was suffocating her. Sara stood out on her balcony and took deep breaths of hot perfumed air. After Alexander had left with Irena she had stood under the shower for ages, trying to cool herself down. Then she had powdered herself liberally with the expensively perfumed talcum powder Alexander had supplied her with, and thrown on a long white silk bed robe – also provided by her husband. At one time she had resented him for owning her so thoroughly. But now, now she could accept it all because it was different. She wanted to be owned by him.

The sky as ever was clear; huge stars hung just above her

head as if painted there. Sara allowed a certain contentment to wash over her. She had a lot to be grateful for. The girls were happy, and delighted to be sharing a bedroom. And Eleni had filled her heart with hope earlier, when she had insisted to Thea that she was her mother too. When she had tucked the girls down to sleep in their beds beside each other Eleni had hugged her as enthusiastically as Thea had. Things were getting better, much, much better.

But not perfect.

Earlier Alexander had thundered up to their bedroom and demanded to know what she had said to Irena, because she was packing her bags.

'I've said nothing, Alexander,' she had wearily answered him. 'If she's leaving, it's definitely nothing to do with anything I've said to her. She did all the talking.'

'She's in tears, wanting to go back to Athens!'

Sara, who had been trying to rest on top of the bed, had suddenly been cross with him for putting Irena's feelings before her own. She'd sat up quickly. 'Well, why don't you take her back to Athens? And while you're there,' she'd screamed at him, 'why not grab hold of some divorce papers in the local courthouse, so we can put an end to this marriage from hell?'

'Divorce!' he had spluttered. 'You think a divorce is the answer?'

'Oh, God,' she had moaned, holding her head in her hands. 'Even that is impossible.'

He had slumped down beside her and pulled her hands from her face before she had a chance to wriggle out of his way. He'd held her wrists and looked at her earnestly, his eyes dark pools of stress.

'We can't go on like this, Sara,' he'd pleaded, his voice thick with emotion. 'We are destroying each other. I never imagined it would be like this.'

And then with a huge choking sob she had clung to him,

buried her flushed face in his chest, because it had all been too much to bear. He had wrapped his strong arms around her and held her, and she had been able to hear his heart pounding in his chest.

And her love had filled her, engulfed her like a huge wave, and she had desperately wanted to tell him how deeply she felt, but she'd been too afraid to do so. For some reason, very probably because of his undying love for his first wife, he couldn't give his heart to her completely. So, how could she add to his emotional stress by admitting how she felt about him?

He'd had years of knowing how Irena had felt about him, and because of a promise to his dying wife he had had to put up with it. Now, to be burdened with her adoration too, it would obviously be too much for the poor man.

'I'm driving Irena back to her villa,' he'd breathed into her hair. 'I'll be back shortly. Wait for me, Sara, just wait for me…hmm?'

And now she was waiting, and hoping and praying that when he did return it would all be different. But she feared it would not. She couldn't *make* Alexander love her.

Her hands smoothed over her stomach. Now there was another life to consider, and this time Alexander would be at the birth. He would see his son or his daughter being born and there would be no twist of fate this time, no tragic blunder to change their lives. This new life, this new member of the family, could mean a new start for them all.

Sara tried to stay up and remain awake. But sheer exhaustion at last drove her to her bed. She had wanted to be on the moon-bathed, flower-scented balcony, quietly waiting for him, the stars adding a romantic backdrop that might make him see her in a softer, gentler light. She had hoped that he would want to make love to her for her own sake, and not just because she was his wife.

'I didn't hear the car,' she murmured sleepily as she felt

the pressure of him on the bed next to her. 'I tried to stay up.'

'You've had a long, difficult day,' he whispered, sliding his body down next to her. She had her back to him and he wrapped his arms around her and pulled her close to him, nuzzling her hair. 'And so have I,' he added thickly.

She supposed removing a mistress from the marital scene took some doing! Sara told herself, before being ashamed of her cynicism. Besides, Irena *hadn't* been his mistress...

Sara swivelled herself around to face him, her arms locking possessively around his back. 'It's over now,' she uttered happily. And she knew that she must never mention Irena again.

She sought his mouth, hungrily, wantonly, and for a second felt she had taken him by surprise. But then he was responding, his hands caressing the warm silky nightdress, and he was groaning in frustration as it got in his way, before eagerly ripping the silk from her trembling body.

Naked, their bodies came together as their heated mouths passionately found one another. Alexander felt different somehow, although Sara couldn't fathom the subtle difference in his caresses.

Physically, there never had been any problem in their lovemaking. Lust and passion didn't need to be cloaked in any sort of deep feelings for it to be good. They had satisfied each other, but for Sara the lack of emotional and spiritual feeling had always left her believing there should be more.

Perhaps it was because her body had a new sensitivity about it now that she was pregnant? But Alexander didn't know she was pregnant, so this new tenderness of his, this new emotional depth, couldn't be because of that.

So why was it different? Did he, too, feel a new release now that they were free of Irena? She didn't know, and, quite frankly, she didn't care. Alexander was loving her with such feeling, almost as if...as if...

'You're putting on weight at last,' he murmured in her ear, and Sara laughed softly and secretively to herself.

And then there were no more words, only soft gasps of pleasure and delight, and long deep kisses, and the mind-bending effect of his tender caresses as he sought and found the hidden and sensitive areas of her body; her flesh was on fire for him, the world spinning wildly on its axis as he entered her at last.

Her husband was inside her, filling her, possessing her with all the urgency and feeling she so badly needed. And as Sara wrapped her legs around him and moved with him she thought he uttered her name, in a way he had never uttered it before. With feeling and with emotion, as if she meant so very much to him, and just to say it would bond her to him for evermore.

Afterwards they lay in each other's arms, limbs lying languidly across each other in spite of the cloying heat of a the humid night. Sara knew that he was still awake, when normally he fell into a deep sleep after their lovemaking. She wanted to ask what he was thinking, because something was obviously keeping him awake, but she was too sleepy to ask. Whatever, she instinctively knew it was something good and positive. She just knew it.

They were both awoken by the bedside phone ringing the next morning. There were other sounds too. Bees urgently gathering nectar from the jasmine outside on the balcony, the girls' sandals clacking on the tiled terrace as they ran across it, shouted to each other. Somewhere in the villa there was the low purring of a vacuum cleaner. Outside in the grounds one of the gardeners had a radio, and Greek music drifted on the air.

They were all new sounds to Sara. She supposed they had been there before, but she hadn't heard them. But this morning was different.

Alexander was still wrapped around her, groaning into the pillow as the phone persisted, hanging on to her and not wanting to let go.

'Answer it, Alexander,' she laughed softly.

He did, picking up the receiver and immediately putting it down again. He hunched up onto one elbow and looked down on her, brushing a whisper of silky hair from the corner of her mouth.

'You're beautiful,' he murmured, 'and you're my wife and...'

The phone shrilled again. Grinning, Sara reached for it this time, and held it to his ear while wriggling out from under him.

'I need the bathroom anyway,' she sighed, and kissed the tip of his nose before getting up from the bed and slipping on her robe.

'Hey, you're beautiful,' she whispered to her reflection in the mirror over the washbasin. 'Your husband has just said so, and he was about to say more when...' She sighed and shrugged and reached for her toothbrush and was grinning so widely she brushed her teeth in half the time it normally took her.

'No, Irena, not again,' Alexander pleaded. 'You are taking advantage of my weakness where you are concerned and it has to stop.'

Sara flattened her back against the bathroom door, tightly holding her breath and closing her eyes. It was Irena on the phone to Alexander. Already she was back in their lives!

'No, I can't go with you. My duty is here with my wife and...'

There was a pause, as if Irena was putting up a million reasons for Alexander going with her, wherever that might be. But Sara could only think how he had used the word *duty*, when referring to his wife, and her heart seemed to turn to stone.

'You don't know the half of it, Irena,' Alexander said wearily, and Sara could imagine him dragging his hand through his hair at the thought of his *duty* and the *half of it* that was the reason for their marriage.

'Listen, Irena, you've had me at your beck and call before. But this time it isn't – You won't Irena…you won't! OK, OK, calm down, sweetheart. Yes, we'll talk, yes…yes I'll come.'

Sara heard the loud click of the receiver being banged down on its cradle, the sound perfectly matching the snapping of her heart in two. Alexander was going to Irena – and that could only mean that he cared for her more than he did for his wife! And love…love was a mocking deceiver, a blinding force that had made her believe in things which didn't exist.

She loved her husband so much she had honestly believed that last night he had finally responded and felt the same way, and now…now she knew that those feelings were nothing but a *duty*.

With trembling hands she turned both taps on so that the gushing of the water into the white bowl would mask the thudding of her heart. She stared at the swirling water and wanted to drown in it. She was drowning in tears anyway.

'Darling, I have to make a quick trip to Athens' – he called out.

He'd never called her darling before.

'Business, I'm afraid. Thea, Eleni, you look after Mama while I'm away.'

Sara came out of the bathroom in a rush to see Thea and Eleni hanging around Alexander's neck while he was struggling into his trousers. He was laughing with them and Sara's blood boiled. What was so damned funny this dreadful morning?

'Where are you going?' Eleni cried, looking so disappointed he was leaving that she let go of him straight away.

Thea still hung on, though, and Alexander swung her around and on to the bed. It wasn't a dismissive gesture and Thea, her good nature prevailing, didn't take it as rejection. She kneeled on the crumpled bed and excitedly asked. 'Can we come too, on the boat?'

'Next time, darling. We'll all take a trip soon, very soon, but Papa has some unfinished business to deal with first.'

'Oh,' the girls groaned in disappointment.

He grabbed at his jacket, which the previous night he had slung carelessly over the back of the chair – something he never ever did. 'I promise you a big surprise when I get back. And there'll be a surprise for Mama, too.'

His eyes locked into Sara's across the room. Just for a fraction of a second he looked uncertain, and then he grinned at her. 'Yes, a surprise for Mama too,' he repeated.

The divorce papers she had demanded? she thought wildly. Please God, no, she inwardly prayed.

Suddenly it was all happening too fast for Sara to take in. Alexander was in such a hurry he wasn't even packing a bag. Athens demanded a stopover, maybe two or three days, and he wasn't taking anything with him! Because he would be staying with Irena and probably already had clothes at her place or his place? He must have a home in Athens, too. One that Sara had never visited and was never likely to see. She, the wife, would be incarcerated here in this backwater, and his real life was in bustling Athens, with her, Irena, and…Sara gulped, her thoughts getting wilder and wilder with panic.

She found herself minutes later standing in the porch outside the front entrance, Thea and Eleni each side of her, clutching her hands tightly and waving and blowing kisses to Alexander as he started the engine of the white Mercedes.

He had said a very perfunctory goodbye to her in the hallway – a kiss on each of her hot cheeks, a light squeeze of both her hands – but his eyes had looked deeply into hers, as if searching for something but not finding it. And, because he was in a hurry, he had not been prepared to hang around any longer to find out what was missing.

He had left her feeling bereft.

'Papa's gone to Athens,' Eleni told Anna as she came out onto the porch, drying her hands on a tea-towel.

Anna looked astonished and glanced anxiously at Sara over the heads of the girls, who were still waving Alexander off down the drive.

'Business,' Sara uttered, and wondered if Anna had guessed at the truth, that Alexander was in fact rushing off to be with Irena.

Sara couldn't meet the housekeeper's worried gaze. Anna was like one of those old family retainers you read about in novels, seeing all, saying nothing but occasionally dropping pearls of wisdom in her wake. And Sara had gratefully gathered up the precious jewels Anna had discreetly dropped for her benefit, but there were no more to come. Nothing Anna could say, or hint at, could make any difference to Sara now.

Anna cleared her throat. 'He'll be gone some days then,' she said matter of factly. 'Not to worry. The best-laid plans of mice and men,' she quoted.

Sara swung on her with a look of incredulity. Anna lifted her chin. 'You girls had better get up to your rooms and make them presentable. We have visitors on the way.'

'Visitors!' the girls echoed, eyes wide with curiosity.

'Don't ask. Wait and see,' Anna said briskly. 'Now, upstairs with you before there is trouble.'

She ushered them inside to the hallway and chased them upstairs before they had a chance to argue.

Pulling her robe around her protectively, Sara asked in a flat tone, 'Am I permitted to ask who the visitors are? Alexander didn't mention that anyone was coming to stay with us.'

Ah…it must be Maria! Had she sent a message to say she was coming for a visit? Sara suddenly felt guilty for neglecting Maria since the day they had spent with her and her family at the taverna, the day Irena had spied on them all and told such lies. But, much as she would love to see her friend, today wasn't a good day. She wouldn't be able to stop herself from breaking down.

It suddenly struck her just how isolated she was becoming. Apart from the girls and Anna, and the other staff she occasionally had reason to speak to, she didn't have anyone else with whom she could have a good heart-to-heart.

'I've taken the liberty of asking my sister to come and stay for a few days,' Anna told her. 'I was going to mention it today, but of course Alexander has had to leave.'

In a way, Sara was relieved that it wasn't Maria and the children who were coming to see her, but a small part of her was disappointed. It was good to have a friend to turn to when you couldn't turn to your husband. She could imagine Anna and her sister gossiping like crazy over those few days, catching up on news, reminiscing, doing what sisters did together.

Sara could feel loneliness closing in around her like an enveloping fog.

'I'm sure there would have been no problem with Alexander,' Sara told her with a weak smile. 'Certainly no problem with me, Anna. I look forward to meeting your sister – and don't feel you have to run around after me and the girls while she is here. Take some time off together and enjoy yourselves.'

Couldn't be better timing, Sara thought positively. She would occupy herself fully with the girls, and the all-seeing Anna wouldn't be around to witness the misery she was sure to let slip now and then. Except she mustn't let the girls see that despair either. For them she must keep a brave face.

Anna nodded and murmured a thank you, and as she

turned away in the direction of the kitchen Sara thought she heard a small sigh of relief come from the house-keeper. As if she had half expected Sara to refuse permission for her sister to come and stay.

Sara hoped she had done the right thing in Alexander's absence. For all she knew Anna's sister might be the sort to run off with the Karakou family silver... But no...she was more than likely a dear sort, like Anna herself. It appeared Eleni knew her and was expected to tidy her room for her.

Sara sighed heavily as she went upstairs to dress. There was so much she didn't know about this household, so much she didn't know about her very own husband.

'Let's go to the sea today?' Thea asked plaintively. 'We never go out nowadays.'

Sara was dressed in her usual shorts and T-shirt and was inspecting the girls' bedrooms to see if they had tidied up.

'There's a beach over the hill,' Eleni told them as she patted her line-up of dolls on the coverlet of her bed. 'We don't usually go because it's a long way and Papa says I will get too tired.'

'You've been spoilt,' Thea laughed.

'I have not!' Eleni shot back.

'OK, we'll go,' Sara said quickly. 'We'll take a picnic with us and stay all day.'

'Yeees!' the girls cried.

And it was one of her better decisions, Sara told herself. The day had been fun, and had successfully taken her mind off her husband's betrayal. Partly anyway. The thought of him rushing off to be with Irena had stabbed at Sara throughout the day, little stabs and prickles of hurt that she had to swallow and try to forget.

The walk to the beach over the hill had turned out to be more a Himalayan trek, but both girls stood the pace wonderfully. Sara realised how much Eleni had changed since their arrival. She wasn't quite the delicate piece of porcelain she had once been. She had toughened up, was striding out with Thea and laughing so much more, and was generally a much more open and relaxed five-year-old.

My child, Sara had to remind herself when at last they reached the cove and flopped down to unpack the picnic hamper and eat and drink ravenously.

As she lay back on a somewhat pebbly beach and watched the girls running in and out of the sea, squealing with happiness and joy, she marvelled at how everything had somehow all merged together. She had two daughters. Eleni her birth daughter, and Thea the daughter she had believed to be her own for five years – till Alexander had dropped his appalling bombshell.

They were both her daughters. And she knew Alexander felt the same. She had watched him with them, knew his love for the two of them was as deep and as profound as her own. It hadn't all been easy but the end result was as if it had. Like a pregnancy: a lot of pain and discomfort but when a mother held her new baby in her arms she forgot the pain and discomfort, which had accompanied the baby's birth. There was only joy at the end of the day, pure joy and ...

'Mama, why are you crying?'

Sara sniffed and laughed and pulled Thea towards her, giving her a hug. 'I've got some silly sand in my eye. Are you having a good time?'

Thea snuggled into her arms and leaned her head back against her shoulder. 'I love it here. Eleni likes it too.' She burst out laughing and pointed at Eleni, who had just been soaked by a large wave. Eleni fell on to her knees, spluttering and laughing.

'Are you happy, Thea?'

'I love our life, Mama. Eleni said she's glad that you're her mama now, and not Irena. She said Irena used to get cross, but you never do. We talk about these things.'

Sara laughed and squeezed her. 'Oh, you're getting all grown-up on me.'

'I'm not,' Thea protested, 'I'm a girl. Alexander calls us his girls. Is he really my papa now?'

'Yes, he's your papa now,' Sara said truthfully.

Thea jumped out of Sara's arms and reached for two cans of soft drink, one for herself and one for Eleni. And, kneeling in the sand before rushing off, she asked. 'But would my real papa mind very much if I called Alexander Papa now?'

Sara gazed bright-eyed at Eleni on the water edge. 'No, he wouldn't mind at all,' Sara said quietly. What was in a name anyway? What was in a piece of paper? It was what was in the heart that mattered, she thought pensively.

'Look! Look!' Eleni suddenly screamed in excitement.

The noise above them was deafening, a thunderous roar that shook through their whole bodies. Thea flew back to Sara, covering her ears and burying her face in Sara's waist. Eleni simply jumped up and down excitedly.

'It's my Grandmama!' Eleni screamed. 'She's come to see us.'

Sara gazed up at the silver and blue helicopter that was juddering over their heads and heading towards the villa. Alexander's mother? And arriving by helicopter!

Eleni ran up the beach and grasped Sara's hand tightly, while with the other she waved frantically at the helicopter.

Sara felt herself turn to ice with a sudden attack of nerves. And Alexander wasn't here to greet his mother. The one that Thea apparently looked like. Oh, Lord, Sara thought. Would she see? Would she know? Did she already know the secret of the girls' births?

She wasn't prepared for this, not one bit. But she should have been, Oh, damn! She would have been prepared and ready to meet her new mother-in-law if she'd had a loving and caring husband by her side to help her cope with the ordeal. But she hadn't. He was too busy with Irena!

'We'd better get back, then,' she told the girls heavily.

What with the imminent arrival of Anna's sister as well, the villa was going to be bulging at the seams. And Alexander wasn't here to support her through a traumatic meeting, one that she had often anticipated but wasn't ready to cope with.

'You are lucky, Eleni,' Thea murmured despondently as they started to pack up their beach things. 'I haven't got a grandmother.'

Sara had to swallow hard. This would never end. Never!

chapter eight

The impressive silver and blue helicopter had long since departed by the time they reached home. As they had trudged back across the green hill it had wheeled over them on its return journey and Sara had gazed up at it in awe, noticing the Karakou logo emblazoned on its belly. She had never really considered the Karakou wealth quite in the terms of island-hopping by helicopter. The yacht, yes – a multitude of Greeks owned yachts – but to have your very own air transport?

Tired as she was from their long trek home Eleni was first in the villa, shrieking at the top of her voice with excitement.

Sara and Thea held back, Thea clutching Sara's hand tightly, Sara wishing they didn't look like a gang of raggle-taggle gypsies after their day on the beach and the long debilitating walk home.

Eleni was already in the arms of her beloved grand-mother as Sara and Thea hesitantly stepped into the hallway of the villa.

Sara hadn't known what to expect, but she hadn't quite imagined Alexander's mother to be so...so like a Greek mother. She was tall, extremely well built, a big woman in fact, but as she swung Eleni around in her arms Sara could see that she had the grace and imperious appearance of a very fine lady indeed.

'What a welcome, Eleni! I have never seen you so exuberant!'

Swinging a laughing Eleni onto one voluptuous hip, she settled her and then gazed fully at Sara.

Astonishingly Sara felt herself quaking with nerves. The

woman was dressed in an outrageously flamboyant outfit of multi-coloured chiffon and, surprisingly for her size, looked very regal in it. Her hair was piled and coiled high on her head, very black and glossy, her make-up was professionally perfect, her whole stance one of an opera diva.

Sara wondered where on earth Alexander had got the idea that Thea favoured the maternal side of his family. There was no resemblance whatsoever between Thea and this grand lady.

And then the diva smiled. Her liquid brown eyes softened and her mouth widened and Sara's stomach clenched fearfully.

It was all there, the open honesty, the up-front confidence of Thea. Thea to a T.

'So you are Alexander's wife,' she breathed, her voice filling the air.

Sara swallowed hard as Alexander's mother set Eleni down on the ground and stepped towards her, at the same time resting her dark, dark eyes on Thea at her side.

As well as Sara could read Thea, she could read this regal lady. She didn't know. She didn't know the little girl she was reaching her hand out to was her very own granddaughter.

'And you must be Thea.' She smiled warmly.

Thea nodded and took her hand shyly, subdued for a change, completely overwhelmed by Eleni's grandmother, who seemed to be larger than life and towering over her.

She then took Sara in her arms and hugged her briefly before stepping back to gaze at her again.

'Anastasia,' she boomed in introduction. 'And before you ask what I am doing with a Russian name – '

'Byzantine,' Sara couldn't help interjecting, and immediately knew she had made her first mistake. This was a lady who liked to be on top, in charge.

Her dark eyes narrowed. 'Brains as well as beauty,' she murmured, and then turned around and raised a commanding hand. 'Anna, get these children bathed and changed for dinner, they are filthy. Where's Joanna?'

'Unpacking for you, Anastasia.'

'My usual room, I hope,' she said baldly. 'We seem to be crammed in here like sardines!'

'I hate sardines,' Thea said strongly.

Sara's heart sank. Thea was so quick to pick up on attitudes, so quick to butt in, sometimes getting it all wrong but at least having a go.

Anastasia looked down her regal nose at her, and Sara held her breath. Suddenly she grinned.

'So do I, dear. Horrid bony, fishy things, only fit for the gulls. I hope Anna isn't going to dish them up for dinner tonight.'

'No fear of that,' Anna muttered as she beckoned to the girls. 'It would be more than my life is worth. I've mixed your martinis,' she told Anastasia. 'They are out on the terrace.'

'Join me, Sara dear, after you've showered and changed,' she directed pointedly at Sara, but Sara saw the glimmer of a twinkle in her eye and smiled hesitantly.

Sara followed Anna and the girls up the stairs, not sure of Alexander's mother at all. Would she get on with her mother-in-law? Would the formidable Anastasia get on with her?

A woman came out of the guest suite when they reached the landing and smiled broadly at them all. Eleni hugged the woman and Anna introduced her as Joanna, her sister. Sara's eyes widened with shock.

'Companion, lady-in-waiting, general slave and untiring servant to Madame Karakou,' Joanna joked as she took Sara's hand warmly.

'Pleased to meet you, Joanna.' Sara smiled. 'Anna and Joanna, I bet you were always getting muddled as children,' she laughed, to cover her surprise that Anna's sister was the companion of Alexander's mother.

'We have two other sisters as well. Sylvanna and Glorianna.'

They all laughed together and Sara felt some of the tension drain out of her, but not all of it.

Later, when Anna was in the bathroom running the shower for the girls while they kicked off their clothes in the bedroom, Sara asked why she hadn't told her that Alexander's mother was coming to stay. The more she thought of it the more she was convinced that Anna had been interfering here.

'I would have liked to have been prepared, Anna. You said you had invited your sister to visit, nothing about her being Anastasia's companion and she would be coming too. And Alexander knows nothing of this visit or he would have said something before he left. Did you invite them both?' Though why Anna should have done so she couldn't imagine.

Anna shrugged. 'They were due for a visit anyway,' she answered evasively.

'Maybe so, but not while Alexander is away!'

'I didn't know he was going,' she said shortly. 'Thea, Eleni, the shower is ready.' And she turned away from Sara's accusing gaze.

Sara stormed out of the steamy bathroom, feeling totally undermined yet again. She didn't even have any authority over her housekeeper. She was now convinced that Anna was solely responsible for her mother-in-law's arrival. She could see that Anna's status as staff was slightly different from the usual because of her sister being a close companion to Madame Karakou, but she had no right to go behind Sara and Alexander's back by inviting them here!

Fuming, she stripped off in her own bedroom and ran a cold shower, letting the water beat fiercely down over her head. There was only one good point to consider here, with the diva in her house, looking down on her from an imperiously grand height. Sara would be fully occupied looking after her, and not dwelling on the fact that her husband was in Athens with a former lover – who only had to pick up the phone to bring him to heel!

Sara took more time than she had ever taken in her life to blow dry her hair and apply her make-up. She had to look her best. She'd never had a mother-in-law before, but there was obviously some truth in music hall jokes. They were to be dreaded, they never looked kindly on the daughter-in-law who had snatched their adored son from their bosoms, and of course daughters-in-law hadn't the first clue about bringing up children. Anastasia must have been smugly satisfied to see Eleni and Thea so scruffy after a day out at the beach.

'I must say, Sara dear, the change in Eleni is astounding since you have come into her life. She has blossomed.'

'Like a hothouse flower,' Sara uttered under her breath, drinking ice cool orange juice and wishing that she could share a martini with her mother-in-law. But, of course, she couldn't, not when she was expecting Alexander's baby.

'All credit to your influence, but I can imagine that Thea has had something to do with it as well. Children learn so much from each other.'

Well, that was something at least – a compliment, even if diluted by the suggestion that Thea deserved some of the credit as well.

Sara eventually lifted her head to see why Anastasia wasn't speaking any more. Since Sara had joined her on the terrace for their pre-dinner drinks, she hadn't stopped for breath.

But now Anastasia was gazing at her thoughtfully, taking in the silky pale lilac of Sara's palazzo pants that hung in folds down her slim crossed legs, the flimsy sleeveless top to match, softly draping her tanned shoulders, her long glossy dark hair with its sun-bleached highlights curving against her throat.

'You are not at all what I expected,' Anastasia told her without preamble.

'What did you expect? Someone more like Celeste, serene and wistful?' Sara asked softly, and held her gaze bravely.

But Anastasia didn't get the chance to reply as Thea and Eleni stepped out onto the terrace to say goodnight. They were exhausted after the day, and rather than keep them up for a dinner that might have them nodding off into their soup bowls Sara had asked Anna to serve them a light supper on their balcony upstairs.

Eleni, in pink silk pyjamas, was hauled up onto her grandmother's lap and hugged tightly. 'Papa tells me you can swim now. A whole length of the pool. You couldn't do that the last time I was here.'

'Sara taught me, and Thea too,' Eleni told her. 'Papa said Thea is like a fish in the water.'

'Not a sardine, I hope!' Anastasia rumbled with laughter.

Even Thea laughed at that.

'Come, Thea, give your new grandmother a hug and a kiss goodnight, and tomorrow I have all sorts of tales to tell you both.'

Sara knew Thea well enough to know that it was on the tip of Thea's tongue to deny that Anastasia was her real grandmother. But, whether she was too tired to argue or not, it didn't happen. Thea went to her, and together the girls hugged Anastasia. Sara thought it showed a kind and caring side to Anastasia that she didn't want Thea to feel left out.

'Ah, dear, sweet girls,' Anastasia murmured. 'Sleep and dream well.'

Sara felt a lump well in her throat. If only she knew the dreadful secret that Sara held deep in her heart.

'I have prepared moussaka for supper. Is that acceptable, Anastasia?' Anna asked as the girls slid off her lap and went to Sara for a last kiss and a hug.

Anastasia had certainly taken over already, Sara thought. Instead of asking *her* if the dish she had prepared was suitable Anna had asked the Grand Dame.

'It's fine with me, but this isn't my home, Anna,' Anastasia said, 'You should ask Sara if the food is acceptable.'

Sara bit her lip. Oh, hell, it was getting worse. Now she was being patronised.

'Sara loves moussaka, and would eat it for breakfast if it was on offer, but I know how particular *you* are,' Anna retorted with a grin.

'*Touché*,' Anastasia laughed as Anna took the sleepy girls away.

They sat in silence, a long yawning silence between them, in which Sara gazed blindly ahead of her and tried to concentrate her thoughts. On the scents of the night, always more heady and musky once the sun had gone down. On just how many cicadas were buzzing out there like mini-chainsaws.

Idle conversation was out. Anastasia wasn't the sort for small talk. How well Eleni was doing was another subject Sara wished to avoid. She didn't want to find herself in a situation where she might blurt it all out. And in her acutely nervous state, hurt and bewildered by Alexander's defection and with pregnancy hormones rushing around her body, she might just do that.

'You mentioned Celeste just now. Do you and Alexander talk about her?'

Sara was surprised by the question. She swallowed before answering. 'Hardly at all. I've just built up an idea about her from snippets here and there. He obviously loved her very much.'

'Yes, he cared very deeply for her. She was always rather fragile, and there were times I wanted to shake her for being so…well, so feminine. My son is a physical man, and at times I felt…' She sighed suddenly and lifted a heavy hand

and waved it in the air. 'It's all in the past now, and God rest her soul.'

Sara swallowed hard again and lowered her lashes, glad that Anastasia didn't want to say any more about her former daughter-in-law.

'Did my son know you were pregnant before he left with Irena?'

The question came like a bolt of lightning out of the velvet black sky.

Sara jerked her head up. Anastasia knew her son had gone off with Irena and she also knew she was expecting his baby!

Sara cleared her throat. 'No, he didn't,' she said quietly. 'I barely know myself. I…I'm just a few weeks pregnant.'

'But long enough to have told him, Sara.'

It was a reprimand rather than a statement of fact.

'That is something between me and my husband,' Sara replied softly but firmly.

'You're right.' Anastasia said shortly, and took a long breath. 'Never underestimate your staff, Sara,' she went on, completely changing the subject. 'If you choose wisely they can serve you well and become trusted friends, enriching your life. Joanna has been a trusted companion to me for many years, ever since my husband died. And Anna could do the same for you.'

'And what are you trying to tell me, Anastasia?' Sara demanded. 'That now my husband has gone I should seek solace with my housekeeper? That I should forget that he is a cheat and a liar – and that he's left me for another woman?'

Sara immediately regretted her outburst. This was Alexander's mother she was talking to. She would hardly endear herself to the other woman by attacking her son.

The other woman looked her straight in the eye. 'Anna didn't know Alexander was leaving with Irena when she called to ask us here. She thinks the world of Alexander and…'

'So she *did* invite you. And she's asked you to come here and speak up for him because she's guessed that I'm pregnant and she's seen the state of this marriage?' Sara breathed quickly, suddenly seeing where all this was leading and appalled at the thought. She had always thought how well she and Anna had got on. But all those damned pearls of wisdom falling at her feet hadn't been for her benefit, but for Alexander's. Anna believed that the reasons for this failing marriage lay with her, and not Alexander.

'And is your marriage in a state?' Anastasia asked gently.

And it was because she asked softly, as if she actually cared, that it brought tears to Sara's eyes. Slowly she stood up and lifted her chin, because if she didn't she would crumble. But she would have to be so, so careful what she said here. She had no idea what Alexander had told his mother about their swift, unexpected marriage. Certainly not the truth. But, whatever he'd said, it must have come as a shock to the older woman.

'We have a proverb in England: marry in haste, repent at leisure. We rushed things, Anastasia, and …and we need more time and…'

'And he isn't here. According to you he is a cheat and has left you for another woman and…'

'Stop it, please stop it!' Sara cried in anguish. Her palms came up stiffly to ward off the hurt. 'I shall work it out. *We* will work it out. We have to.'

'For what reason, Sara? For the sake of that terrible mistake all those years back? For those two little girls?'

Sara gasped with shock, and her hand flew to her mouth. She swayed, utterly dazed, and then she fell back into her cane chair with a thud.

'You…you know?' she croaked so faintly she wasn't sure if she had been heard.

Anastasia poured the last of the martini from the iced jug for herself and orange juice for Sara.

'Alexander desperately needed to share it, and we have always been close,' she told Sara gravely. 'And you might as well know that I thought it best that he didn't involve you.'

Sara's heart gathered pace, thudded so dangerously she thought it would stop altogether.

'You...you didn't want to know your very own granddaughter?' Sara asked, shocked.

Anastasia waved a large but elegant, bejewelled hand. 'Don't forget I'm one generation away from the real emotion of all this, Sara. I had a granddaughter – Eleni. It came about that she wasn't a true Karakou, but she was in my heart nonetheless. I could see only heartache for everyone involved if it all came out, and I advised Alexander against contacting you.' She shrugged her fine shoulders. 'He just couldn't live without meeting Thea.'

'I know,' Sara whispered. 'He said that, when I accused him of being selfish for sharing it with me. For a time I...I wished I had never known.'

'And now?'

Eyes brimming with tears, clutching her hands tightly in her lap, Sara said what was in her heart.

'And now I am glad I know,' she whispered emotionally. 'Nothing will ever change the way I feel about Thea. I love her very deeply and always will. If I had more love inside me, I would love her even more because she is Alexander's.' She laughed softly through her tears. 'That sounds crazy, I know. And Eleni?' She shook her head from side to side and closed her eyes and lifted her head. 'I was so damned scared when Alexander told me the truth. So afraid that there wasn't room for her in my heart. So terribly afraid that I wouldn't be able to accept her.'

She snapped open her eyes and looked at Anastasia. 'It was all such a shock, you see. I looked at her and knew the truth – but didn't feel it. She was mine, my child, the baby I had nurtured inside my body for nine months. And yet if Alexander hadn't found out the truth I would never have known. I might have passed her in the street, seen her playing on some beach, and never have recognised her as my own.'

Anastasia nodded, seeming to understand the state of her emotions at the time. 'And now?' Anastasia prompted with a crack in her voice.

Sara let the tears spill then, she couldn't hold them back. 'I love her very much – so, *so* much,' she croaked. 'They are *my* girls, both of them, *my* girls.'

'They are Alexander's girls too,' Anastasia reminded her gently.

Sara nodded her head vigorously. 'I know. I know he loves them very much. And even if I hadn't fallen in love with Alexander I would fight for this marriage. I'm going to make it work. I'm not going to take it lying down, though,' she said grittily. 'When Alexander gets back – and he damned well *will* come back, because the girls are here,' she ranted on, 'I'm going to lay down some ground rules and…and there will be no more…'

She felt Anastasia's arms around and realised she was sobbing uncontrollably. She heard Anastasia's soothing voice through the rushing of the blood in her ears.

'Just tell him you love him, Sara. All you have to do is just open up your heart and tell him. It's what he is waiting to hear.'

The rush of blood suddenly receded. The tears dried and Sara blinked her eyes, feeling she had just come out of a coma and was wondering where she was and what she might have admitted. Oh, God, no, she had admitted to Alexander's mother that she loved him!

Shakily, Sara got to her feet. 'I'm all right. I…I really am. I'm sorry, I take it all back,' she tried to smile. 'I'm tired…I need to rest.'

She went hurrying up the curving stairway to the sanctity of her bedroom, praying fervently that Anastasia wouldn't tell her son what Sara had said. She wouldn't be able to live through the humiliation of him knowing that she cared for him so deeply. That was if he ever came back.

'Eleni, leave Grandmama alone, ' Thea laughed. 'She's tired of seeing you swim.'

'I used to swim myself when I was younger,' Anastasia told them both as she lay by the poolside in a lounger, watching the girls play in the shallow pool the next morning, Eleni demanding her grandmother's approval of her new-found skills. 'I qualified for the Olympic team, but my papa wouldn't allow me to take the place. He said I had to study instead.'

'Were you disappointed?' Thea asked with interest as she curled up at Anastasia's feet, rubbing at her small feet with a towel.

Anastasia took the towel from her and started to gently rub at Thea's sopping wet hair. 'At the time I was heart-broken, but my papa was right. Study had to come first, and in those days there was no future for swimmers.'

Sara stood back from the balcony and listened to the girls and Anastasia talking below. Thea had swum since she was three, had always loved the water. She must have inherited that talent from her grandmother. There was a lot to be said for genes.

Sara sighed and went back into her bedroom to tidy up. Thea had a family now, a real father and a real grand-mother. It was wonderful, of course, but it made Sara feel so isolated, as if *they* had taken over and the little girl didn't belong to her any more.

She shivered and wondered if this new life inside her was the reason why she was feeling so very sensitive.

But if Alexander was here beside her, to give her strength,

she knew it could all be so different. They would be a family together, something she and Thea had never had.

'Mama, when is Papa coming home? I miss him. Grandmama isn't watching me swim; she's laughing with Thea and I feel lonely,' Eleni pouted.

Sara had swung round in shock on hearing Eleni calling her 'Mama'. It struck such a deep chord of emotion within her that she felt quite weak. At the same time she felt angry that Alexander wasn't present, to hear what Eleni had just said.

Sara smiled and went to her, taking a freshly laundered towel from the pile on the bed, where Anna had left them earlier, and wrapping it around Eleni.

'He'll be home soon, darling,' she said warmly, giving her a hug and then rubbing her gently with the towel. 'He has work to do, but when he gets back we'll have a lot of fun together. Come on, let's get you dressed.'

'Shorts like Thea's,' Eleni insisted once they were in her bedroom and Sara was peeling off her wet swimsuit.

'Don't you like your pretty dresses any more?' Sara laughed, thinking how much Thea had influenced her.

'My real mama liked to dress me up. She called me her little doll and she used to comb my hair for hours and hours. She used to sing to me as well. You never sing to me.'

Sara held out a pair of shorts for Eleni to step into and laughed to quell the lump in her throat. 'You wouldn't want to hear my voice,' she joked. 'Thea says I sound like a cat and she was always embarrassed if her friends were there and heard me.'

Eleni giggled and let Sara do up the shorts. 'Mama didn't like cats, so I never had one. Did Thea have a cat in England?'

'No, but there was one next door and it used to visit.'

'Can we have a cat now you are my new mama?'

'We'll see, when Papa gets home.'

'He will come home, won't he?' Eleni asked plaintively. 'Mama went away, to the hospital, and never came back.' Her lovely blue eyes suddenly filled with tears. 'Pa…Papa said she had gone to be a star in heaven. I…I used to look for her in the sky every night but now…now I can't see her any more.'

Sara held her tightly, feeling the child's tiny frame shuddering against her. It was all she could do to control her own vulnerable emotions. 'Oh, she's still there,' she murmured softly, so grateful that Celeste had given Eleni, *her* daughter, such love in the short time she had her.

'Thea and me look for them every night,' Eleni whispered into Sara's hair.

'Them?'

Sara drew back to look at Eleni's suddenly smiling face.

'Thea's papa and my mama. Thea says her papa is a star too, and they must be together, and she says that we have a new papa and mama now, and that they would be happy for us.'

Sara smiled through her tears, so very proud of Thea, so very proud of Eleni. 'So these are the secrets you two have at night? No wonder you wanted to share a bedroom!'

'You and Papa share a bedroom,' Eleni laughed. 'Do you share secrets too?'

Sara kissed her daughter on each warm cheek and wished with all her heart that they shared more than the one secret that had brought them together. She wished they shared a life instead of endured it for the sake of these two adorable little girls.

'Yes, lots of secrets,' she said with a laugh. 'Now, let's go and see what everyone else is up to. Poor Anna, she has so much work to do with her sister here as well. I think I'll cook lunch today.'

'Can I help?' Eleni said with excitement as they ran downstairs. 'I bet I could make cakes like you.'

'I'm sure you could. I guess cooking is a skill, like swimming, passed down through the generations,' Sara muttered to herself.

Sara didn't get to cook the lunch. Anna and Joanna were firmly entrenched in the kitchen, laughing and gossiping, and had everything under control. And after lunch Anastasia held court with two adoring girls who hung on every word she uttered. They toured the gardens, Anastasia sweeping down a gravel path between roses and geraniums, as flamboyant as the flora itself, the girls skipping happily beside her.

Now siesta had passed, darkness was about to fall. Anna and Joanna, back in the kitchen, were preparing mountains of food for dinner tonight and Anastasia still had two appreciative little girls trailing her and begging for more stories, of which there were an abundance.

Sara dressed for dinner in a soft creamy crepe dress that fitted perfectly now but wouldn't for long, feeling a mounting anger that Alexander hadn't even telephoned from Athens to see if they were all right. Which was why she snatched at the telephone, suddenly ringing in the hallway. She was so bereft of company all day she'd have been grateful for a deep meaningful conversation with the speaking clock!

'Hello?' she said. 'Hello...?' she repeated, when there was no response.

Sara stiffened and clutched the receiver tighter. 'Who is this? Alexander, is that you? Where are you?'

There was soft feminine laughter coming from the receiver. And then, in the background a long way away, a man's voice saying, 'Irena, put that damned phone down!'

Icy chills ran down Sara's spine. She slammed the receiver down with such ferocity that it nearly broke in two. She *knew* that laughter! She knew the voice in the background!

The telephone rang again and Sara, so angry that her mind was whirling like a tornado, snatched it up.

'How dare – ? Maria?' she breathed in astonishment.

'I…I hope you don't mind me calling, Sara. I…I know that our lives are…well, different now,'

'No – it's nice to hear from you, Maria,' Sara responded quickly. She was shaking from head to toe. There was a lot of background noise on the phone in the taverna. 'Did…did you just call me, a few seconds ago?'

Maria laughed softly, but it wasn't the laughter of the previous caller, and Sara knew she hadn't been mistaken. She only wished she had.

'No, I am calling now. I have such news! And, although I haven't seen you lately, I knew you would want to know, and to share it with me.'

Sara's hand went to her clammy brow. Guilt swamped her for not keeping in touch with her friend.

'I am pregnant, Sara,' Maria told her excitedly and happily. 'I only found out today, and we are so happy.' She laughed. 'Forte is making a party right now, and Sara…we would very much like you and Alexander to come. The whole village will be feasting, and we would be very proud for you to join us,'

Sara's head was swimming. Tears filled her eyes as she feared she wouldn't be able to express her congratulations. The words jammed tightly in her throat. Suddenly her own awful situation hit her in the pit of her stomach. She had news, too. Exactly the same as Maria's. But here in this house there was no celebration, no party in a taverna, no joy, no happiness. Maria's husband, Forte, was preparing a party, overjoyed that a new baby was on its way to enrich their lives. Whereas *her* husband, Alexander, wasn't with his wife when she needed him. He was in Athens with his mistress!

'Please say you will come, Sara, it will mean so much to us!'

Sara lifted her head, closed her eyes, bit hard on her lip and heard the echo of Irena's soft laughter in her ears, and Alexander in the background, impatiently urging her to put the phone down.

'Yes, of course we...I'll come,' she heard her own voice saying.

And then, in a dreamlike state, Sara found herself picking up the car keys from the marble-topped table in the hall and walking out of the villa. And why shouldn't she damned well go out? Her husband didn't care. He wasn't here. He might never come back. Damn him to hell and back!

Anna suddenly appeared at the open window of the car as Sara, stiff with pent-up anger, fired the engine.

'Where are you going?' she asked anxiously.

Sara retorted sharply, 'I'm going to a party. And don't tell me that Greek wives do not go to parties without their husbands, because *this* Greek wife doesn't have one!'

'Sara, don't do this,' Anna warned anxiously. 'Alexander will be very angry.'

'Hah! In case it has escaped your notice, Anna, Alexander isn't here. That's because he's in Athens with his mistress – who, incidentally, has just been laughing at me on the phone – and as far as I am concerned he can stay there!'

'But the girls!'

Sara didn't hear any more. She accelerated away, her confused mind assuring her that a night away from her daughters would do them no harm. They had an adoring grandmother to put them to bed, an adoring housekeeper to see to their needs. And as for tomorrow...?

Tomorrow, when this anger and frustration and pain abated, she would return. And she would take her girls back to England. And no defaulting Greek husband, no damned court in the land, was going to stop her!

chapter nine

Sara shielded her eyes from the sun to look up at the cliff top. She had heard the car grind to a halt almost an hour ago, just three metres beyond the last olive tree on the dirt track road above the villa, which nestled in a rocky cove.

He was still there, gazing down. Not a stranger any more, but her husband. He was still as strikingly beautiful as ever, and he still had the power to quicken her breath.

Sara hadn't slept all night. At first she had just sat out on the terrace of the beachside villa to which he had summoned her what now seemed a lifetime ago, staring out into the space of a hot, dark night.

Like a wild thing she had driven away from her home… no – correction!…*his* home, knowing in her heart she could no more stomach a party that night than bungee-jump off the cliff above. But she'd had to get away.

It had come as no surprise to find herself on the cliff top over which Alexander was now pacing. She'd had nowhere else to go. And it seemed fitting that it should be here, where they'd first met, that she would try and lay the ghost of her love for him. A poignant, masochistic sort of an exorcism, because this was where it had all started.

Thea and herself reading on the terrace overlooking the sea; Thea drawing while she prepared the vegetables for their supper, and Alexander…Alexander watching them from above. And then that all-seeing, all-knowing stranger had finally walked into her life – and completely and utterly blown it apart.

She should hate him, but she didn't. Although last night she had been filled with rage and anger, enough to drive her out of his home. But now, in the clear early brightness of a new day, she felt very matter of fact about it all. Almost detached, as if it was happening to someone else and not her at all.

There had been pain at first, but that had receded during the balmy night. And now a strange sort of resigned numbness had overtaken her. No, she didn't hate Alexander. How could she, when he had given her something so very precious? Another daughter. And a new life inside her, which would have the same love she felt for Thea and Eleni.

As she watched him pacing up and down the track, hands plunged into the trouser pockets of the same suit he'd been wearing when he left, she wondered if anyone had told him she was pregnant. It didn't really matter, of course. Like Thea and Eleni, this baby was all hers too. He couldn't have it all…his mistress and the children. No way.

Sara went inside the villa to put a pan of water on to boil. No one had occupied the building since she'd left, and there was still coffee here, and sugar.

She saw his shadow fall across the doorway, but didn't turn to face him.

'How was the party?' he asked.

Sara spooned coffee into a glass jug as she murmured. 'I danced all night. Barefoot, out in the street with a hundred drunken tourists. It was the most wonderful night of my life!'

The shadow from the doorway disappeared and the kitchen was bright again. Surely it hadn't been that easy to be rid of him? she wondered as she took the tray outside.

He was sitting under the cane shades, slumped wearily into a chair and gazing out – where she had gazed all through the long night – out into space. He looked drawn and tired, and she supposed that what he had come to tell her didn't sit too well on his shoulders. Perhaps, in his own way, he thought he had done his best for this marriage. And, loving the man as she did, she knew that any sort of failure for him would be difficult. But then he had his mistress to comfort him, didn't he?

'Maria said you hadn't turned up at her party, so I guessed you were here,' he told her wearily.

Sara sat down and poured the fragrant coffee. She sighed. 'What a very small, insignificant life I lead. Anna guessed I was partying at Maria's, because I know no one else on this island. And you knew exactly where to find me, because I didn't have anywhere else to go.' She sighed again and added, 'If you knew I hadn't been to the party, why ask how I enjoyed it?'

'Why make up a ridiculous lie?' he countered.

'Wishful thinking, I guess,' she retorted sarcastically.

'Is that what you want out of life, Sara? Parties, dancing the night away?' he snapped at her.

That stung. Since meeting him all she had ever wanted was him, their daughters, and a happy and harmonious family life.

Sara forced herself to give a careless shrug. 'I have little choice when my husband chooses to leave me for another woman.'

'I escorted a disturbed woman home to her estranged husband, a woman who was threatening yet another suicide bid if I didn't go with her. If you had stayed at home, as I expected you to, I would have explained all on my return.'

Sara wanted to laugh out loud at that. 'Oh, *she* has a husband now, does she? How convenient! And where did he suddenly spring up from? The eternal well of poor excuses, used by adulterous husbands like yourself?'

His eyes flashed with anger and he shook his head wearily. 'If I wasn't so damned tired of all this, I'd lash back at you for that.'

She pushed a cup of coffee across the wooden patio table to him. 'Well, get some caffeine inside you, Alexander.

You're going to need all the adrenaline you can get hold of, because you are going to have to do a lot better than that!'

'If I needed an excuse for my behaviour recently, I'd clearly do better to make up a sackful of lies, rather than trying to get you to hear the truth.'

'Lies or truth. Neither interest me, Alexander. This has all gone too far. You should have stayed in Athens with Irena and made my life a whole lot easier.'

'After living with you since our marriage I'm beginning to wonder if there *is* anything in the world which would make life easier for you.'

Sara sipped her coffee and hoped the caffeine didn't wipe away *her* weariness. Under a blanket of exhaustion she was safe from more anguish. Fully alert to all this, she would be really suffering the pain of his caustic tongue.

'So, I haven't been the perfect wife? Is that why you took so long to come down here and join me this morning? Were you up there on the cliff path, reflecting that you should have left well alone? That you should never have tried to claim your daughter, Thea?'

He stared at her darkly, so darkly and menacingly she had to look away.

'With a heart as cold as yours, I doubt if the truth would go even part-way to softening it,' he drawled coldly. 'You were determined from the start that this marriage wouldn't work.'

She lifted her eyes then and, damn it, the caffeine was doing its job. Feelings and emotions she wanted to keep dead inside her were flaring up to wound and hurt her. Looking at him now, she realised that she must have started falling in love with this man right from the moment they'd first met. She had completely lost her heart to a man, who had only married her to secure his true daughter.

'I had no choice but to agree to this marriage, Alexander,' she told him wearily. 'You had no choice but to ask me. We were both trapped.'

Slowly he stood up. He couldn't bring himself to look at her and she knew why. Because he recognised the truth of what she'd just said, and had as many regrets as she had.

Watching Alexander as he gazed out to sea for a long time, Sara wished that something catastrophic would happen – like a thunderbolt from the clear blue sky? – something capable of piercing his heart, and changing his indifference to love. But this was real life, not a fairy tale. And miracles were in short supply these days, she told herself wryly.

He finally turned to face her, his eyes hooded with the same exhaustion that must be etched on her own face and weary body. He leaned on the table towards her, as if he hadn't the strength to support himself any more.

'You are right, Sara, You had no choice but to marry me, after what I told you about our daughters,' he told her movingly. 'But I had a choice – and that is the difference between us.'

'You had the same choice as I had, which was none at all,' she retorted.

He shook his head. 'No, I had the choice of whether to make this happen or not. I had a week to decide. A week that you didn't have.'

Sara shook her head, brushing a weary hand over her brow. 'I don't know what you mean. You're confusing me now.'

'I had a week up there when you first arrived here.' He nodded his head towards the cliff top. 'A week to decide whether or not to leave it all alone. The first day I couldn't take my eyes off my daughter. I was looking at my own flesh and blood, a complete stranger to me, yet my very own daughter. Yes, I wanted to claim her, but when I thought of all the suffering it might cause I told myself I should walk away and forget what I knew.'

His voice had risen, and Sara stared at him in confusion, wondering what was making him so angry now.

'But then something happened. I kept coming back because there was another pull, another attraction. *It was you*! I couldn't keep my eyes off you, Sara. Watching you, day after day, as you talked and played with Thea, I knew that I wanted you, more than I'd ever wanted any woman in my life. More, indeed, than I had ever desired my first wife. I wanted you...I wanted my daughter...I wanted it *all*!'

Sara gasped, her red-rimmed eyes widening as her heart began to thud. But she couldn't seem to take in all he was saying. Was only capable of noting the deeply rueful, sardonic twist of his lips, and the bleak unhappy expression in his dark eyes.

'And sadly – and bloody ironically! – I am the reason for the failure of this marriage. Because, I was selfish and arrogant enough to believe I could make you love me.' He sighed and shook his head. 'I was wrong. It didn't happen, and now I realise that one-way love isn't enough to hold a marriage together.'

In total confusion, Sara could only stare at him in astonishment. Had she heard right? Was he *really* saying that he had always wanted her...?

Oh, God – now he was walking away!

Sara was on her feet in an instant. 'Alexander!' she cried out. Her head was whirling. He stopped dead, turning to her in anger, the pulse at his temple throbbing, his eyes black with rage.

'I can't suffer the humiliation of this marriage any longer. You can have your divorce, Sara. I give it to you on a silver platter.' His hand came up and he directed a fierce index finger at her. 'One condition, though. The girls are mine. I want you out of my life, but I'm *not* parting with my girls!'

'*Alexander*!'

His name, called out in a frenzy of awareness and grief, took wing and was gone on a breeze from the sea.

Transfixed, shocked and frozen in time, Sara watched him stride away along the beach path and up to the cliff-top above. Without looking back he climbed into his car, reversed…and was gone.

Sara knew she had no chance of catching him up, so she didn't try. She moved around the villa tidying up, stiffly, mechanically, willing herself to do something…anything…because to dwell on what she now knew would cause her to totally collapse.

He *did* love her. He had *always* loved her! He had tried to make her love him and…and she had failed him, utterly and completely.

How could she rush after him now and tell him she loved *him*? That she always had and she always would? He had just offered her what she'd demanded in a fit of temper a few days ago. A divorce. He would *never* believe her if she fell at his feet now and admitted her true feelings. He would accuse her of wanting to save the marriage just to keep the girls.

And all this could have been avoided if she hadn't been so stupidly blind and refused to read all the signals he had given her.

Sara went outside and stood on the sun-bleached terrace, letting the heat of the sun scorch her face. Her fists were bunched tightly at her sides. Why hadn't she seen those signs and acted on them, made it easier for him to open up his heart to her? Why hadn't she swallowed her own pride and been honest with him from the start?

Her head whirled. Anastasia had said, 'Tell him you love him, it's what he wants to hear.'

And it was *precisely* what she had wanted to hear from him. A declaration of love. But neither of them had been able to say it. They were like two children, saying, *No – you first*! Both of them too proud and too afraid of ridicule, too cautious to open their hearts, just in case the other partner didn't feel the same way.

Sara hugged herself tightly and gazed out across the waves lapping the shoreline. And guilt had also played a big part in their reluctance to admit their feelings for each other. She had felt it the first day she'd laid eyes on him. Guilt for feeling attracted to another man when she felt she should have been more faithful to the memory of Spiros.

And it must have been just as difficult for Alexander. He had been married to Celeste. He'd loved her, certainly enough to have committed himself to her for life before losing her so tragically. And then to find that there *was* someone else, to whom he was drawn, even more strongly... . Yes, knowing Alexander, she realised that he would also have found himself wrestling with feelings of guilt and self-reproach.

Sara shivered in spite of the heat. She could understand how he had felt. In a way, she should be thankful that her commitment to Spiros had not been so entrenched. A planned wedding that had not had the chance to take place couldn't be compared to one that had. But she had loved Spiros, and had suffered his loss. Just as Alexander had mourned the death of Celeste. And yet, when they had both been given a second chance, they'd made a complete mess of it.

Sara locked up the villa at last, and put the key back into a niche in the back wall. She drove home slowly, carefully, giving herself time to think and plan what she was going to say to Alexander, how to make it all right. But she knew it would be an up-hill fight, and by the time she reached home her head was throbbing worse than ever.

And then, as she came to a halt in front of the white villa, even more guilt was added to her misery. Last night she had sped off like a crazed thing, with no thought for anyone but herself. But now she must immediately make atonement for her stupidity.

'Anna,' Sara cried as she entered the villa. Anna was on the stairway, on her way up, and immediately turned as Sara ran across the hall to her.

'Anna, I'm *so* sorry for last night,' she told the house-keeper sorrowfully. 'I had no right to speak to you like I did. And rushing off without a thought…it…it was un-forgivable.'

Anna smiled and reached out and patted her hand as it clenched the banister. 'You're all right, that's the main thing.'

Sara smiled weakly. 'Thea and Eleni? I'm so ashamed of just rushing off and…'

'And you wouldn't have done if you hadn't been sure they were in safe hands. Yes? Well, I take that as a com-pliment,' Anna told her softly.

Sara's eyes filled with tears. 'Oh, Anna!'

'Now, there's no need to cry.' The older woman smiled at her. 'Everything was just fine here.'

'But Anastasia. She must think me the worst mother on earth!'

'Anastasia thinks nothing of the sort, Sara,' Anna re-assured her quickly. 'When I told her that you had flown off into the night, she rose to the occasion and took on the role of adoring grandmother with a new energy!'

Sara couldn't help but burst into tears, and threw herself into Anna's arms. 'I've been so stupid, Anna,' she sobbed. 'You sent for Anastasia because you could see the mess I was making of everything, and…'

'Anna!' A roar thundered down from above. Sara jump-ed. Anna didn't. They both looked up.

Alexander stood on the gallery above, naked apart from a skimpy towel tied around his waist. He was dripping wet – and very, *very* angry.

'Where are the bath towels?' he thundered at the house-keeper. 'This house has gone to rack and ruin lately. My staff spending their time gossiping when they should be seeing to their household duties! Have I no authority in my own home any longer?'

With what sounded like a bullish snort, he turned and stormed off.

Both Anna and Sara sighed, and then smiled widely at each other.

'I'll get them,' Sara whispered, and sniffed away the last of her tears. She looked at Anna as she smoothed a hand over her stomach. 'I hope this one is a boy. I have a feeling that my husband is going to need some male support in this all-female household in the future. Does he know, Anna?'

Anna shook her head. 'This wily old housekeeper knows where to draw the line. And his wily mother knows not to come between husband and wife.' She grinned. 'He has no idea he is going to be a father again. It's all up to you now, Sara! And don't forget the towels,' she called out as Sara ran up the stairs.

Alexander was in the bathroom when Sara stepped into the bedroom, clutching a pile of springy soft towels and a clean bathrobe, which she had taken from the linen cupboard on her way. She crossed the room on tiptoe, gingerly opening the bathroom door and flinging them in, before quickly closing the door. She heard a muffled grunt, and smiled softly to herself as she gazed around at the disarray of their bedroom.

It had never been like this before. Alexander had always been almost clinically tidy. Except once, of course. She remembered the last night they had spent in this dream of a bedroom. On that occasion he had been so eager to come to her that he had flung his clothes aside without a thought.

She had known that night had been different from any

other, warmer, more giving, but she hadn't known why. Now she did. He had felt her love for him, realised that his plan to make her love him had worked, and that was why he had responded so passionately. And if Irena hadn't called to spoil it all, their marriage wouldn't have fallen apart again.

Well, she was going to put all that to rights. She was going to open her heart to him. She was going to bring him back to her if it was the last thing she did. That was if he ever emerged from the bathroom, of course!

Impatient with waiting, she nervously smoothed her crumpled dress over her hips, wishing she didn't feel quite so dishevelled. But, damn it, she wasn't glossy Irena; she was his wife!

Her heart did a double-take as she picked up a sheaf of papers from the dresser and glanced at them quickly. The piece of parchment that stated they were man and wife lay on the top. Underneath was a sheaf of other papers. From Athens. Official documents that suddenly made her feel sick to the pit of her stomach. Especially when she saw the embossed logo of an Athens lawyer.

Dear God – *no*! Surely he hadn't already started divorce proceedings while he'd been in Athens, and brought the papers back with him?

Sara heard movement from the bathroom. In a flash of fury she ripped the papers apart. Oh, no, Alexander Karakou, she thought grimly. You're not going to get rid of me *that* easily!

He caught her tearing the papers into shreds. His face darkened in a fury, and determinedly tightening the belt of his robe, he strode towards her.

'Just *what* in the hell are you doing?' he bellowed.

She flung the papers at his chest. 'Saving this marriage, Alexander. You might think it is all over – but as far as I'm concerned you've got another think coming! I *refuse* to be divorced.'

He stopped dead in front of her. 'What are you talking about?'

Sara kicked at the shredded papers at her feet, but continued to stare fixedly up at him, her blue eyes glinting with obstinacy and very, very determined.

'I'm not going to let this marriage slip out of my fingers, Alexander,' she breathed quickly. 'And it has nothing to do with our daughters. This is about us – *and us alone*. The night before you left, we were both beginning to get the message about our feelings towards each other. And I'm not going to stand back and let some ghost from your past haunt the rest of our days. Last night Irena called here, and laughed at me down the phone. Yes…she laughed at me. And then I heard your voice in the background…'

Alexander shook his head adamantly. 'Impossible. I was already on my way back home.'

'I know. I know.' Sara waved her hand dismissively. 'I realised that just as soon as I saw your car up on the cliff top last night. But I'd got myself into a state, what with your mother here and the house full, and…and just about everything else. I thought she'd won and that I'd lost you forever!'

He reached for her, but Sara took another step back. 'Don't touch me, Alexander!'

His whole body froze, and Sara so desperately wanted to reach out to him. But she couldn't. Not yet. She had to clear away all obstacles between them before she would be able to fall into his arms and tell him what had lain so deeply in her heart for such a long time.

'Not yet,' she pleaded. 'There are things I have to say, and if you touch me they won't get said. You…you said you were bringing Irena back to liven things up, and I naturally thought…'

'You thought I was trying to make you jealous?'

She nodded.

'We had genuine business to deal with. But I won't pretend the idea didn't cross my mind.' He sighed and shook his head. 'I wasn't intending to act cruelly towards Irena. But when you clearly *were* jealous of the woman, I'll admit that I wasn't sorry. I…I hoped it would make you think about me as *a man* – not just the father of Thea and Eleni, who'd forced you into an unwelcome marriage.'

Sara looked deep into his wonderful eyes and a small smile trembled on her lips. She nodded. 'Yes,' she whispered hoarsely. 'I was jealous. Poor Irena.'

'No not "poor Irena", Sara. Greedy, manipulative Irena, who already has a husband.'

Her eyes widened. 'So…so that was true?'

Alexander nodded. 'It's been one of those on-off marriages for some years now. Irena goes crazy at times, threatens suicide to get her own way. She'd come running to Celeste, and Celeste always fell for the latest sob story. She made me promise to look after Irena, when…when she knew she was ill.' He sighed deeply. 'I made that promise, Sara, and…'

'I know,' she murmured softly. 'I do understand.'

'And do you now understand that by taking Irena back to Athens I considered that I was free of any promise I had made to Celeste? That I never intend to see Irena again?'

Sara nodded.

Suddenly he was holding her shoulders, warmly and possessively, and she let him.

'I couldn't stand any more of her demands. I put up with them for the sake of Celeste, but now *you* are my wife, and my life is complete. I delivered Irena back to long-suffering Marios, and left them to get on with it. If she called you it must have been in a fit of pique. Because I left her in no doubt of my feelings for you, and for the place you hold in my life.'

Slowly Sara lifted her head to look up into his deep dark

eyes, but she could hardly see him for the tears in her own.

'And what have I become in your life, Alexander?' she asked tremulously. 'Because if it's one fraction of what you have become in mine, there is a chance that we could be happy together. I know this is all my fault,' she added helplessly, 'but…but I found the situation with our children so difficult to cope with that there was scarcely room in my heart to see what was happening between us. And when I realised that I had fallen deeply in love with you, I didn't know what to do…or say…'

She suddenly felt his strained, tense body relaxing against her, and then his strong arms were closing about her trembling figure, his tall frame shaking with emotion as with a low groan he buried his handsome face in her hair.

Sara clung to him fiercely, her arms locked tightly around his neck. 'I didn't know,' she whispered. 'I didn't know that you loved me. I thought that I was the only one who cared. I've been so afraid of letting you know how I feel. I was in despair. So certain that you would never be able to love and care for me.'

'I adore you, darling. I always have done – and I always will. And the relief of finally hearing that you feel the same… . Oh, God!' he groaned. 'I thought I had lost you when I came back and found you gone.'

He possessed her lips in a long, lingering kiss of total commitment, and Sara's heart sang, her whole body throbbing with the wonderful knowledge that she loved, and was loved in return.

He scooped her up in his strong arms and they fell on the bed, Sara clinging tightly to him, laughing and crying at one and the same time. He pushed the hair back from her face with hands that trembled with emotion, lowering his mouth to kiss away her tears.

'Say it,' he murmured. 'Tell me that you love me! I want to hear it a thousand times. Tell me that you will love me forever – in this life and beyond the grave!'

'I love you,' she whispered huskily. 'Oh, Alexander – I love you so much! Of course our love is forever. How could I ever stop loving you?

'And I love you so deeply that I want to marry you,' he said, with such seriousness that Sara laughed softly.

She was about to remind him that they were already man and wife, but it was too late. He was already impatiently removing her clothes, before equally swiftly disposing of his own, and she was glorying in the hard, firm lines of his muscular frame, his tenderness and strength as his mouth and hands sensually caressed every inch of her body.

His fiery kisses as he trailed his lips over her quivering flesh were definitely *not* what one would expect from a married couple who were already the parents of two-point-four children! Yes, she must tell him about the 'point four' addition to their family. But not…not just at the moment…

Now she was at the new beginning of something very precious, something deep and beautiful. A new freedom, a new glory, a new start. And a new Alexander inside her, moving so deeply and intensely, giving her everything she had wished for and wanted for so long. His love. And she responded as ardently, touching him, pressing kisses to his deeply tanned skin, almost eating him alive with her love.

And as their passion rose steeply and fiercely with each deep thrust inside her, Sara murmured 'I love you' again and again, never wanting him to forget how much he meant to her.

Sara awoke later to feel her wedding ring being tugged at. Once it had been loose on her finger; now it fitted snugly.

'Alexander,' she laughed sleepily, and then felt a chill of realisation. He was taking her wedding ring from her!

His warm mouth covering hers stilled the anguish on her lips. When he had calmed her fears, and she was soft and passive in his arms against the downy pillows, he lifted her hand so she could see what he had done.

Sara gasped in astonishment. In place of her wedding ring was a wide band of gold, encrusted all the way around with large sparkling diamonds.

'Alexander, this is an eternity ring!' she squealed. 'You don't have one of these until you have been married for simply ages.'

Curled up on the bed beside her, he leaned over to kiss the top of her head. 'I'm not taking any chances! And besides, I feel as if this marriage has stretched into eternity already,' he teased. 'You make me feel like an old man.'

With laughter sparkling in her eyes, she twisted her face to look at him properly. Yes, the strain was beginning to show. He looked as if he had fought a long hard battle and only just come out the victor.

Sara snuggled up against him and took his hand. Tenderly she lay it against the faded scar on her stomach. 'Darling,' she murmured softly, 'do you remember that first time, our wedding night…?'

'The night after,' he corrected her. 'I was too terrified to come near you on our wedding night. You made me feel that my misspent youth had all been in vain, and I was like a novice starting a new life.'

Sara laughed softly, before pressing his hand to her stomach. 'OK,' she breathed, 'the night *after* our wedding night. You touched me and said…'

'I said that I wished it had been mine, meaning that when you gave birth to Eleni that stormy night, I wished that she had been *our* child.'

Sara smiled. 'She *is* our child, and so is Thea, and, well…your wish is going to come true.'

He frowned.

'That first time we made love…well, I guess you weren't such a novice after all!' she teased, grinning lovingly at him.

'We have Thea, and Eleni, and…if you're very lucky, there's good chance that in about eight months' time we'll be able to give you some male support in this all-female household. Although of course,' she laughed, 'there's an equally good chance that it will be another girl!'

The frown of puzzlement lifted as he gave a heartfelt groan of sheer happiness, before kissing her so deeply and tenderly that Sara knew she couldn't have given him any better news in the world.

'I can hardly believe this,' he whispered as he finally lifted his mouth from hers.

'So, you're pleased?' she laughed softly.

He looked deep into her eyes and she drowned in his. 'Ecstatically so. I can think of nothing more wonderful.'

With new feeling he ran his hand over her stomach, and then lowered his mouth to kiss the soft, warm plane beneath which his son or daughter nestled.

'It's only tiny yet,' she whispered, 'just a few weeks. But soon I'll be so fat you'll have to buy me a whole new wardrobe of clothes!'

'Dear God – the wedding dress!' he suddenly exclaimed, leaping off the bed and scrabbling on the floor for the shreds of paper she had so furiously torn apart earlier.

'Alexander, what on earth are you doing?' she laughed.

Suddenly their bedroom door was flung open, and two small girls shot into the room like rockets. Sara quickly grabbed hold of the sheet to cover her nakedness, relieved to see that her husband had taken the trouble to slip into his bathrobe.

The girls flung themselves onto the bed and hugged Sara tightly.

'Mama, it's so exciting,' Thea squealed with delight.

'What is, darling?'

Anastasia suddenly swept into the room in a gargantuan purple silk kaftan, deftly stepping over the mound of torn paper on the floor that Alexander was trying to sort out.

She looked down her nose and said huffily, 'Well! I can see that little surprise went down like a lead balloon!' Her shrewd eyes quickly took in the sight of the rumpled bedclothes, and the fact that her daughter-in-law was clearly naked beneath the sheet wound tightly about her body.

'Clever girl!' Anastasia murmured as she leaned over to quickly press a kiss to Sara's cheek.

'What an earth is all this about?' Sara asked, totally perplexed.

'Another wedding,' Thea and Eleni chorused in her ear.

'Dear God, are there no secrets in this house?' Alexander growled.

'None that matter any more, Alexander dear,' Anastasia boomed. 'Does Sara know what those papers are yet? Or have you been too busy to tell her?' she asked with a twinkle in her eye.

Alexander sat back on his haunches, glaring up at his mother. 'She thought they were divorce papers – and tore them to shreds in a fury.'

'What's a divorce?' Eleni asked.

Anastasia, who had plopped herself down on the bed, quickly patted Eleni's head. 'Nothing you'll ever need to know about, sweet child. Not in *this* household, anyway.'

'Will someone tell me what is going on here?' Sara cried.

Thea and Eleni started to giggle helplessly. 'We've just told you,' Eleni told her excitedly. 'It's a wedding! We are all going to Athens to be married again.'

Sara's mouth dropped open.

With a smile of resignation Alexander got up from the floor, the bed creaking ominously as he added his weight to it.

'Could you bear to go through with it again?' he asked with a grin. 'Next week, actually. The full works: church, bridesmaids, interfering mothers-in-law,' he added over the multitude of heads. 'While I was in Athens I arranged it all. I feel that I cheated you first time around – some silly civil ceremony with…'

'With a funny man with glasses on the end of his long nose,' Thea shrieked, and Eleni clung to her, helpless with laughter.

Choked with emotion, Sara tried to gather her whole family into her arms, but it was nearly impossible. Everyone was laughing so much, all except Alexander – who was looking at her so lovingly it brought tears to her eyes.

'I do,' she mouthed over their heads to her husband, and he simply responded with the sublime smile of a man who has it all, and knows that love is forever…

Start a new romance today with
Heartline Books™

Tell your friends that they too can enjoy *Love is Forever* absolutely free of charge from Heartline Books. All they have to do is:

• Call the Heartline Hotline™ on 0845 6000504
• *or* look up our website at www.heartlinebooks.com
• *or* enter their details on the form overleaf, tear off the whole page, and send it to:
  Heartline Books, PO Box 400, Swindon SN2 6EJ

Romance at its best from Heartline Books

If you've enjoyed *Love is Forever*, over the coming months we can promise you a variety of thrilling, often sensual, sometimes humorous but always heartwarming and satisfying new books from our talented authors, who are waiting to welcome you into the special world of Heartline.

Travel to exotic locations, or visit the tranquil countryside and busy cities of Britain; fall in love with charismatic, exciting and gorgeous heroes to be found within the pages of Heartline Books' titles such as *Beguiled*, *Red Hot Lover*, *Jack of Hearts*, *Dangerous Rapture* and *Heart & Soul*.

Heartline invites you to live the romance along with our engaging modern-day heroines, who face such dilemmas as … the sudden and dramatic reappearance of a long-lost love; coping with life as a single parent, or busily carving out a career in a male dominated profession. A great read is guaranteed as our heroes and heroines engage in a sparkling battle of the sexes – experience for themselves the highs and lows of discovering that *love is forever*!

Please send me my free copy of *Love is Forever*:

Name (IN BLOCK CAPITALS)

_____

Address (IN BLOCK CAPITALS)

_____

_____

_____

_____ Postcode _____

If you do not wish to receive selected offers
from other companies, please tick the box ☐